Advance praise for *HOME*

"There really is no place like home. Reminiscent of blockbusters like *Summer of Night* and *Needful Things,* Ben Young's *Home* invites the reader to become a part of small-town life. Pull up a chair, join the local HOA and watch as death and destruction bears down upon all you hold dear. Because everything dies. Everything."

Leigh Kenny, author of Cursed

"Reads like one Stephen King's better small-town horrors. Ben Young delivers 'can't-look-away' dread. And I LOVE these characters. Every time I put the book down I was excited to get back to them."

Ben Farthing, author of I Found Horror series

"You'll find plenty of creepiness and blood. Words that are nightmare worthy. Each character could produce a book unto themselves, as they are multi layered and hold deep secrets only the reader knows about. The way Ben brings life to each one is masterful and shows his commitment to the craft."

Edmund Stone, author of Tent Revival and Within

Praise for *STUCK*

"This is an intelligent, carefully crafted novel that explores death, guilt, expectations, and fear in a unique and bare-bones way. It details claustrophobic settings and equally claustrophobic emotions, and demands that you shine a light on your own traumas and fears."

MJ Mars, author of The Suffering

"I took my time because I needed time to process each chapter. It shifts through so many emotions like grief, loss, loneliness, hope, and despair that one sitting feels like an emotional rollercoaster. One thing is for sure, this book is guaranteed to have you thinking about what death really means."

Kayla Frederick, author of Voices and After the Devil

As someone who is claustrophobic, the idea of being stuck anywhere is terrifying. This book made me really rethink what being "stuck" means and I'm so emotional about it. I'm so glad I read this and I truly believe everyone else (especially those experiencing grief) should too!

Asia Brito Guerrero, author of Butterscotch

HOME

BEN YOUNG

For Welles

My strongest symbol of all

INTRODUCTION

When I first met Ben Young, he was an aspiring indie author running around the second ever AuthorCon in Williamsburg, Virginia, pitching a short story to any author who would read. I'm happy to say he gave me a copy. Since then, our friendship has grown. We are even sharing two tables at the biggest indie cons of the year. I've worked with other authors in the past, but with Ben I felt a cohesiveness I didn't find with others. We are now discussing other upcoming plans and projects. One thing you'll find in Ben is a drive for excellence, in writing and reading. He also does something I greatly believe in; he pays it forward. Those are some of the best attributes an author, indie or otherwise, can exude.

He got some praise for the story he pitched at AuthorCon from some noted authors, namely Laurel Hightower, who added a blurb to the short story. I also had the chance to read and fell in love with his writing style. "\system" was one of the best body horror stories I'd ever read. Definitely read it yourself if you get a chance.

After reading that story, I saw something in Ben that impressed me. Sure, his writing is phenomenal, as you'll see firsthand in this book, but other things caught my attention as well. Notably, his ability to seek all the knowledge possible about the process of producing a book.

Putting together your own book is not easy. You are not only the writer but also an agent, a publisher, and manager, all rolled into one.

It can keep you up all night sick with worry and fretting over the finished product. Then there's marketing and building buzz for the book. You also must find a dedicated group of people who not only want to read and review, but wait with anticipation for the next release. These are people who not only enjoy your book but will share that praise with others as well. Depending on your level of comfort, this can be a daunting task unto itself.

A Facebook group called Books of Horror has helped Ben and I both in finding an audience. It's such a great community. Where else can you find a group of dedicated readers and authors all in one place supporting indie horror?

But even without that help, Ben is one of those authors who will always rise to the occasion. His prose, as you will see soon enough, will wrap you up and make you thirsty for so much more. He's a writer who is here to stay.

Ben Young is one of those authors you want to root for, because he gets it. Putting yourself out there for the scrutiny of readers and reviewers is never easy, but Ben handles it all with dignity and grace. He does this because his writing backs it up. You'll see once you begin to read, characters like Lloyd Mnemic, Myrtle Fallsworth, Preston Clark, and Walter Sterling and his dog, Cowboy. Even the unsure and apprehensive mother, Katherine Yost. Each character could produce a book unto themselves, as they are multi layered and hold deep secrets only the reader knows about. The way Ben brings life to each one is masterful and shows his commitment to the craft. An impressive feat, this being only his second book.

His first book, Stuck, released last year, has already garnered fantastic reviews and praise from many readers and reviewers. Also, some notable authors. In it, he weaves a tale of some characters you'll root for and hate at the same time. The premise will have you guessing to the very end and make you want to read again to make sure you didn't miss something. Also, though, because the entertainment value is impressive.

You, my friend, are about to be entertained at a level you can't imagine. This book starts with an ominous back story of a house going through several owners and a checkered past, then quickly evolves into a world of mystery and dark dealings with the sole proprietor, Lloyd Mnemic of the infamous haunted house on Asher Street.

Every town needs a funeral home to allow those in mourning a place to give their last respects, but do they need a friend? Mnemic seems to think so and he'll soon find a cast of characters who are seeking so much more.

The town of Oak Hollow, Ohio, is not much different from where you live. I've been to a few small towns in Ohio since the state is right across the river from where I live. Ben captures the warmth of everywhere USA with an ease you'll find inviting, even with the ominous tone he presents. You will see, as you read along, what I'm talking about is true. Ben will not only entertain you, but he'll keep you enthralled.

I'm no stranger to small town aesthetics and writing those in my books. This story will give you the sense of cohesiveness a small town exudes, but also an underlying dread. The uneasiness presents itself when you read the premise. A house in a town with a dark past and lore everyone knows about but only half believes in its validity.

Finally, I'll leave you with some added information. This book has horror in it. Some of the scenes are cringe worthy which, for me, helps to get me salivating. Going through an entire book and getting very little in the way of things that make me look around the dark room to see if I'm alone would be unsatisfying. This book, however, is not one of those. You'll find plenty of creepiness and blood. Words that are nightmare worthy. Just the way a horror story should be.

Be thankful, my fellow reader, you picked this one up. When you feel as though you can't put it down, as I did, realize you are taking a journey with an emerging talent in the genre of horror, and this is only the beginning of all the great things to come.

Edmund Stone, March 2024

*I suppose I've passed it a hundred times, but I always stop for a minute
And look at the house, the tragic house, the house with nobody in it.
I never have seen a haunted house, but I hear there are such things;
That they hold the talk of spirits, their mirth and sorrowings.
I know this house isn't haunted, and I wish it were, I do;
For it wouldn't be so lonely if it had a ghost or two.*
—Joyce Kilmer, "The House with Nobody in It"

*"If decomposing bodies have disappeared from culture (which they have),
but those same decomposing bodies are needed to alleviate the fear of
death (which they are), what happens to a culture where all
decomposition is removed?"*
—Caitlin Doughty, *Smoke Gets In Your Eyes & Other Lessons from the
Crematory*

*My ma's so sick
She might die
Though my girl's quite fit
She will die
Everything dies
Everything dies
Everything dies
Everything*
—Type O Negative, "Everything Dies"

THE HOUSE

You have one too.

That's right, boils and ghouls, ladies and germs. Yes, even you, my young friend in the back. I realize you're not all from our quaint little town of Oak Hollow, so I feel it worth pointing out that there's one just like it in your neighborhood, wherever that may be. And I'd bet good money you know where to find it. Yes, it's right there in your town and I'd stake my reputation on that as a fact. I'm *that* sure. Because it's known. It's accepted. It's there.

Whatever you do . . . don't think about that house right now. Yeah, you know the one.

Are you doing it?

Are you picturing it?

I think you'd better stop. You know nothing good ever happened there.

Yes, there's a house just like it in every town. And in every town, the stories are told with a momentum all their own. Feeding the undertow of our shared innate fears. Fear of our own mortality. Fear of the unknown, and of the inexplicable.

The terror nearby.

The cancer inside.

We think we can contain or overcome these fears by giving them form, then placing them safely on a shelf or across the street, and keeping our distance. Using them as mere props to caution those less informed than ourselves.

"Look, but don't touch," we say.

"Oh, I wouldn't get too close if I were you."

The truth is, however, these fears *can't* be extracted or removed. They won't be controlled or made docile. And that is why it will always exist, this place. In every town across this great nation of ours.

It will never fade.

I'm talking, of course, about the house. Yes, *the* house.

The haunted house.

Folks, as we're approaching our final stop, it seems fitting to point out that, back when I started planning these walking tours, there were plenty of unknowns. Yes, I was awash in a sea of options. There were endless decisions to make and questions to be answered, lots to figure out. But amidst all that uncertainty, there were three things I knew for sure.

First, I didn't want this to be like every other "ghost tour" out there because I've been on my share of those, and most are quite forgettable. Which is why I *don't* dress in period clothing carrying an oil lamp, and I *do* talk about far more than just spooky stories on this Midnight Mysteries tour. My goal isn't simply to scare you, no. I want to make a deeper impact than just tonight. I want to expand your minds to the hidden parts and secrets of the world around you.

Second, I didn't want to use lies or embellishments to sensationalize my stories. Which is why I keep telling you things other tour guides won't. You may feel that takes some of the punch out of these stories, but I would argue instead that it gives the ones that *are* true a certain . . . gravitas. I aim for credibility first. I'd rather you believe what I tell you, even if it's not the most exciting version, because I think it makes the spooky parts all the spookier. You can trust they're real and I'm not some barnyard tour guide who acts like he's channeling Amelia Earhart every time he picks up a pair of dowsing rods.

And third, one thing I knew for sure from the very start, one thing I never doubted or reconsidered, was that *this* needed to be the end. The grand finale. The last stop on the tour.

Gather 'round here, on the sidewalk, please. Can you . . . can you folks at the back scooch in closer? Thank you. I can't have my groups spilling into the street. Mr. Spellman doesn't like when we block his pharmacy's parking spots. Plus, it's a busy intersection. Well, busy for a place like Oak Hollow, of course. And if I'm being quite honest, this isn't the best part of town to be in after dark. Even a few months ago it was different, but that's Oak Hollow these days, I'm afraid. Things are getting dire, in a hurry.

It doesn't help that the county sheriff's office is understaffed, police presence is nonexistent, and response times are abysmal. Plus, everyone at city hall is distracted, caught up in their scandals and finger-pointing. I guess if someone wanted to get away with something big, now would be the perfect time. Hell, if they were slick about it, they could go days without being detected.

You've probably heard about the recent increase in drug-related activity and the rampant break-ins around town too. Then there was that slashing on the bus line last week, and . . .

Well, no. I'm sorry to startle you, and I wouldn't bring you here if I didn't think it was safe. But this town has seen better days and I just need to make sure we all stick together, that's all.

And maybe keep a good grip on your purses and wallets.

Now, where was I?

Ah, yes . . .

As you're trying your damnedest not to think about that spooky abandoned house in your own town, let's talk a bit more about the mythos of the haunted house, shall we?

This one you're familiar with, lying in wait back in your neck of the woods, coiled like a snake; have you seen people deliberately cross the street to avoid it? What kinds of rumors have you heard about it? Come on, don't be shy . . .

. . .

Okay, we're a quiet group tonight. That's fine. In case you haven't realized it yet, I like to talk . . .

. . .

Hey, these are the jokes, folks. They won't get any better.

Well, since you're not going to tell me what you've heard about your local haunted house, I'll take a few guesses.

I bet you've heard tell about strange noises coming from the house late at night. And someone once told you about the time they walked by and there was an odd smell in the air, like rotten eggs or maybe like nothing they'd ever smelled before. I see a few nods already.

People claim unnatural sensations when they're near it, right? Like the hairs on their neck standing, or cold flashes, even a blip of déjà vu or two. Bad vibrations, *doo doo doo*. They say they've seen lights on when there shouldn't be, perhaps shadows moving inside the windows even though it's been abandoned for years. Some time ago, an investor purchased the place and sent contractors to flip it, but one worker went into the basement alone and was never seen again, so the work just . . . stopped.

When you were in school, you heard one upperclassman broke off a small piece of the house and took it home as a souvenir. Maybe it was a splinter of wood or a cobblestone from the walkway. Maybe they were particularly ballsy and took the antique brass door knocker right off the front door?

More nods and a couple of shocked looks this time. Tragedy befell that brave upperclassman, didn't it? Something came for them and took its own gruesome souvenir, like a finger or toe.

I see we have a general agreement on this point as well.

Folks, I could go on with more examples, but I think you take my point, so I'd rather pause there and explore this little phenomenon we've just uncovered together, if you don't mind indulging me yet again.

It's something we've all contributed to, you see. I like to call it the "Schwartz effect," after the author of those books with the creepy artwork that were just a little too intense for their intended age group. Which, of course, made them wildly successful and popular. Then that got them banned, which made them even more popular.

Anyway, as rampant as those books became, none of the stories were his, you see? His main goal was to distill and share folk tales he felt deserved to be retold. He did it so well that he ended up contributing, in a big way, to a cultural touchstone.

And while we don't all make the sizable mark he did, still, it's something we're each guilty of. Heck, I do it for a living now. There exists that healthy of an appetite. You see, we all add to those whispers in the hallways. We keep the tales aloft around the firepits, hanging up there with the tufts of smoke, droning along with the crickets. We pass the torch to the next storyteller, leaving our own little imprint or signature on it somewhere. It's become a means to cope with a mortality we can't face head-on. Instead, we try to cover it up, like underage kids on a corny sitcom wrecking a parent's car and then hiding the evidence.

Stories are culture, but we've become a culture of death-deniers despite being specifically evolved to survive. That's increased our fear of death, so we turn death into a fantasy so we can have some illusion of control over it.

But by doing that, it's all of us, together, lending the thoughts that give it power, that perpetuate the cold, shuffling, shambling life of it. We're creating our own demons.

We are the story.

We *are* the haunted house.

If you'll look to your left, across the street, you'll see Oak Hollow's prime example. The big one, the reason you're here, I suspect. All our previous stops, though interesting in their own rights, pale in comparison to the most haunted house in Oak Hollow. Some would even argue it's the most haunted in all of Ohio, perhaps even in this vast flyover void we call the Midwest.

Please note, I've conducted three separate high-tech, overnight investigations inside this house, along with running these tours and the subsequent photos shared after. I've also spent a few hundred hours researching official records, interviewing subjects, and poring over any related documents I can find about the place. And just as I have with each previous stop, I'll tell you the same stories as the other tour guides, but I'll also tell you the verified facts, along with my personal interpretations, and leave you to make your own determination about what's real, what's embellished, and what's a flat-out lie.

Boils and ghouls, I give you . . .

432 Asher Street.

Its official name is the Koenig House. Hans Koenig was a Bavarian immigrant who bought ninety-eight acres of land to establish a farm. Construction of the house was finished in October of 1826, and though it took him six years to finish building, nearly bankrupting him along the way, Herr Koenig himself only lived in that house for three months before dying of tuberculosis. He breathed his last right there in the master bedroom with his wife, Aloise, by his side. Allegedly, their marriage was filled with tension because she never bore him a son, and this much, I believe is true. Aside from that, I don't think Hans Koenig was a *remarkably* bad guy by any means, despite what you've probably heard. A bad guy, yes. Closed-minded and self-righteous, racist and sexist, sure, and xenophobic, no doubt. But no more so than average for his time period, certainly not enough to stand out in the history books or to cause a tremble in a storyteller's voice a hundred and ninety-some years later.

They say Aloise and their daughters disappeared in the middle of the night, leaving no trace. One of those daughters was recaptured a few days later, bound and tortured by her father (before his death), then left flayed and on display in the front window for passersby to see.

Chilling, isn't it?

Well, it's also a lie. His wife and daughters each lived full, happy lives after his death. Aloise stayed in the house for just over sixteen years with their four daughters, remarrying one scant year later for purely financial reasons. Aloise and all four of her little girls moved in with her brother's family in Pennsylvania once her second husband became abusive. The records are easy enough to find. His youngest daughter even took some college courses toward the end of her life.

As you can see, the house itself is a unique architectural combination of Greek Revival and Federal style, with some decidedly Victorian features added in for character. It's enough to make me wonder if anyone in its series of owners ever realized they were making it a magnet for the kinds of myth and speculation it's accumulated based on its strange appearance alone. Maybe you agree? To me, it makes a natural scapegoat because it looks so . . . alien. If Frankenstein's monster were a house, am I right? Even more so these days, with all the plain neighboring buildings for contrast. Like it fits the subject's description. Call the Asher Street storefronts in for a police lineup and we'd all point the finger here.

Count that platoon of six-panel windows, starting with the dormers up on the third floor there. You should get fourteen total, and they say that's because Aloise Koenig was superstitious and couldn't abide a home with thirteen of anything. I'm not so sure about that, because if it were true, then wouldn't one of those windows seem crammed in or unnecessary?

The house has been vacant for close to twelve years now, so I'm sure you're noticing all the flaking paint, warped boards, failing fire escapes (not original, of course), even that giant scar in the brick over there near the second-floor window. Other tours include a story about that being caused by a lightning strike at the culmination of a bizarre cult ritual. The version I hear most often is something akin to the scene in the first *Child's Play* movie, when the dying villain transfers his consciousness by chanting and invoking a sinister higher power. It's not true, I'm afraid. Nope, that was caused by nothing more exciting than time, neglect, and decay. No great story behind it. But it sure looks cool, doesn't it?

The expansive, wraparound front porch is one of my favorite features: very Victorian with its intricate latticework, which is all original, but the iconic Greek columns and a few other embellishments—like that three-part transom above the door—were added by the second owners in the 1850s. Around the time that Oak Hollow was growing at its fastest rate and became the county seat for a few years. If you live here or have been paying attention to our local economy lately, it's strange to picture this place growing at all, but at that time, it was blooming because of the new railroads and its proximity to both Cincinnati and Columbus.

A great fire in the 1860s took out nearly a third of Oak Hollow's buildings, including the original church and schoolhouse, but the Koenig House was spared and for almost fifty years, it stood alone again. I can confirm that three people died on Asher Street the day of that fire, but none of them were inside of this house. Although one of them, a ten-year-old boy, is said to wander around this porch when we're in need of a good summer rain.

A remodel in the 1940s is responsible for that whole wing you see on the right side, including the octagonal turret with the wrought iron spike on top, like some bizarre weapon aimed at the sky.

I know, I know, you didn't come here to learn about architecture and home building.

On with the ghost stories.

While we're all still looking at the turret, a man supposedly killed himself in that room, which I can neither confirm nor deny. At least one person I trust has told me they've seen a shadow moving in there, but I don't have any firsthand evidence of a spirit in that room from my own investigations. And if it is true, I have no information about who he may have been or why he was here. So we'll have to leave that one as a question mark.

Let's talk about the first story that I believe *is* true. Those arterial-red bricks were all handmade by slaves. If you look closely, you can find fingerprints here and there, and anyone with psi-sensitivity gets flashes of those slaves' lives when they place their own fingertips in the prints. A good friend of mine did this once and was shell-shocked after. Once she had time to recover, she told me the sense of loss and grief she got from it was enough to make her cry uncontrollably for days.

The most common stories about this place all stem from the rumor that it served as a field hospital during the Civil War. I desperately want that to be true, but I have found no records or credible sources to prove it. I'm still looking, though, so let's say the jury is out on that claim for now.

By my count, there are at least ten unfortunate souls buried under the cellar's dirt floor: everything from Confederate amputees to hatchet murder victims, tuberculosis or yellow fever patients, unfortunate pirates, one decapitated midwife, and a few more outlandish examples. I think it's plausible there could be human remains in there, but I haven't been able to confirm that.

The Civil War and plague stories are the most likely to have some truth, and I can rule out any of the hatchet-wielder tales for you. This place is not Amityville. In all my research, I have found no substantive evidence of domestic murders in this house. But it seems likely there were several disease-related deaths, counting Koenig himself. And it's plausible some of the blood from the Civil War washed its way inside this house.

Oh, and don't believe anything you hear about pirates. Come on, we're in Ohio, for Spock's sake.

I'll leave you to pick which of these things you believe. Assemble your own demons from there and use them as a flimsy buffer against your own inevitable death.

This brings us to the last few decades. It was around twelve years ago when the Christian bookstore folded, which was the last time the building was in use. I was inside about eight years ago and can attest that it had become home to a few squatters and resident wildlife in that time.

There was buzz just two years ago about the current owners: descendants of the Koenig family, I'm told, but they haven't answered any of my emails petitioning to register it as a building of historical significance. Given that, no progress was made.

So here it sits. Empty and brooding and full of mystery.

To wrap things up, I'll remind you that I've tried to prove my healthy skepticism and that I'm not just saying things to sell more tours. Instead, I'm out here most nights trying to counterbalance all the exaggerations and embellishments coming from the other tour companies in town. This house has a tragic and fascinating history, that much is true. But most of the juicy details about it are not, and I'd much prefer that the real stories be retold.

I've been doing this for years, have traveled much of the world researching the supernatural and the paranormal (yes, there is a difference), held hundreds of interviews, conducted dozens of high-tech investigations, and written several books. By the way, if you purchased a copy I'll be glad to sign it before you go. I've hosted or appeared on dozens of radio shows and podcasts too. And through all that, I've had three, and only three, genuinely inexplicable experiences myself. One was in Savannah, Georgia, and if you want to hear that story, you'll have to buy me a few drinks first because I hate to think about it, even all these years later. The second was at Stonehenge during solstice, and the third was a simple dream that foretold the unexpected death of a family member.

I've never seen a ghost, and I have never, *never* had a supernatural experience at this house, even though I've certainly *tried* to have one.

There are some entertaining stories about this place, some of which I desperately want to believe, but it's my humble opinion this house is not actively haunted. At most, I believe there may be a few residuals—by which I mean, recurring sounds or leftover energy that a strong medium could sense and interpret. But nothing I would consider an actual ghost or apparition, and certainly nothing threatening.

If that feels like a letdown, I apologize, but I'll say again that my goal is to tell you the truth as I see it and not to sensationalize as a form of marketing. And maybe it's some consolation to think that the worst things to happen at 432 Asher Street . . . are yet to come . . .

I mean, who knows what could happen in there next week, even?

Why, anything could happen.

Anything at all.

We already know what allegedly occurred in those fables and legends we've heard whispered about this place. Those are the demons we *know*. What about . . . the ones we *don't know* . . .

. . .

. . .

Ahem. Well, folks, that concludes the Midnight Mysteries tour tonight. Gratuity is always appreciated, and don't forget to leave a review on Tripadvisor. You've been a great group, and I hope you enjoy the rest of your— I-I beg your pardon?

What sign?

Oh.

Oh, I hadn't seen it before tonight, actually. I didn't realize the place had finally sold. That's pretty cool. We haven't had any new businesses come to Oak Hollow in years. But I hope the new owners won't have a problem with me bringing tour groups by.

Yeah, it's hard to read from way over here, but I think the sign in the window says *Coming soon, Mnemic Family Funeral Home*."

FRIDAY

SHAWN HANGS

It's almost time, Shawn Yost thought. *Almost time to go.* He walked to the far side of the basement, stepped through the door leading to the unfinished storage room, and stood under the bare *I* beam that crossed the house at length, holding everything steady, keeping in place the tons upon tons of material above him. He reached up, touching the beam with two fingers, then unfolded a short stepladder.

For weeks, as things worsened all around him and any effort he made to right his ship failed and burned into more wreckage, he had been drawn to that enormous iron beam, pulled toward it. Because he knew, unlike himself, that it would never fail, would never budge. His family could spend years bringing ever more weight and objects and expectations to set atop that beam without fully testing its strength. It could hold the bulk of their entire life, their possessions, their experiences, their bonds, and memories, without wavering one inch. Not even a fraction of an inch.

An earthquake wouldn't move that beam.

It was strong enough to hold everything in place for centuries without flinching.

Shawn was not.

His own strength had failed in every way that mattered, except one. He was still here, in Oak Hollow. But that last thread was giving way too sharply now to be denied. It was all about to come down. He had to leave his home.

The Yost family had called the town of Oak Hollow "home" for generations. They were embedded in its every facet. You couldn't travel more than a few blocks without tripping over the name Yost on some building or sign or other, without reading the name in a news article or spotting it on a flyer somewhere. The Yosts symbolized everything that had once made Oak Hollow great, everything that gave it life. And their roots run deep here.

Shawn's grandfather (Frank Yost, Sr.) was often credited as the principal founder of the Banana Split Festival, the town's biggest annual event, now in its fifty-seventh year. His Uncle Felix owned the Hideout Tavern on Main Street. Uncle Paul ran a tire shop on the outskirts of town. His cousin, Margie, a gossip queen if Shawn had ever met one, delivered mail to most of the Oak Hollow homes.

Within Shawn's extended family, his own wife, Katherine, was the only one not originally from Oak Hollow. They'd met at a company picnic of all places. Katherine's father and Shawn both worked for Blue Sky Logistics (BSL to the locals) at their air cargo hub. Hell, half the town did back then.

Of course, that was prior to BSL relocating their operations to the Cincinnati airport—an hour and fifteen minutes southwest of Oak Hollow—taking away 8,000 jobs, Shawn's included.

The callous decision of BSL to leave the town that spawned it was devastating to the local economy, and since that day, Oak Hollow had crept ever closer to living up to its name. It had grown truly hollow.

As had Shawn Yost.

Losing his ability to provide had been the first crack, breaking the seal, and everything he cared about seeped out after that. He'd muddled through for a while, between his severance, unemployment benefits, odd jobs, and the accumulation of debt. But the damage to Oak Hollow's economy was too great, and there had been no new business or jobs in years. Recovery was not happening.

Even in its darkest hour, though, Oak Hollow was home, had always been home, with the broader Yost clan presenting a united front, refusing to leave when their beloved homestead needed them most. But now things had changed. Katherine did her best to be understanding of this, but it was clear from the start that she did not share his attachment to this town. She had been ready to leave months ago, but Shawn was holding her back. And she wouldn't stay here forever. She couldn't.

It became a decision point between leaving his home or losing his family. Those were the only possible outcomes now. He'd either be the first Yost in generations to desert a sinking ship, or a man left behind by his own wife.

Until the day, three weeks ago, when Shawn found himself in their basement storage room, looking through photos from his childhood, each page rife with smiling faces and Oak Hollow as the backdrop in every shot, and then he noticed the beam.

He had first seen it as an ideal, something to strive for, because of its unwavering strength. But that changed quickly as he realized the beam was a paragon no human could ever reach, especially one as pitiful as himself. It was stronger than his very bones, more influential than any dream.

Then it became his way out, his third option. Rock, hard place, or beam. Shawn may not have the strength to change these awful circumstances, but the beam damn sure did.

"All things serve the beam," he thought distractedly. It was a phrase both familiar and odd, and he couldn't place its origin in that quiet moment.

The beam's strength could carry him away. Set him free. It could save him. Save them all.

Katherine had been so pleased when she told him this morning about her new job, and for a space of heartbeats Shawn felt relief. Dread washed away like silt in a cleansing rain, and he glimpsed light in their future again. Perhaps he'd even be able to find firm enough footing to start his own business and help breathe life back into his cherished hometown. He wanted to believe Oak Hollow could rebound, given enough time. And he longed to be part of that while his ancestors smiled down.

Then she told him, with clear trepidation, that she'd be working as a paralegal for a large, established, multi-partner law firm. Shawn's heart sunk; he knew there was no such place within twenty-five miles. He recovered a bit, supposing she had made peace with a substantial commute. But then Katherine confirmed his fears by adding—her trepidation morphing into something bordering an apology—that the new employer was in Indianapolis.

A different place, a new city. A different state entirely. Factoring in traffic, it would be a three-hour trip from Oak Hollow, one way. Shawn had screamed at her, and she had cried. Then came the worst argument of their marriage and she had stormed out of the house. Within minutes, Shawn was overcome with guilt, knowing that his screams and jabs had all been borne of his own failings and insecurities.

The beam was forefront in his mind. He needed to act before the kids got home from school. This was his last chance.

Standing under the beam now, he snapped the hinges on the step stool, locking them into place. This was a habit concerned with safety, and the irony was not lost. Another time, it may have caused him to smile, perhaps even to chuckle. But he felt no trace of laughter.

Shawn felt as hollow as his hometown had become. Like there was a chasm inside himself, opening wider and pulling him down. The only thing he had left to give his family was freedom. Freedom from his inadequacy and from his stubborn attachment to Oak Hollow. His absence and his life insurance payout would make the move to Indianapolis much easier on them.

He picked up a length of rope from his tool bench, tan and thick and harsh enough to give splinters, not like the white nylon kind that was sickeningly smooth and unreliable. Surely, this would work. Shawn checked the knot, consoled by its strength as well. It occurred to him distractedly that this knot looked nothing like the ones used at the gallows in the movies, not a flashy and gruesomely picturesque one. It was, instead, simple and sturdy. It would work. This knot would get the job done. The knot and the beam.

Shawn put a foot on the ladder's first step as the base of its legs gritted against the concrete floor like a knife scraping cold bone. He shuddered, then lofted the rope up and over the beam, directly above the ladder. It cleared, dropping back down beside him, hanging inches from his cheek. That brought a tear. He sobbed, silently at first, shoulders lunging forward once, twice, stopping briefly, then three more heaving sobs, loud and wet.

Shawn climbed. Pulled the loop of rope over his head. Dropped his hands to his sides.

And then, as if the oxygen from those deeply pulled sobs had reignited his rationality, he stopped. Moved his left foot down, off the top step of the ladder.

What am I doing? he thought, scolding himself. He had considered this option dozens of times since noticing the beam, but not in any serious capacity. Surely, this was an overreaction to Katherine's news and their fight. Hanging himself was a fleeting impulse. It was crazy.

Of course it was. She'd be home any minute. They would talk it out. They would figure a way through, like they always had. She needed him, still. His children did too. No one wanted this.

Another tear rolled down his cheek, refracting an image of the photo album he'd left lying on the floor, and before Shawn could descend the ladder, he felt a presence with him. Not in the room, but close. And sinister. As panic gripped Shawn's heart, a man's voice came to his head, one he did not recognize.

Face it, Shawn, this voice said. *Life in Oak Hollow will never be like that again. Never.*

Then it was as if his feet weren't his own, moving without his command. He stepped forward, the ladder toppling sideways, a sound like a sigh mixed with a scream escaping his throat as he dropped.

He clawed at the knot, but it held.

Within his meagerly lit basement storage room, the strength of the beam came for Shawn Yost and carried him away.

MNEMIC ARRIVES

Inside the house at 432 Asher Street, which had been still and silent for twelve years, the basement stairs creaked at a slow, steady pace. These creaking sounds traveled up toward the main floor of the home, one after the other, and pausing between. When they stopped, a figure emerged from a darkened doorway, seeming to take shape from the very shadows as it moved outward until it resembled a man.

Were there a witness to his coming, they may describe him as a well-dressed and clean-shaven Santa Claus halfway through a crash diet.

He had wispy white hair, oversized ears, and knotted, lengthy fingers like insect legs. His face was coin-like, flat and round, with a hint of jowls forming where his jawbone ended. He wore a trim, well-fitting charcoal suit over a white collared shirt with a deep purple necktie, and a warm smile. Above that smile he had large, wide-set eyes behind wire-rimmed bifocals, topped with bushy white eyebrows that were upturned in their centers, giving him an expression that bordered on surprise, as if awaiting the punchline of a joke.

Lloyd Mnemic had arrived in Oak Hollow.

With a steady grace that may be unexpected given his poor posture and size, he moved through a back room that had once housed the Koenig family's grand piano. More recently, it had contained only clumps of dust, stray leaves, and ample cobwebs, until a massive executive desk and three antique chairs were delivered early in the day.

Lloyd Mnemic stood near this desk for a length of time, eyes closed and rubbing his hands together as if they were cold. They weren't. This was a conditioned mannerism he had adopted long ago, an attempt to fit in. To look more like *them*.

A few stitches' worth of sheep's clothing.

He opened his eyes and walked in a circle around his desk, pulling off the cloth sheet covering it, floorboards creaking as he stepped, each with a unique voice. It was good the furniture had arrived ahead of him because his first customer was calling already.

Events were beginning, right on schedule.

Mnemic sensed a man approaching death down the street from his new outpost, this being one of his many talents. Death reverberated through him whenever it loomed close, sent a pleasing tingle through his limbs. All his limbs.

It stoked his hunger.

When it was strong enough, he could tap into its stream, pirating signals. The reason for this ability was lost to time, but perhaps it had begun as a survival mechanism.

Death's signals were strong in Oak Hollow, a place rife with fear.

In this instance, he needed only to send a trite suggestion, short-circuiting a moment of indecision, then induce a single, forced step forward. Four minutes later, it was done. He had all the information needed to proceed and had turned an obstacle into an open pathway.

His true work had begun.

A service would be arranged soon, and Mnemic needed to be prepared. He would contact the widow shortly after she discovered the body.

He could sense both of his new agents nearby, as they should be. Waiting to cross paths with him.

Yes, there was much to do, and he was on a tight schedule. He'd left little margin for error this week. His time above ground was always limited (by necessity, not choice), as was his range of influence, and before anyone in this expiring little town realized what was happening, it would be too late. He'd be gone, taking with him everything he'd ever worked toward.

He scoffed to himself, thinking about their flimsy illusions of control and authority. Their regulations and laws, their licensing and politics and kickbacks and closed doors. He'd found a path through all these, although it meant adopting more of a smash-and-grab approach in this final phase than he'd prefer.

Their fear, which was the strongest it had been in generations, through his patient, timely, and undetected influence. He'd spent so long sowing the seeds for exactly what this specific town had become at this precise moment.

Now was the time to reap, and their fear would be his scythe.

Approaching the office's window, he looked down Asher Street. It was not quite dawn, the air was still, and the sun peeked from the horizon, infusing the clouds with an array of colors, pastel pinks and blues like a mix of cotton candy sweeping down from outer space.

He walked out through the office door, scanned the short hallway and two adjacent rooms. All traces of the years-long vacancy and bouts of vandalism had been erased.

His eyes returned polished, hardwood floors; a fresh, neutral paint scheme; controlled, tempered lighting. The space was warm, welcoming, and dignified. Televisions hung in several corners to display slideshows of the recently deceased in their best moments. Mnemic smirked a second time at how the families never included photos from the other real moments. The ones that would round out a life and make it three-dimensional.

In life, they have a cacophony of emotions. A spectrum of feelings and experiences. In death, though, they distill it down to one misleading and oversimplified component. Happiness and nothing else. They are quite eager to reduce themselves to such shallow and heartless displays when it's all over. And what would happiness be without pain? A diluted, unformed notion. A vague, untouchable distraction. Pain is a necessary part of the human experience. Yet they make such an effort to remove or deny it. Just as they deny death. They try to forget, but they are born to die.

It was not the first time he reminded himself of that, for this was the exact reason he'd come. Whereas the rest of his kind were content to wait for scraps, Mnemic was more proactive. More inventive. More planful.

Death as a business model is ingenious, he reminded himself. *Because* everything *dies. Everything.*

PRESTON CHEWS

D usk was gathering around the confines of the small park, and Preston Clark grew nervous as his perfect moment approached. This was his chance, his first real opportunity to pull it off and he couldn't lose sight of how important the timing was. The lighting, the movement, the surprise. Each had to be handled precisely or he would blow the whole thing.

He crouched behind a water fountain, positioning himself carefully to ensure he was ready when the time came. Of the options for hiding places, he'd decided this was the safest, the least likely one to be guessed. And there would only be one shot. It all came down to timing. Too slow and his target would slip by. Too fast and he'd divert attention to himself. He needed to do this . . . just . . . right.

Preston stared at the bride's face, some twenty feet away, walking toward him with her long white gown flowing and swishing behind her with each step, arm in arm with her groom. Checked his watch. Gauged the height of the sun as it faded over the horizon. Everything felt right.

He pounced, firing off a quick series of ten shots, all in one fluid motion. The newlyweds stopped in their tracks when they saw him move.

A few tense moments passed as the three of them stared at each other. Preston dropped the camera to his side, holding it one-handed.

"Well?" the groom asked.

Preston held the camera up to his eye, checking the small screen to review the shots. The first three were blurry, which was not surprising. The fourth was clear, but off-center. The composition of the fifth picture was close, but not good enough. The sixth was even better, but the effect he'd hoped for hadn't worked. His heart sank in his chest. He clicked the <**ADVANCE**> button once more and saw that the seventh shot was perfect. He smiled broadly and met the bride's eyes, then nodded.

She squealed and rushed to his side to check for herself.

Even in the thumbnail-sized picture, it was clear that what he'd promised her was true. He'd pulled it off.

The picture showed a completely authentic, candid moment between the newlywed couple, strolling through the park at dusk, and with the sun positioned at a precise angle behind them, her dress looked like it was glowing, as if lit internally.

The bride (whose name Preston couldn't quite recall anymore, Kayley or Kaylynn maybe?) gave him a hug. An actual hug from another human. Preston melted in her arms for an instant, a feeling he'd forgotten existed in this life.

"Thank you!" she said, her voice high and squealing. "It's perfect, thank you. It's just like you said."

The groom (whose name Preston didn't recall hearing once) clapped a hand on Preston's shoulder and he fought the urge to pull away from it. "I gotta say, man, when you told us you wanted to hide and jump out, and you wouldn't even tell us where you were gonna be? I just thought you were nuts. Gave me a definite stalker vibe."

"Th-that's . . . it," Preston said, stuttering. He tried to recall the last time he'd experienced physical contact from another person. "It's the first time. That it worked, I mean."

He had started his photography business recently, following months of job searching, and was close to giving it up already. In that time, he'd only had a handful of paying gigs: four in-home newborn shoots, a round of class photos for a middle school a few towns over, and one studio session involving a grown man and his three pet iguanas, all of them wearing matching capes (the lizards *and* the man). This was his first wedding, and he'd only landed it by promising the bride this one amazing, glowing-dress shot. Now he could add it to his portfolio and hopefully land more weddings, where there was actual money to be made. That would keep him from losing his apartment and being back on the streets.

Homeless was a familiar place, and though Preston knew he could survive it again, he feared what it would do to his already-weak resolve. The first time he found himself with nowhere to live was when his mother had abandoned him. The second time was when he fled from the house of his aunt (and legal guardian). He feared a third time would break him and end his burgeoning chance to live a normal life, permanently.

Kayley/lynn, still gushing, extended her hand to give the camera back to Preston. As she did, it slipped away, but she caught it in the opposite hand, pressing the shutter release and triggering the flash directly into Preston's eyes.

In that flash, he saw a clear mental image of himself smashing a claw hammer into the side of her head. It lasted no longer than the camera's flash, but it was complete. Fully formed. He saw the violent impact knocking her head sideways, contorting her neck before the momentum had traveled down to her shoulders. Heard the distinct *crack* of her skull fracturing and caving. Smelled the coppery blood released by the hammer. Sensed the obscene pleasure that such an act would provide him.

"Oh geez, I'm sorry," she said, breaking the daydream and bringing Preston's attention back. "Such a klutz."

He smiled at her, downplaying the full-body shudder that followed these violent images conjured by his mind and said, "No problem. You didn't even drop it, really."

Then there was a brief discussion of what came next (proofs, edits, final gallery, timing for all these). The young couple thanked him several times, the bride far more vocal about it. As their business concluded, he handed them his card, said he'd be in touch, and left.

As he walked out past the park's entrance, carrying three bags full of photography equipment and seeing streetlights turning on along the road leading toward his apartment a few blocks away, he steeled himself against the clicking sound in his head. It shouldn't be back yet, he knew this. It was far earlier than usual. But he also knew that flash-vision had awakened it.

Click . . . click . . . click . . . click . . .

This was the beginning of a predictable pattern, one he'd dealt with as long as he could remember. He walked faster, as if he could outpace it, and his focus wandered back in time to his first such flash-vision. It had been equally violent but more surprising and more exciting. He was a child, it happened at school during recess, a teacher calling his name, turning his head in response, sun reflecting off a metal playground slide and blinding him. In that instant he saw himself grabbing a female classmate (Pam Graeter, he still remembered her name) by her hair and slamming her face onto the blacktop, over and over, smiling while he did it.

He did not know where it had come from or what was wrong inside him to cause it. He had learned since that first time, though, that it was not normal for him to have these flash-visions—these violent, inhuman urges—and that after each one, came the clicking in his head, like a metronome of mounting rage and destruction. No, not a metronome because it wasn't that steady. It was more like a countdown timer, and with each *click*, a pressure built between his ears until he felt like his head would pop.

The clicking sound was the fingers of some shadow inside himself, tap-tap-tapping for attention.

That first recess incident was on a Friday, and the clicking had stayed with him throughout the weekend. Even as a child, he knew there must be something wrong with himself, something important was broken or missing inside, so he was too afraid to speak of it (especially to his single-parent mother, who terrified him despite not being around much).

It lasted all weekend and he went back to school on Monday, frazzled, exhausted, and aggravated. He'd smacked another boy across the face and been sent to the principal's office. As he sat awaiting punishment for his actions, he'd noticed the clicking was finally gone.

A violent vision triggered the clicking, and a violent act had stopped it. Like he was merely a capacitor: violence comes in, violence goes out, and in between he provided storage. The inner shadow craved violence, and each successive clicking episode became harder to end. Preston waged a steady war to keep from straying over the line separating man from monster.

He'd once pushed a teacher, nearly knocking him down the stairs, and that was the closest to causing a severe injury. After that, the clicking had stayed quiet for almost a year, causing Preston to wonder how long his peace would last if he brought a knife to school and used it on someone. Or if he went after his mother with a baseball bat. If he drew blood, would the clicking stay away longer than a few months? If he did permanent damage to someone, if he made scars, would it leave him alone for years? If he broke bones, would it be silent until he grew up? What would it take to get rid of the clicking permanently? If he killed someone, would it be gone or just come back stronger, craving more?

Click . . . click . . . click . . . click . . .

Preston arrived home, unlocked the building's front door and walked down a short flight of steps to his apartment on the lower level. He set his photo equipment down just inside the door and walked to the weight bench near his only window. Lifting weights didn't change the clicking at all, he'd learned that years ago, but it helped distract him in a minor way. He'd often marveled at how, even when it dragged on for days at a time, he never got used to that incessant noise in his head, as if it was less a sound and more a scraping along his live nerve endings.

Click . . . click . . . click . . . click . . .

Once he sat on the bench, he felt stronger. His muscles were tanks beneath flesh, primed and ready. He picked up one of his largest dumbbells, forty-five pounds of black metal, and started curling it toward his shoulder. Twenty reps, then switched arms, then back to the first arm. He completed six sets without slowing, feeling validation in his strength and slight distraction from the clicking for a few moments. It was early in this round of clicking, but the sound was already stronger than it should be. Soon, the lifting was not working as a distraction any longer, so Preston turned on his radio and tuned to a religious talk station, hoping the white noise of steady chattering voices would help. He sat cross-legged on the bare linoleum floor and stared ahead.

The voices swam in and out of his awareness, one male and one female, their discussion centered on a particular verse from Ephesians.

Click . . . click . . . click . . . click . . .

It was louder, faster, drowning out the voices now. Preston looked to the corner across from his bed, resigning himself to a different strategy to abate the sound. He was confident this one would help for at least a few hours. Perhaps he could even sleep awhile. But he usually preferred to save it for later in the cycle.

Click . . . click . . . click . . . click . . .

At this rate, saving it wouldn't be an option. In that corner was a stack of four shoeboxes, each a different brand. He'd fished these boxes out of a dumpster behind a shopping mall recently, transferring his collection from grocery bags with delicate precision. It was around the time Preston dropped out of high school that he realized he could collect certain special items to keep the clicking at bay temporarily, and since then he'd amassed quite a few samples. The top three boxes were full and easier to distinguish, even when closed—a row of damp discoloration formed a line around the bottom of each full box. Only the fourth box, underneath those, was still clean and dry. He would prefer to switch them to plastic containers, but most of his possessions (besides the camera equipment and weights) had been recovered from the trash, and he hadn't yet found any suitable tubs that were both opaque and still had their lid. That was also assuming he could keep his collection and add to it without getting caught. He hated to think what would happen if he got caught.

Click-click-click . . . click-click-click . . . click-click-click . . .

Preston stood, tilting his head slightly toward the right, away from the sound, and felt a small pain deep in his neck. The large muscles in his chest and arms clenched as he fought to maintain focus on the boxes.

The neck pain was commonplace, but leaning away from the sound was a more recent compulsion. It was involuntary, and if not for the pain, he may not even be aware he was doing it. He slapped the left side of his head a few times as if trying to reset a skipping record on a phonograph. His head stayed tilted.

He grabbed the filled shoebox from the top of the stack. It was a bold red-orange color, with a leaping jungle cat logo on the top and sides. The latest additions to his collection were inside. The box and lid were one attached piece of cardboard, so the lid folded up and down rather than coming off completely like most of the other boxes with separate lids. He put a hand beneath it, shuddering with pleasure at the damp, slick feel of the bottom. Its scarlet color became bloodred along the bottom few inches around the box. Its weight was already comforting him. This one was quite full. He lifted it up and down in the air with both hands a few times, admiring its heft but being careful not to drop it.

He folded the lid open and moved the box toward his face until his nose and cheeks were inside it, touching the still-moist contents. They were best when they hadn't dried all the way yet. The smell was stronger. Preston breathed deeply and smeared the contents of the box in a slow circle against his face. Breathing and smearing. Smearing and breathing. Feeling the texture, the coarseness. Smelling the muskiness of them all combining into a new but somehow primal and ancient scent.

Click . . . click . . . click . . . click . . .

It was already helping. Experience told him the sound would not leave completely, but he could dampen it for at least a day if he just kept giving it a taste of what it wanted. And when that wore off . . . he'd just have to acquire a new piece.

He turned and set the box down on the stained, bare mattress. Delicately, like one would set down a newborn baby. His eyes grew wide as he looked at the contents.

Preston licked his right thumb and index finger and reached into the box, pulling out a fiercely knotted clump of raven-black human hair, placed it in his mouth, and chewed as the crickets sang outside.

KATHERINE FINDS

Katherine Yost stood outside her home, blank-faced and unmoving. It was the first time she had ever stormed out of her own house. This act struck her as the type of dramatic farce some people may make frequently, but that was not her nature at all. She was known for being calm, good-willed, and even-tempered. So unfamiliar was she with the concept of storming out, that the second her soles had touched the driveway, she hadn't known what to do next.

For several minutes, she played back the fight with Shawn in her mind. As was typical, she blamed herself for how she had delivered the news more than blaming Shawn for his reaction to it. Surely, she had misrepresented it, or her enthusiasm had made him feel small, like she was making a major life decision without his input. Perhaps he'd felt attacked, he had always been sensitive about Oak Hollow, his home, and she should have known that asking him to leave would seem to him like she was insulting not just Shawn himself, but his whole family, their legacy, all their decisions and values. Her family was not originally from Oak Hollow, and during the years they'd been together he'd impressed on her how much the town and its community meant to the Yosts and vice versa. She'd never really internalized this, didn't feel how he felt, and it was easy to forget how sensitive he was about it. As if just using the town's name in the wrong context could serve as a trip wire to his worst defense mechanisms. So in an instant, they'd be in a heated debate she wasn't aware had begun, and he'd be shifting blame and taking cheap shots.

Yes, yes it must have been her fault things got so heated so quickly. He'd been on edge more than ever lately, unable to score any consistent income, convinced he was failing as a husband and provider. Even the odd jobs he'd been finding, helping neighbors and family mostly, had dried up weeks ago. He'd made a comment about it feeling like charity, with a pained look on his face and a crack in his voice. He'd run out of means, tapped the last of his resources. His home, his source of strength and identity, had turned sour.

And then she'd come sailing in, acting like she didn't need his help or his birthplace anymore. It must have been emasculating.

Soon, her anger had faded and she felt ready to face him, to apologize and try again, but she gave him a bit more time. When he was upset, he took longer to cool off than she did.

So she'd gone to the grocery store, knowing she'd have just enough time to pick up a few things and be home before the kids were out of school. That's what she did on her Tuesdays off, anyway. Yes, she'd make it up to Shawn with an elaborate dinner. A seasoned roast with russet potatoes and gravy from scratch, plus a few bottles of his favorite beer—a hazy IPA from the local Birdseye Brewpub. He'd love that, and with money having been tight for so long, they hadn't splurged on anything for months. It would be a treat, and with her job news, this should be a night to celebrate.

She returned home less than an hour later and set the bags of groceries on the kitchen counter.

"Shawn?" she called out, noticing how quiet the house was. She'd expected him to be playing some music in his study, a Zane Grey novel in hand, or maybe watching TV in the basement. "Shawn, honey? I'm sorry about before. Can we talk? I brought a peace offering."

When he didn't answer, she shrugged and started preparing the meal, wanting a head start before the kids came charging in from the bus any minute. Once the oven was preheated and the broiling pan inserted, she went to find Shawn, figuring he was still sulking, avoiding her to spare his pride any further wounding.

"I'm not mad anymore, really," she said, walking over to the study and seeing it empty. On his desk was a stack of receipts from the hardware store next to an open can of Diet Coke, implying he'd been there recently.

She called upstairs. "Honestly, Shawn, it was my fault."

No answer.

"Shawn?"

Most times when she came home, if he wasn't in the study, he was upstairs watching TV in bed. She didn't hear him, though, and walked up there to check. Their room was empty, as were both kids' rooms.

Could he be in the backyard?

She looked out a few windows but saw no sign of him outside, either.

"Where are you? Shawn?" she asked, louder than before.

She was about to try his cell when she remembered he'd been spending time in the basement recently. Their troubles had brought out a nostalgic streak in him and she'd found him down there again yesterday, looking through his old family photos, earbuds in, listening to grunge rock CDs.

She headed for the basement stairs.

"Shawn?" she said again, as she descended the last few steps. With no warning, the hairs on her neck stood. The basement air was charged, as if an electrical storm were approaching. Something was wrong, definitely wrong. Katherine looked toward the storage area at the back of the house's footprint, where she'd found him pining over those old photos and softly crooning along. Shawn was a terrible singer, but it didn't stop him from trying.

The door was closed, light spilling out from underneath, but it was still and silent. No, almost still and almost silent.

"Shawn? Are you down here?"

As she neared the entryway, she saw movement within the light coming from under the closed door. A shadow swinging side to side. She heard a small, rhythmic creaking noise.

Katherine pulled the door open, then screamed.

SATURDAY

WALTER CHATS

"I hate this damn town," Walter Sterling said, spying his neighbor, Mrs. Baker, tending her garden. It was true, at least in that dichotomous way where things can be true while the precise opposite is also true.

Walt loved Oak Hollow. It was home and always had been.

Everything familiar was here. Everything that mattered. It had been his late father's favorite place, and he'd lived all over the country. Right before Dad's death, he'd told Walt he was writing a book about Oak Hollow (most of his unfinished notes were still in the house). That's how strong his bond to the town was. Naturally, that endeared it to Walt himself.

But it was also claustrophobic, nosy, and judgmental. Most of the people living here were so interested in what everyone else did that it was difficult to leave his house unnoticed, like entering a minefield of gossip and listlessness. There were times he loathed the town and dreamed of leaving, but also times he wondered how it would be possible to live anywhere else. One moment, he admired it so intensely his chest would swell as he surveyed memories, and the next, he'd wish for a secret fault line to appear deep in its bedrock and reduce the whole fucking place to a crater. More than once, he'd pictured a massive sinkhole opening in the center of town and swallowing it all.

Coincidentally, many of those times were shoved together in small spaces and would toggle quickly back and forth. For instance, he looked forward to the Banana Split Festival every summer and was longing for someone to attend with later this year. Alone, he was easy prey for the busybodies who would say things like, "What rock have you been hiding under?" Or "We should catch up!" Or "Did you ever get that raccoon out of your attic?" as if it was any of their goddamn business.

This would be the first festival since his father died, and going had always been something they did together. They'd buy a few bottles of light beer, then meander down the rows of vendor booths, listening to live bluegrass music coming from the nearby bandstand while regarding the variety of homemade recipes (all prominently featuring bananas), craft items (most prominently featuring bananas), and vintage clothing (at least several prominently featuring bananas).

If he went to that festival without Dad's company, it wouldn't be long before someone pounced and started making small talk. Walt was terrible at small talk. Terrible at most talk.

Oak Hollow, being so small and tight-knit, set his comforts against his discomforts in just that manner frequently. They were often adjacent despite their contrast, like salt and pepper shakers in a closed cabinet.

Right now was one of those toggling moments.

The doorknob was half-turned in his hand before he noticed Mrs. Baker hunched over her rose bushes with her gardening visor on, gloved hands, holding a pair of shears and wobbling her wide ass like it was on a spring.

He was aware that waiting for the mail every day was catapulting him into the old man stratosphere, but today the latest issue of *The Magazine of Fantasy & Science Fiction* was out there. And he didn't want to get trapped with Mrs. Baker for twenty minutes, chatting about the weather or what her second cousin had seen his barber doing at the grocery store. That toll was a bit too high today.

Dad had loved that magazine and cultivated Walt's own deep admiration of it over the decades they'd lived together. The stories in it were one of the few things they could speak about at length. In all their time together, Walt and Dad hardly spoke. To most that may seem odd, but to Walt it felt natural, a by-product of their joint personality.

Dad (Walter Sterling, Sr.) had deftly handled the role of single parent all of his son's life, giving his only child (Walter Sterling, Jr.) everything he needed with a constant smile on his face. Dad washed and dried. He disciplined and he coddled, when each was needed. He worked and he cooked and he fixed the plumbing and he sewed torn clothes. He was always there.

To be fair, Walt was not a difficult child to raise, and by the time he was an adult, he had never considered living anywhere else. He wanted to be there for Dad the way Dad had been there for him. Through it all, there was little that needed to be said between them; most everything went unspoken.

Agreement was unspoken. Appreciation was unspoken. Respect too.

Love was unspoken.

These were all present, just not aloud. Not in words because those weren't needed, or so Walt had thought.

But now that he *couldn't* speak to Dad, now that it was no longer within his control, it left a gaping hole.

Yes, unspoken had been fine. But now, unspoken had mutated into *unsaid*, and that was different.

Unspoken could still be interpreted through nonverbal cues, or it could wait for later. Unspoken was in the present. Still within reach.

Unsaid was in the past. Permanent.

In an ironic twist of fate, an overactive part of his subconscious had taken to filling this hole by using Dad's voice to narrate moments of Walt's life. Just last week, he'd been watching TV when one of those obnoxious drug commercials interrupted, and just as the scene switched from a sunlit horseback ride to a boisterous high-five in a bowling alley, came Dad's spectral commentary.

Possible side effects include anal leakage, increased philology, and explosive onomatopoeia. Ask your pharmacist about Phonyalis today!

Whenever this happened—with increasing frequency the last few weeks—Walt would either shake his head in mock embarrassment or chuckle, depending on how effective the one-liners were. But he would also marvel at how Dad's absence was affecting him in ways he'd never have imagined, and being more vocal after death than he ever was in life was certainly a surprise.

Here Walt stood in the house, eight months after finding his father dead of a sudden heart attack in bed, wondering how the man had truly felt about his only son. What Walt had meant to him. If he'd been enough. If Dad was proud.

Compounding these regrets, Walt had also spent those eight months grappling with that most frequent of demons: grief.

One clear truth Walt had found was that grief didn't exist in stages as all the conventional wisdom holds. His grief wasn't a process, and it damn sure wasn't linear. It also wasn't a problem to solve or a chapter to close. Those were all too simple concepts. Grief was far more complex, more long-lasting, more omnipresent. It was a black granite orb sitting in his stomach. And with time passing, it wasn't getting any smaller, but maybe Walt was learning to grow larger around it to accommodate its permanent presence in his home. He hoped that much, but some days it was so hard to tell if he was making any progress.

At first, that orb had weighed him down constantly, making it a struggle to move most days. After the first few weeks, it morphed from a steady gravitational pull into erratic, crippling bouts, like a piano dropped from floors above. His legs would give and he'd fall, blind, dizzy, reduced to a blubbering mess. And this state lasted anywhere from a few minutes to half a day. More recently, these bouts were waning, but their severity and unpredictability had resulted in him spending all his time inside.

Having lived with Dad most of his adult life allowed Walt to retire early from BSL—luckily, just a few months before they announced the whole operation was moving away—and the house was now his, bought and paid for. Amazon deliveries took care of damn near every material need these days. He had TV, boxes of vinyl and CDs, a treadmill for exercise, and books, of course. Mountains of books. He even had groceries delivered to his door now.

He didn't want to think about words like *agoraphobia* or phrases like *crippling social anxiety*, but how far off were they?

So it seemed a small victory that he wanted to go outside to get the mail today.

"Damn it, she'll be out there for hours now, Cowboy," Walt said, looking away from the window to his eight-year-old greyhound, lying with his broad and lean frame on a dog bed shaped like a small green sofa, his head spilling off the side, fully perpendicular to his chest, and his tongue lolling out of his long snout. As usual, the dog had barely moved all morning, causing Walt to marvel at how a creature so sedentary could maintain something like two percent body fat underneath his white and brown-spotted fur. Cowboy's slim cheeks puffed out with the steady rhythm of his breath as he slept. His front feet twitched slightly and his one visible eyelid fluttered.

"Help me think of a way to slip past her, big guy."

Cowboy's only response was sleep.

Walt had met Cowboy at an adoption event three months ago. He'd never considered owning a dog, let alone one as deceptively large as a greyhound, but the dog's stillness had spoken to him.

He said something to the volunteer about greyhounds needing a ton of exercise, but she told him they were affectionately referred to as "40 MPH couch potatoes" because they slept eighteen hours a day and didn't even like going on walks over a mile long. Cowboy had looked up with big, soulful eyes without even moving his head, which was brown except for his long white snout. Then Walt had noticed his ears. One was pointed straight back, flat against his narrow skull, but the other appeared to be permanently creased across the middle so that it folded forward, pointing toward his nose. The pair sat atop his head opposite each other, like furry helicopter blades. Inside each ear, tattooed in blue ink, was a series of numbers and one letter, which the volunteer said signified Cowboy's racing number (66233) for tracking and betting purposes, and his birth date and whelping order (45B, 45 for April 2015 and *B* for second dog in the litter).

Walt had surrendered on the spot, signed the papers, bought a crate (which sat unused since) and a bag of dog food, and Cowboy came home with him that night. It didn't escape Walt's notice that, despite his inherent laziness, Cowboy was always nearby when grief took the upper hand. He'd lean against Walt's leg or stand by his head or lay down close enough so they were touching one another.

"Look at us," Walt said to Cowboy now, who had started woofing softly in his sleep while his feet twitched. "Just a couple of old retired dudes watching the mailbox."

He looked out the window again and was presented with an opportunity. The mail truck, having made it around the cul-de-sac and back to the front of his house, stopped. The mail carrier stepped out and Walt noted it was Margie Arnzen, one of two who typically brought his mail. She crossed the street, back to the side Walt's house was on, and approached Mrs. Baker. Walt knew Margie was a talker, and she'd previously told him this was the last street on her route. The two of them could chew the fat out there for much longer than it would take Walt to sneak out, grab his mail, and bolt back inside.

"Aha, that's it, boy!" Walt shouted, waking the dog up. Cowboy's head raised, his eyes glassy with sleep, one ear shooting straight up while the creased one folded sideways across the top of his head. Before he'd set his head back down, Walt was outside.

He ambled down the walkway toward the mailbox, an actor in a prison break scene, trying to look nonchalant and wholly aware he was failing because he was hurrying too much. He opened the mailbox, removed a bundle of letters and the *F&SF* magazine wrapped in a thick rubber band, turned back toward the house, and heard Mrs. Baker call to him.

"Walt Sterling!" she said. "What rock have you been hiding under?"

He gritted his teeth before looking across the yard to see the two women standing together, Margie waving him over.

His heartbeat became a *thud*.

"Good morning," he responded, then walked toward them, stopping six feet away, feeling like a small boy caught playing hooky and already flipping through escape plans in his head. One of his feet pointed itself back toward the house and safety.

"I haven't seen you out in weeks," Mrs. Baker continued. "How have you been?"

"Just fine, thank you."

"Well, how have you been holding up since, you know? Since your father passed." Margie asked.

"It . . . it's getting easier now," Walt said, hoping the lie would stymie a long line of potential questions related to the thing he least wanted to discuss with these women. *Just me and grief over here, like a predictable prime-time sitcom.*

"What have you been up to?" Mrs. Baker asked, then before he could answer, "Did you hear the big news, at least?"

"News? No, I don't think so."

"Oh my, you have been under a rock, then," Margie said, giggling in a manner unbefitting her age. "There's a new business opening, right over there on Asher Street."

"That's right," Mrs. Baker added. "Oak Hollow's recovery is finally starting."

The two women exchanged nods and mm-hmms.

"Everyone's talking about it." Margie continued. "It's the first new business to open here in years. Isn't that exciting?"

"Sure is," Walt answered, already questioning if it was as exciting as she implied.

"Times have been tough for so many, for so long," Mrs. Baker said. "And now there's hope again."

"That's right," Margie responded. "This town can get its spirit back, its work ethic. You know, as one of the few folks who kept steady work through this whole crisis, I'm glad to see others able to be productive again."

"All those BSL severance payouts dried up a long time ago," Mrs. Baker declared. "And if none of the able-bodied folks can find work, what's a person to do?"

Margie turned toward her so the two women faced each other, showing they'd forgotten about Walt standing there. "That's what I've been telling Bill, don't you know? All the old folks like us have just been scrimping by on Social Security, but the younger ones are all turning into miscreants. That's why there's so much drugs now. And all the theft."

"It's been getting scarier as the weeks pass," Mrs. Baker agreed. "That's for sure. Getting so a person can't even walk downtown alone without fear of some junkie or an out-of-towner showing up."

"That's why I carry this," Margie said, producing a small plastic rectangle from her pocket. She pushed a button on its side and electricity popped between two metal studs. "Pepper spray wasn't cutting it anymore."

"What kind of business is it?" Walt asked. While he waited for the answer, he wondered how many people Margie had pepper-sprayed, and why.

Mrs. Baker made a confused face for a moment, then looked to Margie for an answer. It occurred to Walt they'd probably been so busy talking about other people and the crime rates (which he agreed were more of a concern lately, even if these two squawking flamingos were exaggerating and acting on assumptions) that they'd missed the point of their own story.

"It's a funeral home," Margie answered.

"Oh. Well . . ." Mrs. Baker said.

"And it's right in that spooky old Koenig House, to boot." Margie continued.

"Oh. Well . . ." Mrs. Baker repeated, appearing to Walt like a dumbfounded parrot (more so than usual, even).

Walt, finding this notion to be clearly absurd and normally in great control of his impulses, said exactly what he was thinking before he could stop himself, "You think a new funeral home means the town's economic problems are ending?"

Margie gave him a wounded look, then stood more upright, clutching her canvas mail bag tighter. "I certainly do. Of course it won't happen overnight, I know that. But it's starting. It's a sign. A hopeful sign."

"Yes, it's the first pinprick of light at the end of the tunnel," Mrs. Baker added.

"Of course, you're right," Walt said, recovering his self-control along with his flight impulse. "I didn't mean to be rude. It's just, a funeral home didn't sound like a business that would mean new jobs. But I agree it will just be the first of many."

"Yes, yes it will," Margie said. "Business owners from all around will see that we're still strong here."

"Exactly," Mrs. Baker agreed.

"Well, if you ladies will excuse me, I need to go feed my dog."

"It was good to catch up with you, Walt." Mrs. Baker gave a small wave. "You should come outside more often."

Margie smiled. "Yes, it was good to see you."

Walt held up his bundle of mail and said, "Thanks." He was halfway back to his house when Margie called out to him.

"Oh, hey, Walt. You know my cousin Shawn, don't you? Shawn Yost?"

"Yeah, I do. Tell him I—"

"Well, he hanged himself the other day," Margie said, her voice flat and indifferent. "The viewing's at the new place on Asher, and the owner asked me to help spread the word because he hasn't even finished fixing it up yet. Monday at nine a.m. Hope to see you there."

MYRTLE STEALS

The doll caught Myrtle Fallsworth's eye before she was halfway down the aisle. She felt the urge to jump, but her old bones wouldn't appreciate that, so she settled for a single clap of her hands, along with an enormous, cheek-splitting smile. The doll wasn't there yesterday, it must have just arrived, and now sat on a shelf at eye level with a two-inch buffer of open space surrounding it, as if it had been waiting for her, shoving the neighboring junk aside for fear of being missed.

But how could she miss such a beautiful piece?

She reached forward, the back of her fingers gingerly grazing its rosy porcelain cheek, greeting it like she would a small dog, giving it a chance to get accustomed to her before she approached it in earnest. Its hair was perfectly curly and chestnut brown, a direct match. And its darling white dress with the ruffled collar and billowy sleeves, lacy socks, and shiny shoes, all these were just what she had pictured little Rosita wearing.

Sweet Rosita.

Her angel-child.

The cherubic doll even had her green eyes.

Myrtle picked it up, turning it over in search of the small paper price tag. This thrift store usually either attached those with a bit of string or wrote the price somewhere discreet with a black marker. *Please, no,* she thought, *don't mark this gorgeous baby anywhere.*

But she needn't worry, the price tag was attached to the back of its skirt with a small safety pin. Myrtle breathed a sigh of relief. The pin would not leave a noticeable hole. She looked the doll over thoroughly, inspecting for any blemishes, scratches, or other indignities it may have suffered from previous careless owners. She sneered as she considered what horrible things may have befallen this one before today, or what terrors could pass had she not found it now.

No one will care for this like I will, she reminded herself. "Don't worry," she said to it. "You're safe now, dear heart. You'll come home with me to get all fixed up."

She left her cart in the aisle—no sense in risking any harm to her new prize—so the doll sat cradled against her chest as she walked to the checkout. Along the way, she stopped twice to adjust the anti-embolism stockings around her calves.

The store had just opened for the day several minutes ago—her favorite time to hunt for treasures, when the best items were still freshly displayed and undiscovered—and there was no one in line.

Cassie was behind the counter because it was Saturday, and Myrtle smiled like a victorious fox safe in its den as she eased the doll onto the counter, so proud of her find. Without speaking, Cassie moved her hand toward it as if it were any random tchotchke off the rack. Myrtle gasped, startling the cashier who gave her an annoyed glance.

"I was just—" Cassie said.

"Well don't!" Myrtle interrupted, her voice a small blade through the air. "I know just where the price is and I don't want you soiling this."

"Fine," Cassie replied, pulling both hands back from the counter and holding them at shoulder height with her palms facing the customer, surrendering in apathy.

Myrtle used two fingers on her good hand to gently pull the price tag from under the doll's pristine white dress. When she checked for the tag before, she was so relieved it hadn't marred the doll or its dress that she neglected to look at the amount written on it. Seeing it now caused a panic.

Six dollars was more than she had to spend.

"Oh no," Myrtle said, more to herself than not. "I only have four and some change left for the week."

Cassie made another move to grab the doll, like a bullish man reaching for some filthy socket wrench or a woman's thigh. Myrtle shot her hand out, stealing the doll away without a second to spare. That bitch had almost touched it.

"No, it's mine."

"Myrtle, I'm sorry, but it's *not* until you pay for it. I can hold it for you. The usual forty-eight hours?"

Myrtle glared, hunching over with the doll clasped to her chest. She made a small hissing noise as she turned and walked back to the toy aisle.

Cassie stooped down to pick up some plastic bags and placed them on the metal rack next to the register. Then, with no other customers in the store, she stepped through the door behind the counter and into the office.

Seizing the opportunity, Myrtle whisked by the checkout and out the front door, the doll still clutched to her chest.

She didn't have far to go and was glad the doll did not need any preparation. It only needed that dirty price tag removed; the rest was immaculate. Pristine. It was ready.

Her bus arrived quickly, which was a relief. She didn't think the cashier saw her stealing, and the doll held far more value for her purposes than to sit on that filthy, crowded shelf a moment longer, but still, she wanted to take no further chances. God had seen fit to send her this gift and she would let no one take it away.

Soon, she pulled the stop cord and got off the bus, stood on the curb, and held a hand to her forehead to block the beaming sun so she could check the street name. Vine Street, the 400 block. She was in the right place and smiled to match the doll's porcelain face.

She strode down the sidewalk, careful not to swing her arms or jostle her dear cargo. Little Rosita would wait for her, most certainly.

The house came into view, and Myrtle heard children's voices—no better sound in the world. It rejuvenated her more than any substance or sensation, quickening her pace as she approached the walkway to visit with her sweet Rosita once again. She paused, only to adjust her stockings once more.

"Hello?" she called out, waving one hand and cradling the doll in the other. "Hello? Rosita?"

The girl was in the driveway, crouched by a toy car. Dressed in jeans and a T-shirt again as if she were a boy, but that was a matter for another time. She heard Myrtle's voice and turned slightly toward it, then caught herself mid-motion, stopping abruptly and staring ahead with the eyes of a squirrel waiting until the coast was clear.

"Rosita, sweetie, I have something for you."

The girl gave another glance around, but as Myrtle neared, she stood and ran toward the house without responding. When she got to the porch she yelled, sounding panicked, "Momma! Momma! She's back. That lady is back again!" She opened the door and ran through as if being chased.

Myrtle remained in the driveway, in the same spot Rosita had been playing, holding the doll out and humming quietly as she scoffed at the blue toy car near her feet.

She'll be right back, Myrtle thought. *Probably went to get me some juice or a piece of butterscotch like last time.*

The house's screen door shot open, and it wasn't Rosita coming out, but a grown woman. Her eyes were wild with fury, tight curls bouncing as she came down the front steps.

Myrtle sneered, pulling the doll back toward herself to protect it.

"How many times do I have to tell you?" the woman yelled, as she headed toward the driveway. "Stay away from my family, you crazy old bitch!"

Myrtle looked puzzled and opened her mouth to speak.

"No. Don't," the woman said, cutting her off. "I don't want to hear it anymore. I've tried to be nice to you, lady. I really have, but you just don't get it, do you? Her name is *not* Rosita, and you are *not* her mother. How many times do I have to tell you that? Just turn around and leave right now, or I'll call the police." She held up a cell phone demonstratively.

Myrtle was confused, unsure how to respond to this unexpected scene. She had arrived with such a perfect, beautiful gift, expecting to be welcomed, not shouted at. Whomever this woman was, she at least had to appreciate how much the doll resembled the sweet little girl. But Myrtle could see this person had no grace. No interest in discussing it like civilized adults. Myrtle turned and left, choosing not to validate the other woman's insane rambling with a response. She had nothing but time and could come back tomorrow when this belligerent, interfering person wasn't around. Then, she could give the doll to her precious baby girl. She scolded herself for rushing over here, but she had been too excited about the doll and acted brashly. That caused this scene, nothing more.

She walked away, pulled the doll closer to herself, and turned her chin up triumphantly, already knowing the perfect time to return and try again. A time when Rosita would be all alone.

As she left the property and moved a few houses away, back toward the bus stop, the other woman called after her. "Next time, no warning. I'll dial nine-one-one before you set a foot near my daughter. You hear me?"

Myrtle headed around the corner to make sure she was out of sight. She walked past a few buildings, then sat on a bench outside the spooky old house on Asher Street.

The one all the schoolchildren whispered about.

She had never been afraid of that house, like most others were. In fact, she felt drawn to it, as she walked by frequently on her way to church. She realized she had never noticed a bench there before today. It seemed a perfectly good place to sit and gather oneself after such a humiliating display and the indignity of it. Yes, it was a delightful little bench. Maybe she would come back with her knitting soon.

She felt better quickly, and a wonderful thought occurred to her, seemingly out of nowhere, as if someone was speaking to her. There was no one around, but this thought arrived in a man's voice, strangely.

Rosita needs you. She is just confused; you know how easily children can become confused. You can rescue her from that woman's influence. Make it right. She needs you now more than ever.

Well, yes, she thought back. *I must make it right.*

Your baby girl is counting on you, Myrtle, the phantom voice confirmed. *Don't give up. You mustn't fail. Come back and save her.*

"A girl needs her mother," Myrtle said. She sat on the bench for hours without moving, except to blink and stroke the doll's fine hair. Then she walked back around the corner to Rosita's house, gave the doll a kiss on the cheek, and left it on the porch.

As she walked away, she hummed the melody to "You Are My Sunshine."

KATHERINE VIEWS

Minutes after finding her husband's lifeless body hanging from a thick, coarse rope tied around a support beam in the corner of their house's basement, Katherine Yost received a helpful, if not unexpected, phone call from a man named Lloyd Mnemic.

She'd answered in a haze and this Mr. Mnemic—in a voice like honey, smooth and clean and reassuring—had identified himself as the owner of a new funeral home nearby. He then offered his condolences, which felt sincere even through a cell phone speaker. And though his words held more suggestion than authority, she had done what he said with a measure of unearned trust. It was a relief to be told what to do just then.

"The children should spend the night with their grandparents," he'd said. "Have your mother pick them up from school."

"Okay," she'd answered. (Probably. Hard to recall her own side of the exchange now.)

"You don't want them to see what you've seen. And it will give you time to think about how to best break the news to them."

Hey, kids, pause that YouTube video for a sec. I've got some bummer news about Dad.

That thought had stayed with her since, but before it could break her, he'd continued speaking through the phone, "You should stay there, too, of course. In the morning, come to my funeral home on

Asher Street. You'll know which building, I'm certain. We can start making arrangements then. One thing I'd like you to know right now, is that I do not charge for my services. Not a solitary coin. I'll take care of everything. You don't need to call anyone else. I'll notify the authorities for you. Go be with your family, Katherine. That's all that matters right now."

It was only after she'd hung up that it occurred to her how odd it was that he'd known exactly when (and how) to call her. Her phone rang in her pocket practically before Shawn's body was done swinging.

If not for the received call from Mnemic Family Funeral Home in her phone's history log, she might have thought she'd imagined it.

She left her parents' house before dawn while everyone else slept. Mnemic was right, she knew which house she'd find him in. But first, she drove aimlessly up and down every street along the way, trying but failing to organize her thoughts. Hesitating to process these events, or to face what she must, or even to approach that monstrous house.

But her own home was far more monstrous now.

Wasn't it?

Which was why she ultimately decided to go to Asher Street. To listen and trust this Mr. Mnemic, rather than process or handle Shawn's death on her own. And wasn't that what funeral directors are for? The handoff? They deal with all the grisly bits and tedious details so you can grieve, can heal?

Even though she decided to take his offer, she felt unsettled by the timing and nature of that phone call and decided she'd at least ask how he knew when to call. She supposed there could be ways to find her number if he was industrious enough, but how had he known what Shawn had done?

He couldn't have been dead for more than a few hours, and he was in their basement. There was no way anyone could have seen him before she did. The past twelve hours had been a gauntlet of shock, tragedy, and turmoil. Every cell in both her head and heart seemed to scream incoherently, but this sense of unease lay overtop everything like a blanket.

How had this Mr. Mnemic known?

She parked and walked to the porch, rang the doorbell.

When he answered the door, Mr. Mnemic appeared quite similar in person to the image in her mind when he'd called.

"Mister—" she made to address him, but he waved her words aside.

"Please, call me Lloyd," he said.

The first thing she noticed was his height. Katherine was not tall, perhaps an inch or two below average by her own estimation. Yet she felt like she towered over this man, at least a full head taller.

She guessed his age as late seventies, and his expression was pleasant, calm, almost grandfatherly. There was a deep stillness about his face. An implication that he could stay that way until you were ready. And rather than offer a hollow platitude like "I'm so sorry for your loss" or "God needed another angel," Mr. Mnemic (Lloyd) said nothing, letting his expression and stillness speak for him.

His face read, "Take all the time you need. I'll be right here."

They stayed that way for several minutes, perhaps longer. Katherine breathed deeply, in and out, searching for words without the conviction to find them. She had no energy for introduction or small talk. This was no normal greeting, and she didn't care to pretend it was.

Her gaze settled on the warped floorboards of the porch, moved to the scant traffic up and down Asher Street, to his eyes briefly, then away again. Her own eyes were heavy and drained, like coral left in the sun. She felt no pressure from him, no expectation to move or speak.

Instead, there was something growing in her heart that could actually be a micron of relief.

Eventually, he reached to put a hand on her shoulder and she leaned in closer. His touch felt different, in a good way, open and unassuming, as if he were simply conveying his presence and respect, rather than urging her to give anything in return.

"I'm glad you came," he said, breaking the long silence. "This must be so difficult for you."

She collapsed forward then, sobbing so loudly it was more like screaming. He kept his hand placed firmly, right there on her shoulder until she could stand upright again.

He said nothing else as he brought her inside the house (the remodeled interior a stark contrast from the way it looked outside) and led her to his office. Lloyd gestured toward a pair of chairs on the near side of the desk. They appeared both high-end and antique, made of pristine cream-colored upholstery and elaborately carved, dark wood clawed feet, gnarled ends at the armrests, and scrolling along the back.

Katherine sat, and rather than going behind the desk, Lloyd took the adjacent chair and leaned toward her with his elbows on his knees and his hands folded. It seemed an informal posture, warm and welcoming, as if he intended to ask about her upcoming vacation plans, rather than discussing how to haul her husband's dead body from their basement and put it in a box for their family and friends to stare at.

As he spoke, his voice was more soothing in person than on the phone and somewhere in the first part of their conversation, she forgot to ask how he'd known about Shawn's death so quickly.

"I hope the exterior of the home wasn't too off-putting," he said, once they'd sat down. "I have the renovations all planned, but of course, these things take time."

Katherine nodded distractedly.

"But again, I'm very glad you came, and I want to say that I appreciate the trust it's taken just to meet with me. There is much to be done, but I assure you, if you're willing to allow me, I intend to take care of nearly everything for you. This is what I do, and I've done it for a very long time. And as a quick reassurance up front, I've taken the liberty of contacting all the proper authorities. The necessary steps are already underway, the paperwork and official matters dealt with. Custody of your husband will be transferred to me soon, so that I may transport him here and begin caring for his remains."

The word "remains" struck her like a fist and she fought against a fresh bout of sobs. While she did, Lloyd took her hand in his, leaning forward so far it looked like he may fall out of his chair if nudged. It was an awkward and humanizing pose, which he held while speaking, "You've taken such amazing care of him, Katherine. And of your children. Let me help you now."

She nodded again and managed a choked "Th-thank you."

"Before we discuss anything further, I just want to confirm. Are you comfortable with me taking over from here? You have my word that I will consult you on any matters that should require a decision, and I reiterate that I've done this many, many times before. Also, as I explained over the phone last night, it is my personal mission to provide everything needed free of charge. So, are you comfortable proceeding that way?"

She considered this question more so than the rest of his words to this point. Did she have trust in this man? Sure, he spoke with confidence and displayed both knowledge and expertise. Finesse, even. And having everything provided for free was more mercy than charity, under the circumstances. But did that mean he had no agenda of his own? He was a stranger, albeit a compelling one. It would be so easy to trust him given the circumstances, but was that a sign of a con or was she truly so lucky to have him arrive at just the right time, in just the right way?

"Is that how these things are normally done?" she asked, failing to mask her suspicion.

"You're quite observant," he answered. "That's not exactly the conventional approach. But I'd be lying if I said I put much faith in convention. No, I have my own methods. And while those are a stark change from how these things are 'normally done,' as you put it, I assure you that I have refined every facet of the process through years and years of practice. And I have seen its benefits time and time again. To be frank, you're in no mental state to be weighed down with all the minutiae and tedious details. It's too much, and I'd like to help. That's what I do."

After debating silently for a few moments, her better judgment won out long enough to ask him a question of her own in response, "How . . . how do you know so much about me? About us?"

He seemed taken aback, tilting his chin toward his chest and furrowing his brow. His smile changed to a small pout. She regretted the question immediately and decided not to ask any others. She needed help too badly to look this gift horse in the mouth.

Lloyd regained his composure, and the look of uncertainty faded from his face.

"I know only what you told me over the phone, Mrs. Yost. I apologize if I've come across as too forward, though. It makes sense if our conversation last night is unclear. You were understandably distraught. I've been at this long enough that most of the smaller points are honed to instinct and I tend to act quickly. Not to sound trite, but I could handle many of the details in my sleep." He laughed, deep and strong. More shocking than that, she laughed back. A quick *ha ha ha* that fell just short of morphing into more sobs.

"There, now," he said. "I know it sounds incredible, but you'll see there's still reason to laugh, given enough time."

"So what happens now?"

"Well, the primary decisions at this point are around what type of service to hold. Given the number of Catholic families in Oak Hollow, I would suggest a traditional viewing and burial. Though, we have other options, should you wish to discuss those instead."

"A viewing? Is that . . . is that where the coffin sits in the room and people just walk up all day?"

"That's about the gist of it, yes. We can control how long it lasts, so it doesn't need to be 'all day.' And I expect we'll want a casket rather than a coffin, though I don't think the difference is important at this point."

"A Viewing," she repeated, subjectively capitalizing the word. She knew that was the custom. The expectation. It's what his family would want, surely. She didn't understand why, though. It was an odd ritual: hiring someone to pump him full of preservatives like some gruesome human shaped balloon so they could all stand around and gawk, eating finger sandwiches.

Katherine had been to her share of funerals, but the last was close to twenty years ago. Her Uncle Marvin's during which her mother, clearly overtaken with her own grief, had forcibly dragged little Katherine across the room and pushed her hand inside until it touched his. "If you don't say goodbye now, you'll never have another chance," her mother had sobbed, projecting her own regret. That memory rose now, drawing her eyes through the open doorway toward the chapel across the hall.

This misunderstanding of the dead-body-gawking step was strongest now because she'd been plagued by flashes of Shawn hanging from that beam. Up there, he still resembled himself. His lifelessness was too fresh to change his appearance yet, but that didn't mean she wanted to keep looking. Soon, though, she'd have to stand next to his waxy, stiff doppelgänger for hours and stay focused so she could listen to empty consolations, all the while willing her mind to quit parading images of him hanging in the basement.

For a few moments, while she pondered all this, the room was silent, and if Lloyd was uncomfortable at all, he did not show it. There were a thousand words in Katherine's mind but none would fit in her throat, so she looked out the only window in the small room, away from the chapel, gazing down Asher Street at the fading sun, begging it to burn the image of Shawn's dead face from her retinas.

"I do feel," Lloyd said, breaking the silence to her relief, "this is one of the most difficult parts. Getting started, taking it seriously, deciding. What has happened to your family is … unspeakable, and yet we must speak of it at length. I certainly do not mean to make light of your tragedy. I intend only to confirm that it can be infinitely more difficult to pull your mind away from certain … imagery—

A flash in her mind to Shawn's shadow swinging beneath the closed door, the steady creaking of the rope, the precise moment she … knew

…

—in order to deal with official matters." Lloyd reached toward the desktop, grabbing a stack of papers, "These things"—he waved them to his side in a dismissive manner, shrugging his shoulders— "require attention, but not necessarily yours."

Katherine nodded, still sobbing, while the vision in her head changed back to Shawn's face, wrenched and swollen and purpled, spittle dangling from his parted lips, eyes open wide and filled with burst capillaries.

"Another part of my expertise," Lloyd said, "is to comfort." As he spoke, her mind's eye punctuated each sentence with flashes from happy moments.

There's Shawn, splashing in a swimming pool on our last family vacation.

"That is why I am here . . . to bring comfort."

Now Shawn telling Trevor a dirty limerick and making him swear not to tell his younger brother.

"Oak Hollow needs comfort, as I'm sure you'd agree."

Shawn used to take us on those Sunday morning hikes in the state park.

"I have experience which I can use to help."

We'd all protest, but he knew we'd have fun. And we did. We'd hike for miles and no one complained at all.

"I have been to . . . several towns much like this, you understand, and I feel I can be of some service. To you, most urgently, of course."

The slideshow in her mind shifted back to Shawn's hanging corpse as Lloyd's words slipped past her ears in that silky, lilting voice. She realized his body would be moved soon. Had it been already? Was it lying on a table under her feet right now? Blue. Unmoving. Naked.

"As I've said," Lloyd reiterated, "I can handle the great majority of decisions that need to be made, but I need to discuss one or two smaller matters with you first."

"Sure."

"The announcements for the service will go out immediately, and it will be held the day after tomorrow, assuming you have no objection. I've notified some of his family already."

Why wait until then? she thought as she nodded again. *I'm holding the Viewing right now, if anyone wants to join me. I'm Viewing him while I'm sitting here because I'm Viewing him always while I'm doing everything. I don't want to <u>hold</u> a Viewing, I want to <u>stop</u> it.*

Lloyd smiled and raised one eyebrow as if he'd heard that thought. "It's so unpleasant to think of, I know," he said. "But like all unpleasantness, it is best dealt with swiftly. Is there some specific clothing you'd like him to wear? I will locate it when we pick him up."

"He only has one suit. It should be in our bedroom closet, upstairs, still in the dry cleaning bag."

"Thank you. Is there any sort of personalization you'd like me to do for the viewing?

"Personalization? What do you mean?"

"For example, any pictures you'd like displayed or made into a slideshow. Or perhaps some cherished items we can set near the casket?"

At that, Katherine pictured herself carrying a cardboard box filled with some of Shawn's baseball memorabilia and Western adventure novels, then removing and setting these items gingerly around an open casket in that chapel across the hall. That prompted a fresh, bird's-eye image of him lying dead and nude in a dark room below her, nothing but a few sheets of plywood separating them, an angry ligature mark around his neck. She fought for an answer but couldn't find one.

Lloyd waved his hand as if swatting another question away. "I apologize again. Of course now is not the time to think about that. I'll make sure we gather some items from your home and we can consider them together a bit later. What else? Ah, yes. At the risk of being presumptuous, I've already arranged for him to be interred at St. Mark's, right here in Oak Hollow. Does that sound appropriate? If not, we can easily adjust."

"Yes, actually. I know that's what he would have chosen. He . . . he never wanted to leave this place. It was a sore subject between us."

"Say no more. Now he doesn't have to leave. Ever." Lloyd offered a smile, pulled a tissue from a box on the desk, and offered it to Katherine.

She took the tissue. A detached creaking sound came from down the hall, as if a door had closed on its own. It was probably common in a house of this age, the structure settling or the wind finding a gap to make its entry, yet it startled her. It was too much like the sound Shawn's rope had made.

Katherine was suddenly desperate to leave. Even if none of the old stories and rumors she'd heard about it were true (*What if even one was true?*), it was a place of death now. She didn't want to be inside it for another second, knowing she'd spend ample time here with Shawn's body soon enough. She didn't want to be in Oak Hollow, in this life. She felt like she was in her own coffin already. Or was it a casket? Lloyd would probably explain the difference if she dared ask.

He stood. "I think I have what I need for now, so I won't keep you any longer. I can't imagine how hard this is for you, Mrs. Yost. Or for your children. And I will do everything that I can to help."

He reached down, looking into her eyes, taking one of her hands in both of his. Katherine stood also, charged by his touch, which was markedly different from when he'd placed his hand on her shoulder before, and the first time he'd held her hands. Her urge to escape multiplied. His eyes were still warm, his smile looked genuine, and yet there was something about the feel of his hands on hers this time that jump-started alarm bells deep in her brain. For an instant, fleeing was all that mattered, and it wasn't about Shawn's death, or about Viewing him and burying him, or about haunted house stories, or about facing her children again. No, it was all about this man touching her, about his intentions for her, whatever those may be. His words offered condolence, his eyes foretold support, his face displayed warmth, and yet his touch conveyed a completely different story now. Something primitive in her cried out that she was in danger. There was a sense of loss, more fresh than losing her husband, this was loss of *self*. A blip of energy passed between their enclosed hands. It felt as if, when Lloyd touched her, he took a part of her into himself. A small part, but a very important one.

She pulled away, hoping he would not notice the urgency in her motion, and then the desire to escape was gone, any memory of it fading *away* and replaced by scenes of her husband's suicide, and Lloyd was leading her, foggy-brained and bleary-eyed, back through the hallway and onto the porch of 432 Asher Street.

He said something about contacting her tomorrow, but most of his words were lost amid the residual creak of the rope she'd seen wrapped around Shawn's neck.

PRESTON RESISTS

Despite the early reemergence of the clicking inside him, like a socket wrench connected to his central nervous system that kept twisting all night, ratcheting him tighter, Preston slept. Some. It wasn't much, but it helped, and it came only after he spent hours pinching and smelling wads of discarded human hair, then chewing each like a cow with a mouthful of cud.

Click . . . click . . . click . . . click . . .

When he woke, the sun was cresting, and he assumed he'd been asleep no more than two hours. He walked to his bathroom, cold tile underfoot, pulled the Percocet bottle from the medicine cabinet, shook out three, and swallowed them dry. He did this because, although it was partially satiated by exposure to the hair, he knew the clicking would not leave. And each time it came back he would attempt to take away its power by interfering with its vehicle. He couldn't touch the source of the sound, but he could muddle his brain so it received less efficiently. It would only get stronger until he gave his inner shadow what it really wanted, but sometimes the pills would turn its volume down for another few hours.

The next stalling tactic was acquiring a new sample for his collection, which would last longer. Doing so required careful planning. And patience. Without those, he was likely to be caught, arrested, and then there would be no turning it off.

Click ... click ... click ... click ...

Discarded hair fascinated him, for two reasons. The first, and more basic, was the texture. In particular, the variety from one ... donor to the next, but also the way it felt against his most sensitive parts. Inside the mouth was his favorite, but there were others, and he expected to use them all today as he fought against the inclining and inciting drone of the clicking. The second reason, both related and more fulfilling, was how each individual strand had once been attached to a living, breathing person without ever being alive itself. And in that way, when he touched it, he could also touch them, without the person knowing he was touching them. He spent most of his time with the collection doing just that, touching it. Losing himself in the feel, between his fingers, against his crotch, along his cheek. Inside himself. Sometimes it was enough just to think about the feel of it to make him shudder with pleasure.

Hair was born dead, and that's what he loved most about it.

It was so much like him. It was his kin.

Click ... click ... click ... click ...

And then there was the thrill of the hunt, equally important in its own way. Finding some cache of this wonderful material knitted by another human's body and then shed to become its own separate form of stillborn life. Discarded, so close to life but never enough to become alive itself. Life-adjacent. Humanlike, but also not human at all.

He'd gasp upon seeing a well-used hairbrush in a bedside drawer. Or feeling a dry, coarse clump snarled inside a garbage can. The best was the clean, wet payload inside of most drains. That's where the purest crop was found, and shower or bathtub drains were the most reliable. That was his favorite hiding place, by far, made even more special by the extraction process. When it happened just right, he could pick up one stray piece, tug gently and evenly and patiently like a deep-sea fisherman fighting for that once-in-a-lifetime glory, as the blissful seconds ticked by and all the pressures and stresses and teeth of this world retracted, fell silent in anticipation with him, until that lone valiant piece led to an unearthed and complete artifact of recent human memory and a form of life that was never truly alive nor dead. The sensation of a fine, wet clump finally pulling loose and sliding up from the netherworld into clear view was incomparable.

The first time he had fished inside a shower drain with a dull pencil, he'd brought up a lovely fat clump of his Aunt Vickie's wiry brown hair. How he had marveled at the single gray strand woven throughout like some albino hidden within a herd of wild beasts for protection.

Aunt Vickie never wanted me, he thought. *But when Mom abandoned me in that mall parking lot, there wasn't any other option.*

For hours, he had stood next to an oil stain his mother's car left on the blacktop, made iridescent by the fading sun—the only sign she'd ever been there—waiting for her to come back. Instead, a policeman had come, asked a series of questions to which Preston had no answers, then stuffed the boy unceremoniously into the front passenger seat, handed him a stick of mint gum that was too hard and too old and too strong for a child, and drove him to an office where a series of adults asked him more questions he couldn't answer.

Aunt Vickie was the only family he had, and she had taken him in until he was old enough that she could force him out—sixteen was her magic number.

She said from the start that I gave her the creeps. So when she told me to leave, I didn't bother arguing. I put some clothes and food in a backpack and walked out on Christmas morning.

Since then, he'd been living under bridges or in alleyways and panhandling near highway on-ramps with a cardboard sign, eating anything he could salvage from dumpsters behind restaurants and convenience stores. Three months ago, he had saved enough for a deposit on his apartment and his first camera.

The photography business was his key to a normal life. Maybe his last chance to stay human.

Click . . . click . . . click . . . click . . .

The minimal sleep last night was a small miracle, but the Percocet wasn't helping. There were other stalling tactics he could try, had tried many times: ripping cloth, swinging an ax or hammer, smashing things with rocks, but they would only waste energy and build frustration. As a child, he had killed a small animal occasionally (Aunt Vickie first grew suspicious after his third pet gerbil "escaped," and then caught him just before the act of butchering a garter snake he'd caught in the garage using a glue trap), but somehow there was still a part of him that actively fought against going further down that path. If he didn't become a monster, maybe someday his mom would come back.

If he was still human, maybe he could go home.

He may be broken, plagued by the inner shadow and wholly unaware of its origin, but he was not some inhuman, unfeeling psychopath, and he wouldn't allow the inner shadow to turn him into one.

Clickclick . . . clickclick . . . clickclick . . . clickclickclick . . .

As his resolve wavered, the clicking sped up.

Preston needed a new sample. Today. Luckily, he had done some scouting previously, knowing a day like this would come, eventually. He'd dreaded it, and it was much sooner than he'd expected, but at least he was not completely unprepared.

Tonight, there would be a fresh addition to that scarlet box atop the stack in the corner.

Clickclickclick . . . clickclickclick . . . clickclickclick . . . clickclickclick

A blonde one, from Kayley/lynn, the bride.

Come nightfall, the clicking had evolved from a noise in Preston's head to a physical sensation, a knifepoint tapping at the top of his spine. It had also sped up and grown louder.

Clickclickclickclick . . . clickclickclickclickclick . . . clickclickclickclick . . . clickclickclickclickclick . . .

The wait for darkness to fall outside had been awful, and it seemed no matter how many of his samples he played with, felt, tasted, his inner shadow was urging him further and faster than ever before. He spent the day lifting weights and fighting against flash-images of himself murdering anyone and everyone that arrived in his memory, in increasingly aggressive, violent, and bloody ways. He saw himself hacking at limbs, severing digits, slicing skin, biting and grinding bones, smashing organ meat, ripping muscles and tendons with his bare hands, and all the while, he knew this was what the inner shadow wanted from him. It was calling for its bloodlust to be satisfied and would stop the clicking only when he complied. Maybe for good this time. And he could choose anyone, it reminded him. It would not discriminate amongst targets.

Still, his resolve held minute to minute because he had one last chance to abate it. He only needed to wait for the cover of darkness.

When it arrived, he was quite ready.

Then his mind was a steel trap holding only two images. The Shell station across town—where he could duck into a short alley for cover, climb a chain-link fence and be in her yard before anyone noticed him—and a healthy clump of detached blonde hair.

He was walking through the heart of Oak Hollow and his plan was on track. In less than an hour, all would be well again, if only for a short time. He could keep the inner shadow at bay for another round while he worked to build a normal life.

He turned onto Asher Street, dark storefronts lining both sides as he beelined across town with his objective firmly in focus.

Then a light came on a few buildings ahead of him, on the first floor of that house everyone had sworn was haunted back when he was in school, even if they had never been inside themselves.

Now, in the silence of the late evening hour, when it seemed everyone in town was locked safely inside, Preston saw the outline of a man standing in the window of that house, with the only light on Asher Street gleaming behind him like a noir film poster.

Preston kept walking, feeling only the need to sate his inner shadow, aware his focus was slipping a bit and prodding himself to stay on track. This was too important. He was too close to the edge to fail.

He was about to cross the street to avoid passing close in front of that house when he heard the front door creak open. The man inside called over to him.

"Hello there? Excuse me?"

Preston walked faster, desperate to avoid any delay. His resolve was depleted, he needed to shut the clicking off before he lost control.

He needed to—

Clickclick ...... click ...... click.

Needed to—

Click ...... click.

...

It was gone. The clicking had stopped. Could it do that? It never had before, not on its own like that.

"I'm sorry, I know I'm interrupting you," the man said, now from behind Preston, his tone gentle but his volume louder with urgency. "But I'm in a bit of a bind. Could I just have a moment of your time, young man?"

Preston—stunned by the sudden clarity in his mind and operating on autopilot as if the inner shadow was pulling him backward—walked to the house, noting its time-battered condition, and took the two wooden steps up to the porch with one smooth stride. The man in the doorway was short and somewhat round (overweight but not obese), and he wore a formal charcoal-colored suit. Despite his expensive-looking clothes, the word that came to mind for describing his appearance was "homely." His eyes were large and far apart. He wore wire-rimmed glasses with oval-shaped bifocal lenses.

Though he couldn't place it, there was a near-palpable sense of sameness coming from inside himself, as if the inner shadow had given up the clicking in this man's presence and switched to whispering words of reassurance.

Here is another. He is kin. This guy gets it.

Then the man was talking again and Preston's sense of comfort increased further beneath the gentle weight of his voice. As he spoke, he fiddled with the bridge of his glasses as if they never quite sat in the right spot.

"I hope I'm not taking you away from anything too urgent," he said, "but I was just so glad to see you happen by right now. I really could use some help."

"I was just . . . " Preston said, trailing off. Unsure why he was doing it, he agreed. "Sure, I can help."

"Oh, good. Very good. Please, come in. I promise it won't take long."

Preston, off guard while his inner shadow seemed drawn in, followed him into the spooky old house, fast noticing it was only spooky on the outside now. The rooms they passed were all fresh, neat, new-looking. He stopped to peer in the largest room. It was filled with rows of slim chairs, all facing away from the entrance, with two potted flower arrangements on pedestals near the wall farthest from where he stood. The chairs were pointed toward that wall, and the pedestals were separated by at least ten feet, giving the impression the space was reserved for something a room full of people would want to see clearly. Preston wondered what went there, what that room was used for.

"As you can see," the stranger said, "I've nearly finished setting things up in here. We'll be holding our first service the day after tomorrow, and the place needs to be in order. First impressions matter, wouldn't you agree?"

Preston nodded, intuiting a dual meaning in that question. "Service? What kind of service?"

"A viewing."

"What's that, like a movie?"

"Ah, well I had assumed someone as . . . knowledgeable as yourself would have been to one before. I apologize. A viewing takes place before the burial, wherein family and friends come to pay their respects. Say goodbye."

"So, this is a funeral place?"

"Home. A funeral home. Indeed, it is. And you must forgive the condition of the exterior, but you see, I've had to prioritize the interior so I could be ready in time." His expression turned sour. "One of your fellow townsfolk has died, unfortunately. These things can be quite costly, if you weren't aware, and that means, in towns like Oak Hollow where gainful employment is scarce and every penny matters . . . Well that's precisely what I'm here for. My interest is in ensuring his loved ones can celebrate his life, those closest to him can find comfort, all without adding financial burden to their considerable hardships at a time like this. Monday morning this home will be filled with grieving relatives, friends in mourning, and other acquaintances paying their respects. That's what happens in this room. We in the profession call it a *chapel*."

"Does . . . does that mean there will be a dead body in there?"

"A cadaver. Precisely."

A flash of a smile started on the man's face and leapt to Preston's like the start of a block fire spreading between buildings. In response, something deep inside Preston fluttered, awakening, and he understood what had drawn him to this man, why he had followed without hesitation. His speech about comforting and helping people didn't match the look on his face then, meaning Preston's senses had been spot-on. Why had he stopped? Why had he been drawn in? The answer was beautifully simple.

This is someone who gets it, he thought again. This stranger wanted to bring death as surely as Preston himself did.

They stood quietly for a moment, with Preston looking at the backs of chairs and the gap between the plants, feeling the heavy, somber silence of that room pressing into the hall where they stood. Tomorrow an actual dead body would occupy that space, and his blood surged at the thought. The unspoken connection he felt was looming large enough that he expected the other man to put a hand on his shoulder. Instead, he stepped aside and broke the silence.

"Oh, now. I was so glad you happened by when you did that I've forgotten my manners. My name is Lloyd Mnemic."

He extended his hand.

Preston shook it.

"I'm Preston. Clark."

"I'm most pleased to meet you, Preston."

"You . . . own this house?"

"I do, as of recently. I'm a funeral director, and this is where I'll be working while I'm in Oak Hollow."

"You're not from here?"

"No, I'm new in town. And I offer all my services for free."

"Why?"

"I'd like to change how my profession is seen. We're not all predatory salespeople taking advantage of those in grief. Others may say things like, 'Don't you think your mom deserved the very best Gold Protection Casket with the navy blue interior?' And then they'll charge tens of thousands of dollars just to stick the thing in the ground."

"But how will you stay in business, then?"

"I've been fortunate to have acquired enough money to be independently wealthy—from patents, mind you, not from upselling caskets or burial plots—and I've decided to give back. Now I'd hate to keep you from your other . . . appointments, but I'm afraid there's an urgent task that I'm not able to handle on my own. In my younger days, it would be no problem. But I just can't haul them up and down the stairs anymore, you see? And it must be done tonight. I'll pay you well, of course."

Preston considered this, weighing it against his earlier trajectory. He *had* been on his way somewhere important, sure. But this encounter had changed that. With the clicking gone, his plans for the night were over. Had this man, Mr. Mnemic, truly done that? Or was it the house? If being here was related, plus he could make money, that seemed like an obvious thing to do. Had he just stumbled upon the means to live the normal life he'd wanted all along?

Mr. Mnemic waited patiently while Preston weighed his options, which didn't take long.

"Tell me more."

Mr. Mnemic smiled, showing his straight white teeth. "As I've mentioned, I have an urgent task for tonight. And if you're interested, we can talk about something more long-term as well."

"What's the urgent task?"

"I need you to bring me the cadaver, Preston. And then help move it downstairs so it can be prepared for the viewing. Is that something you'd be interested in doing?"

"Yes." It was one of the strongest truths of Preston's life.

"Good. Come this way, we're in a bit of a rush. I'll need to show you how to use the mortuary cot and load it in the transport van."

Preston nodded. "Why the hurry, though? I mean, he's not really going anywhere, right?"

"Well for one, I don't have a refrigerator to store it in just yet. But the main reason? Let's just say, it's important that we get there first."

"First? Who else is coming?"

"Hopefully, no one yet. But that will change quickly. If certain parties within the funeral industry or government offices find out what I'm up to, they may decide to intervene. Me offering for free what they've grown fat off of? That's going to ruffle some feathers. This industry is surprisingly corrupt and political. But, before we begin our partnership, I'd like us to learn a bit more about each other. Wouldn't you? Let's come to understand one another. That should make for a more . . . mutually beneficial relationship."

Mr. Mnemic narrowed his eyes at Preston, a devious playfulness coloring his features.

"Would you mind telling me what you had planned this evening? Where were you headed just now, so late at night and all alone?"

Preston was taken aback, his defenses rising along with his voice. Years' worth of hiding and following convention told him to protect his secrets, regardless of what he thought about this new person. "Walk. I was just taking a walk. I do it most nights."

Mr. Mnemic shook his head and turned away. He moved down the hall and into another room just out of sight. Preston, compelled to explain himself, followed. In the room was an enormous wooden desk with two fancy old-looking chairs in front of it. Aside from a few scattered papers on the desk, there was nothing else in the room. Lloyd sat behind the desk and motioned for Preston to take a chair on the opposite side.

"Preston, let's have some real talk here. I can drop my customary 'funeral director' face around you, can't I? I'm going to need you to be more forthcoming. Be honest with me. I'm not here to judge."

Preston stiffened at that, but Mr. Mnemic continued talking, "I understand your hesitance. But you may be surprised to hear that we have something in common. Let's call it . . . an inner shadow."

Preston's jaw dropped. He'd never heard anyone use that phrase before. "How did you—" he started, but of course he knew the answer.

Mr. Mnemic waved the unfinished question away like a gnat. "I'm going to ask you to trust me, and I know that's a large thing to ask. So I'll first try to prove myself worthy of that trust. I can sense your dark urges, Preston. The thirst for violence. I see the drive in your eyes, can feel the marauder sheathed in your musculature. And I know how that feels because I have it too. We're like two predators crossing paths in the jungle. Others may not sense it, but I see it in your eyes. Power recognizes power, do you understand? Your secret is safe with me because I'm already carrying it myself. And rather than viewing each other as a threat, we can rise above our savage counterparts in that jungle and help one another. Form a pack."

"I don't know what you're talking about."

"Preston," Mnemic said, leaning forward, locking eyes. Suddenly, his skin looked younger, smoother, tighter. Surely, a trick of the light as they'd moved from the porch, to the hallway, and now this back room. "Look at me."

Preston looked and found Mr. Mnemic was right. It was like someone scratching a bone-deep itch that had been plaguing him. There was a . . . knowledge in his eyes. Predatory, dangerous. A flash of need, a sheen of violence held in tight restraint. Preston surprised himself, and instead of positing further denial, he sought insight. "How do you . . . you know . . . How do you deal with it?"

"Oh, I don't need to deal with it."

"But, you *do* have to. Don't you? I have to. I've always had to fight it."

"Well, yes. I trod that path for a time myself. The temptation grew, and I resisted, tried to beat it back with everything I had, anything that I could use against it. An impossible task, though. An unwinnable fight. How do you combat your very nature? It would be hard enough to defeat your own shadow, something that moves away as you move toward it. But to overcome a shadow that lives *inside* you? You can't even touch it, Preston. It's out of reach. And that fact shouldn't discourage you, it should liberate you. Let me ask this way . . . do you know where this inner shadow comes from? How it got inside you?"

Preston shook his head, then sat in silence, certain Mr. Mnemic was guiding him somewhere critical.

"Of course you don't. Because it's been there from before the beginning. It arrived when you weren't even conscious to sense it. I may as well ask you where your fingernails came from. You've never understood it because it came to you at a point when you weren't capable of understanding anything. Before feeling, before thought. Far, far before movement or language. When you had none of those things, you had the shadow in you. You had this darkness before you had any light. It's in there, deep and wide. Removing it would be like removing your veins. Fighting it is like fighting your own marrow. Pointless. It's in your every cell. A birthmark on your DNA. It's not a part of you, *it is you*. And you are it. Inseparable. *It* was you before *you* were you. Do you see?"

"Yes."

"I was once in your position, filled with temptation. Fighting hardscrabble against it, from each minute to the next. Surviving. How can you hope to resist temptation that strong? It's a pulling tide backed by the force of the moon, the stars, the galaxy. Its grip tightens every second of every day. But I suddenly realized that it didn't need to be so hard. I was the one making it hard. There was a way to beat that temptation, so obvious it was laughable. Beat it permanently, in an instant. And it wasn't hard to do either. Because that's the amusing thing about temptation, Preston. You were feeling it today, weren't you? That's where you were going, isn't it? Trying to get leverage over that awful, never-ending temptation, if only for a few more days, or hours even. Am I correct? Am I? Tell me. Tell me, you don't need to lie to me."

"Yes."

"You see, you've created the temptation. You've chosen it. Inadvertently, of course, but that's the truth of it. Are you ready for the best advice I have to offer, Preston?"

"Yes."

"There can be no temptation . . . if you stop resisting."

MYRTLE NURSES

Once she had sat on the pleasant little bench outside the old house on Asher Street long enough to regain her composure, then left the doll for Rosita to find later, Myrtle returned home to pass the time in her normal day's business until she could come back and catch Rosita alone. Then they could have the momentous reunion for which she'd been waiting so long.

So very long.

Outside her modest single-story house, the yard was a micro-rainforest, lush, unkempt, and wild. The roof was coated in moss and mildew, blending related shades of green like sample palettes for paint shoppers. Both front windows were partially opaque under coats of grime and splintered by long spiderweb cracks.

When she opened the unlocked front door and let herself in, a large gray mouse skittered past her feet unnoticed, disappearing behind stacks of brittle, yellowed newspapers and magazines. Diluted sunlight fell in through sagging, uneven curtains, providing only minimal visibility.

Myrtle made her way carefully down a narrow path that wove through each of the house's four rooms, using her good hand to steady herself as she stepped on and over clumps of plastic bags, discarded packaging, and clothing. The "goat path," as she called it, opened in an inverted *Y* shape, the right-hand branch leading to a tattered polyester reclining chair patterned with orange plaid punctuated by daisies, the only accessible seat in view. The other branch wound past a door that had once opened to reveal the basement stairs, now shut off behind stacks of clutter and garbage. Then the path wove through the kitchen and into the bathroom.

In the kitchen, the stove and counters were buried under crusty dishes and moldy food containers. Somewhere in a forgotten corner of the room stood a refrigerator that had broken down even before the electricity was turned off. Near the sink, just in reach from the end of the path, was a four-inch-square section of counter that held a single blue plastic bowl. Inside the bowl were a fork and a pocket-sized can opener. Behind it were a few dozen cans of store-brand pasta meals.

Past the kitchen, the bathroom was also awash with clutter, a landfill of used adult diapers, milk jugs, and soda bottles filled with dark yellow urine. The pedestal sink was filled with used toiletry bottles. Above it hung a mirror with so many cracks and splotches of muck it was near-unusable. The toilet was obscured from view by the detritus piled on the surrounding floor.

At the far end of this branch of her goat path sat a five-gallon paint bucket with a bent handle, its inside coated with a thick, unspeakable black slime. Once every two days (unless it filled more quickly), she would carry the bucket along the goat path, through the front door, around the side of the house, and empty its contents onto the ground.

Throughout every room in the home could be seen an abundance of cobwebs, black mold, peeling wallpaper, yellowed bubbles in the ceiling plaster, dead insects, and mouse droppings. A visible film of dust coated everything that lay more than a foot away from the goat path.

In what had once been the living room, past the abused orange recliner, openly defying the condition of all else surrounding it like an alien monolith, stood a seven-foot tall, six-foot wide display case, all glass except its base and top, which were made of solid, honey-colored oak and capped with decorative moldings. The wood was polished and gleaming. The glass was spotless, inside and out. Within the case were eight glass shelves, also spotless, and each was lit by three battery-powered LED lights fastened above it. A half-foot buffer of open space separated this case from the nearby clutter as if by a force field.

It was filled with dolls, carefully arranged, smiling in robotic symmetry, held upright on individual display stands—a sea of apple-hued porcelain cheeks and synthetic rooted hair.

Myrtle waved her customary greeting to the dolls, feeling pangs of disappointment because today's thrifting trip had been cut short. She'd brought nothing home to share with them. Then she recalled why it had been cut short and that it was her own choice. She realized there would be plenty more opportunities soon, with Rosita joining her, and that she had very little money left for the week.

She removed a clean tissue from the purse she was carrying, using it to cover her fingers as she opened the case and delicately rearranged several of the dolls on one shelf, closing the gap she had made before leaving this morning. With the doll collection back to presentable condition, she moved throughout the house, picking up several items from the top of any heap, moving down the goat path with them, and setting them down on another heap, indistinguishable from their original placement. She repeated this process, over and over for an hour, reminding herself that if Rosita were to come back and live with her again, she would need to make sure the house was clean as a whistle. It needed to be in tip-top shape for her darling baby girl's return. On one pass down the goat path, she spotted a coloring book peeking out from under a black plastic bag. A thick, yellowish liquid had leaked from that bag and congealed on the book's cover. She used the bottom of her sleeve to wipe this away, also knocking loose the few black mouse turds on it. Then she walked the book over and sat it next to her recliner so it would be ready for use tomorrow. Along the way, she also picked up a small box with a picture of children playing checkers on it, boasting it contained *Over 100 Different Games Inside!* Since she did not have a television, she would need to keep Rosita entertained after school ended.

While doing all this, she continued to hum the melody to "You Are My Sunshine" while holding tight to her plans for the evening.

After a while, she sat in the chair and ate one of her cans of pasta, licking the bowl and fork clean when she had finished. Then she gathered the few items she would need to complete her evening's task, put them in a canvas bag with large handles (and a black stain on one side), and placed it on top of the pile that stopped the door from opening all the way.

With the house "clean," entertainment for Rosita at the ready, and her supplies prepared, Myrtle returned to the glass display case and spent the rest of the afternoon admiring her dolls, removing them one by one from the case, turning them over in her hands, smoothing dress hems, brushing hair, polishing faces, and positioning their limbs.

As dusk arrived outside, and her usable light dwindled, she walked to the bathroom as quickly as she could manage and looked at herself in the cracked, filthy mirror. Near the sink was a makeup case covered in black faux leather that was peeling in spots to reveal cotton-like padding beneath. She opened its brass buckle closure, removed a glass bottle of foundation that was several shades lighter than her skin, and slathered it on her cheeks, chin, and forehead. She applied clumps of bright red rouge to her sunken cheeks and bright red lipstick in wide swoops around her mouth. When she'd finished, she stared approvingly at her reflection in the remaining light. The makeup creased and flaked around her smile, and Myrtle resembled a large porcelain doll herself.

She felt more whole this way, more true, beneath her armor.

Protected from all the awful men who had wronged her in life, knowing she was the only force on this Earth that could protect Rosita from a similar fate. The world made no effort to spare young girls from the horrors of men. No, her daughter counted on her, and her alone, for that, and she would deliver.

Full dark had settled by the time she returned to the house where the rude, furious woman was holding Rosita hostage. Myrtle could not comprehend what power or influence this woman had at her disposal and had begun to suspect that she may be dealing with something that wasn't human, but she could not afford to let Rosita be held under its sway a moment longer. No time for hesitance or subtlety, and there was only one weapon that could break the hold of brainwashing that kept her daughter from recognizing her and running away when presented with a beautiful, personal gift by her true mother. The purest act of motherly love could not be ignored, it could not fail. It would break through and reawaken the true Rosita, and then all would be right again. Myrtle just needed a chance to deliver it.

She approached the house, opened the screen door, and found the wooden door behind it locked. But she was prepared, her supplies in the bag slung over her arm, and a simple plan to execute.

She removed a baseball-sized rock, a bottle of lighter fluid, and a box of matches from her bag, then walked over to the green sedan parked on the street in front. She slammed the rock against the passenger door window. Again and again. On the third hit, the window splintered. On the fourth, it shattered into small cubes. Myrtle aimed the lighter fluid into the car's interior, clamping down with both hands despite the pain, then emptied half its contents onto the front seat and dashboard. She struck a match and threw it in. Then she calmly walked toward the house and before entering the shadows next to the front stoop, she rang the doorbell twice.

Ding dong.

Ding dong.

Within seconds there was a voice inside, shouting. "Who the hell? What? Oh my God! My car!" Rapid footsteps followed as the woman (thing) Myrtle had encountered earlier ran downstairs and shot through the door, leaving it wide open behind her. "Call nine-one-one! Please, someone, help!" she shouted from the street.

Myrtle, taking advantage of the chaos she had created, knowing it might not last long, walked inside the house through the open front door. It was an unfamiliar place, and there was not much light, but years of fumbling down her narrow goat path in the dark had raised her spatial awareness, and she trusted her instincts that the bedrooms were all upstairs. With her good hand still clutching the canvas bag and its remaining items, she strode up the steps. When she reached the top, she saw a faint light down a hallway to her left. *A night-light,* she thought. *Rosita had always slept with one before I lost her. She must still use it, and that means she remembers her old life. Her real life, with me.*

She walked toward the light and found her baby girl sleeping on the bottom of a set of bunk beds. A boy, years older but hard to tell how many in the dark, lay on the top bunk, also sleeping. The noise and disruption must be far enough away, filtered by walls and closed doors. Neither stirred and for a moment, Myrtle was entranced by the sight of her angel sleeping so soundly despite the shouting coming from outside.

The boy on the top bed stirred, rolling sideways. Myrtle snapped alert again, and she assumed the woman would have either regained her composure enough to come back inside and call the fire department or reached a neighbor for help by now. She must hurry.

She climbed into the bed next to the sleeping child, the mattress sagging under her added weight. Rosita lay still, she had always been a deep sleeper. From her bag, Myrtle removed a slim pack of hygienic wipes and a clean cloth diaper with a small pink bunny embroidered by hand on one corner. She unbuttoned her housedress, sliding it off one shoulder to expose her right breast, sallow and puckered. She massaged it with one hand to stimulate the gland inside, and with the other hand, she used one wipe to clean the nipple and surrounding tissue. Then she picked up the diaper, prepared to wipe up any milk that may spill. She gently slid a hand under Rosita's pillow, raising the sleeping girl's head and rubbing Rosita's soft lips around her exposed nipple. As she waited for her baby to latch once again, to pull the sweet motherly nectar that would release her from whatever awful programming and lies she'd been subjected to, Myrtle recalled the most tender moments of their former life together. Her tiny baby, eyes shut, only days old, rooting her head around in search of that life-giving substance. At first, there had been hours, days, where she feared Rosita would not latch, and that she would fail before even giving the girl a fighting chance in this man's world. But, as it always did, her persistence had won in the end and she'd raised a strong, healthy daughter. That child had been stolen from her, but Myrtle was strong; she had not let herself be defeated. Returning to the beginning like this was surely the right way to get Rosita back. She would drink long and deep of Myrtle's milk, and it would reset her mind so they could escape and rebuild. Love would reprogram her.

For one breathless, life-affirming second, Rosita's neck stiffened, her lips parted, pushed outward, moving to accept her true mother's gift of life and memory. Then a shout behind her.

"Hey! Get the fuck off her!"

PRESTON RETRIEVES

Less than a day had passed since they'd met, but Preston was very much enjoying his role as Mr. Mnemic's apprentice. And only partly because the clicking had stayed quiet for hours already.

Is that what you'd call it, his "apprentice"? Maybe "protégé"?

No, protégé seemed too strong just yet. He wanted to learn the trade, but time would tell if he wanted to be like the man himself. Mr. Mnemic seemed odd. But then, who was Preston Clark to judge that?

Come to think of it, he didn't know much about Lloyd Mnemic at all. Their conversation had been short, pointed, fast-paced. Focused more on Preston and their shared connection than on Mnemic himself, then shifted straight to a set of instructions for retrieving the cadaver. Despite covering the topic of their inner shadows—Preston's most guarded secret, which Mnemic had coaxed out with the precision of a surgeon excising a black lump of cancer—they hadn't delved into anything else personal. He didn't know where Mnemic had come from, if he had any family, what was important to him (besides providing his services free of charge), or what he thought about Oak Hollow so far.

Preston decided to find out some more about the guy when he could. Maybe he did want to aim for protégé?

But later, that would come later. Right now, he had an urgent task to complete. And therein lay the real benefit of his new role as Mr. Mnemic's apprentice.

No more fishing clumps of hair out of shower drains in secret, he was now on his way to retrieve an actual dead body. It was a monumental leap. Even better, not only was he allowed to do this, he was *supposed* to do it. He'd been hired to do it; it was his job.

Transporting it at night was an added benefit; under the cover of darkness was where he felt most at home. Plus, it was nothing short of thrilling to drive the sleek, black transport van through the empty streets and use the specialized mortuary cot. It didn't seem like real life, more like some TV drama. Shouldn't he have training for this?

Yet here he was.

To say that Preston Clark was riding high tonight was no exaggeration. He felt needed, purposeful. A functioning member of society performing a necessary but undesirable (to others, that is) service. Like a macabre sort of doctor. Or better, like some clandestine superhero cleaning up the town's streets.

An antihero, perhaps.

Have no fear, Preston is here!

Mr. Mnemic gave him specific instructions, and he'd listened, enraptured. So Preston knew exactly where to go and that no one would be home. He knew how to load the van and use the cot. He knew to grab clothes for the decedent (*mortuary terms are so slick*) and to look for photos or any personal effects the family may want to display.

Lastly, he knew that his fun was just beginning. Things would get far more interesting when the cadaver was in the basement at Asher Street.

At the Yost house, he caught himself peering around like a cat burglar out of habit, before recalling that he was allowed to be here. He was expected. For once, he was supposed to be going inside someone else's house to retrieve their remains. Should anyone stop to question him, he could explain himself with confidence, with assurance.

Preston pulled on a pair of black nitrile gloves, opened the dual back doors of the transport van, and dragged the cot out. It was silver, gleaming in the moonlight, with the general appearance of a hospital gurney but smaller and much more lightweight. His heartbeat quickened as he recalled the most thrilling part of Mr. Mnemic's instructions for the body.

Can I touch it? Preston had asked, knowing the answer already but wanting to hear it spoken.

Yes, indeed. You'll have to.

Just as he'd been told, Preston found the front door unlocked and the cadaver in the basement, where the air hung like cotton, muting the rest of the world.

He was alone with death.

Shawn Yost's body—undisturbed for a whole day—dangled, motionless, from a large iron support beam like a side of beef but far more intact and exotic. All the blood was still in there, but not for long.

The skin on its face was a color Preston had dreamed about but had never seen on such a large surface area: a diluted purple marbled with brown streaks of dried internal bleeding, like a bruise had stretched across the front of the skull. The eyes were open and staring, a milky blue.

A heavy, complex smell permeated the basement, the potpourri of death. In it were notes of old meat, feces, dried sweat. Preston's mind wandered to what that smell would transform into after a few more days. A smile trekked its way across his face.

He wrapped both arms around the dead man's waist, surprised by the weight of the cadaver, hoisting a few inches and resting it against his shoulder before using one hand to cut the noose with a knife Mr. Mnemic had provided. The rope snapped, and the cadaver dropped to the floor as Preston lost his hold, thudding face down and retaining most of its hanging posture. A glop of discharge fell from its open mouth onto the concrete, resembling a puddle of chocolate syrup.

Mr. Mnemic had told him that rigor mortis sets in quickly, and this body had been here over twenty-four hours.

It won't be very cooperative, Mr. Mnemic had said. *You'll need to break the rigor mortis from the muscles to make them livid again. Almost like breaking bones.*

Preston lowered the telescoping legs of the cot, five clicks on both sets, dropping the apparatus to its lowest setting. He laid out a white plastic sheet on the floor, as if preparing to paint the walls, then rolled the body onto it through a jerky series of motions. The cadaver held its position as if inside a full-body cast, so he didn't need to break anything. Yet.

Wrapping the loose ends of the sheet over the top of the cadaver, he grabbed handfuls of the plastic and hoisted it onto the cot, first the feet, then the torso. He secured it in place using the attached nylon straps, one each at the chest, hips, and knees. Preston tightened the belts with an audible, pleasant sigh.

With the cadaver tied down, he stepped back to get a better look at it. Its head was forced up at an awkward angle, locked in place from the time spent hanging. That wouldn't do, not at all.

"Let me take care of that for you, sir," Preston offered. He straddled the cot and its occupant, then used both hands to force the head back into a more neutral position. It resisted, which he enjoyed. The forehead skin loosened, sliding and squelching like bad fruit, and he splayed his hands out to distribute the force across more surface area.

Preston pushed harder, narrowing his eyes and feeling how closely this action mirrored the violent visions cast by his inner shadow.

Once again, Mnemic's words echoed in memory.

There can be no temptation . . . if you stop resisting.

He let the shadow form itself then, looming and overtaking him. For the first time in his life, Preston allowed it to seize control. He surrendered to its current and pressed down. Muscles tensing through his whole upper body. Fingers grasping. Wrists locking. Face hardening. Pushing. Pushing. Forcing the dead man's head toward the cot until it snapped, loudly, like a shot fired in the basement. The neck went limp.

More than limp. The head lolled to the side, moving farther from the shoulders than it should.

Oh shit, Preston thought. *I broke his neck.*

But any panic was subverted by another, entirely different sensation. Something new, and most welcome. A visceral, cathartic satisfaction, like an unclenching of his lungs. Preston was a junkie taking his first hit in years. Discovering a novel, more effective substance.

Off the wagon and loving it.

No longer was he a transient outcast, drifting on the fringe of society and willing an impossible change through every molecule that made him. No more a boy abandoned by his mother, shunned by his guardian, hated by himself for his very nature.

He was transformed into a being with purpose.

He was right where he should be.

For one shining moment, Preston Clark was home.

With a laugh, he pulled back his left hand and slapped Shawn Yost's dead body across the face. The head turned sideways, mouth slack in death's apathy, eyes wide and cloudy and oblivious.

Preston slapped it again, the other direction this time.

Punched it in the chest, his own lungs filling and emptying rapidly as the shadow took what it had wanted all along, in great, leaping strides of freedom.

He pummeled the body, smashing his mighty, antihero fists into its hardened surfaces again and again until he was out of breath and sweating. Then, regaining some composure, he pulled the shadow back, forcing it into a mental cage like a bloodied dog that had won the fight. This body needed to be on display. If he let the shadow reign any longer, that would become very tricky.

He waited until his breath returned, staring into the corpse's dead eyes all the while. Then he stood and pulled a handle toward the head-end of the cot so that it reared upright like a grim hand truck. There was a cloth cover meant to go over the cot once it was loaded, but Preston had deliberately left that in the van.

He knew he wouldn't want to cover the body until he had to. He didn't even want to leave it while he went upstairs for the clothes Mr. Mnemic had mentioned.

With the clothes in the van, Preston rushed back to the basement. He dragged the cadaver up the steps, the cot's wheels lightening the burden significantly, and watched carefully for any more discharge to erupt, disappointed when nothing came out. Atop the steps, he ran his fingers through the dead man's hair. Then he wheeled the cot and its fascinating cargo toward the van, smiling the whole way, his mind silent.

At peace.

SUNDAY

WALTER GOOGLES

In the morning, Margie's parting words were still jangling around in Walt's mind. They had disrupted his sleep considerably, and he'd spent hours tossing in bed, deeply unsettled by both what she'd said as he walked away and how she'd said it. She'd delivered awful news about a member of her own family as if she were telling Walt he had toilet paper stuck to his shoe, or he'd left the stove on. Like she thought it was an everyday occurrence, and also like she was doing him some odd little favor by warning him. All without even looking at him.

Phonyalis treats those pesky symptoms of my stage three flamingo syndrome so I can get back to living my life. Chatting with neighbors about my irrational fear of foreigners while failing to mention how my cousin hanged himself!

Thanks for that, Dad.

More troubling, though, was that Shawn Yost committing suicide was so unexpected. He was considered the unofficial mayor of Oak Hollow by many. Everyone knew him, everyone liked him. He was this dying town's most stalwart champion, the one who never seemed to lose faith no matter how dark the future looked. When BSL had left, and living in Oak Hollow felt like riding in a plummeting elevator, Shawn had not lost confidence. He'd kept to his family routines, shared optimistic words with anyone he encountered, and started taking odd jobs to help make ends meet. His faith in the town's future hadn't wavered, at least not that Walt had ever observed, and Shawn would often talk about all the years of prosperity his family shared here, the strength and resilience he knew Oak Hollow had. Take away Shawn's positivity, and triple the number of rats that would have deserted this sinking ship by now. Then what shape would the place be in? In a way, his death left the town that much more defenseless.

To top all this off, Shawn Yost was likely the closest thing to a friend Walt had since he'd retired (except for his father, of course). He was easily the person Walt had spoken to most frequently, in part because he and Dad had shared a love of their hometown. Dad's house was a few years older than Walt and in need of considerable upkeep despite its small size. So while Shawn took work as a handyman from anyone in town who had the means to pay him (and quite a few who didn't), they'd crossed paths frequently at the True Value hardware store on Asher Street, which coincidentally was two blocks away from the formerly-haunted-house-turned-funeral-home. There were dozens of mornings that Walt had walked the one mile separating his front door from True Value to pick up a few odds and ends—sandpaper and deck screws, most recently. This would take under an hour round trip unless he ran into Shawn. Occasionally, he'd spent so much time shooting the shit that he'd decided it was too late to start a project now and would wait until the next morning. And twice, Shawn had come by to help Walt and they'd sat around a fire behind the house drinking beer and talking about Zane Grey novels—Zanesville being less than an hour's drive from Oak Hollow—or music. They were both par- ticularly interested in drummers, especially progressive, polyrhythmic geniuses like Neal Peart and Danny Carey.

Shawn was good people, he had strong ideals and common ground with both Walt and his dad. His name was included on a short and exclusive list titled *People I can actually hold a comfortable conversation with*.

But Walt could not understand what would have changed so quickly to drive a man like Shawn Yost to suicide, even in dark times. He was strong and determined, a man who loved his family, who loved his town. And even though things seemed bleak, unless everything the man had shown outwardly since BSL left was a mere façade, a pageant, then it was hard to believe he'd given up so much of his identity. It just made no sense.

During that long, sleepless night, Walt's mind was also occupied by troubled (and troubling) thoughts about this new funeral home. Something about Margie's comments wasn't sitting right. Something elusive. Clichéd as it sounded, Walt's sense was that it wasn't just *what* she had said but *how* she had said it. The owner had asked her to "help spread the word" about Shawn's viewing. And the owner hadn't "finished fixing it up yet." These points may not have seemed so strange if she weren't so . . . blindly accepting of them. Was that it? Like she'd been specifically chosen to blab about it, rather than formally announcing it.

Timing could be a factor, urgency. But maybe the owner was lazy or just plain kooky. There were ominous vibes there, like a vulture lurking close behind as you dragged yourself, still alive, through the desert toward safety, but he couldn't discern what was driving these vibes. If pressed to describe its undercurrent, he'd say it just seemed too fast. Funeral homes were a regulated business with a certain amount of governmental involvement and oversight.

While far from an expert, Walt had some knowledge of the ins and outs of the mortuary world from recent experience with Dad. That told him, while it wasn't like opening a hospital per se, it also wasn't like opening a lemonade stand either. There should be some lead time involved if everything was being done above board. Right? On the other hand, look how quickly marijuana dispensaries popped up once legalized. Maybe all the time spent checking regulatory boxes happened before the signs were hung?

Another thing, how could those chatty women think its arrival meant things were already turning around for Oak Hollow? A business like that was unlikely to hire anyone in town, and it was doubtful a new funeral home would bring any money into the local economy from outside or spark a revitalization that would spread to more new commerce.

Walt was naturally open-minded, tending to wait and gather more information before making his own decisions, not prone to jumping to conclusions or following others blindly. Yet, for the first new business in town to be one based around death? Seemed like bad juju. Fuel for the superstitious and knee-jerk types.

Plus, why would anyone want to bring a new business to Oak Hollow and choose that house to locate it in? The expense of making it presentable would be enormous. And even made spotless, it would be a chore just to get most of these closed-minded morons to step foot within a hundred paces of it.

Capping all that off, was it more than a coincidence that Shawn's service would be held there?

Admittedly, he'd been spending too much time alone and that was influencing his thoughts, but there was too much about it that didn't sit well. A primitive warning was pinging out that this would lead nowhere good.

Something had come to pick clean the bones of Oak Hollow, this once-proud and prosperous Midwest town that his dad loved and called home. And suddenly its most stalwart defender was gone.

As Walt set about his usual Sunday morning routine, though a few hours earlier than usual, these two questions hounded him: *What would drive Shawn Yost to suicide? And what did this new funeral home really mean for the town of Oak Hollow?*

They persisted in his thoughts as he let Cowboy out into the fenced backyard, took his morning walk on the treadmill so he didn't have to venture outside, showered, dressed, ate his usual meager breakfast of toast and yogurt, and by that time, as the sun was cresting, Walt felt as if there was some overlap between these two thorns in his mind. The timing was a strong coincidence, but did that mean correlation?

No, he thought. *I'm jumping to conclusions.*

Consult your physician before taking Phonyalis yourself.

Got it, Dad. Thanks again.

Sure, they were both noteworthy occurrences in a place where very few such things transpired, so the timing of these happenings being so close could imply some relationship, but there was no substance to it. No rational reason to think one had anything to do with the other.

Walt put a scoop of food in Cowboy's bowl and, as usual, the dog looked at him for approval before he started eating. "Yes," Walt said, "it's your food and you can eat it." Cowboy kept looking, unmoving. "Good boy," Walt said. "You're a good boy." The dog finally lowered his head, taking several pieces of kibble in his mouth, then began chewing as most of them spilled onto the floor. That gave Walt a bit of relief from the thoughts troubling him all morning. He walked over and patted Cowboy's head, flipping his creased ear upward.

"You goof. All this time off the track and you're still not used to eating dog food like a dog. Good thing I don't have any stairs around here."

When Cowboy first came home with him, Walt was informed by the adoption group that he might still need some help adjusting to retired life in a house. Walt had scoffed at first, but it quickly became clear just how deep the chasm was between Cowboy's former life and that of a house pet. They told him that greyhounds, while living and racing at the track, eat only raw meat, have never seen a flight of stairs, and depending on which track and each dog's personality, they may not even understand how windows work at first (as in, they'll try to walk through the glass repeatedly before realizing they can't). They also have been exposed to very few other animals, including different breeds of dogs. The world outside of racetracks was entirely foreign and could be quite overwhelming. Cowboy, from every sign available to Walt, had adjusted quickly, though, with the hard kibble being the one exception. The dog could certainly consume, so he must enjoy it, but it was a little like watching a toddler eating soup with a fork.

When he'd finished, leaving a smattering of crumbs spread on the floor around his bowl, he trotted over to the couch where Walt was sitting and held his nose a half-inch away from Walt's hand, gazing up. Walt stroked the top of his nose twice, then adjusted Cowboy's custom Martingale collar (which he'd learned was a necessity for the breed because their heads are too narrow for other collars to remain on), with its pattern of little Stetson hats, and said "You're welcome, boy." He still marveled at the dog's obvious display of gratitude after every meal. The ritual complete, Cowboy walked slowly over to his bed, where he'd likely spend the rest of the morning and most of the afternoon.

With the dog fed and the latest *F&SF* finished yesterday evening, Walt wondered what else he could do to take his mind off the portents regarding Shawn and the new funeral home. That didn't require leaving his house, at least.

He walked to his study, lined with bookshelves on two walls and windows on the fourth, and sat at his small desk. If asked, he wouldn't have been able to say what he intended to do on the computer just then, but he soon looked for information related to 432 Asher Street.

Like most people in town, he'd heard the stories. Koenig slaughtering his own kids. The construction crew plagued by disappearing equipment until one day the foreman himself went missing. The heavy metal band that had filmed a music video and conjured a demon in a bedroom. He didn't believe any of it, but Dad had his own theories on several tales.

At one point, Dad had even talked him into going on a "haunted walking tour" that stopped by the house. That was years ago, far enough back that they may have been in one of the first groups to sign up. At one point, there were a handful of those companies to choose from.

During the tour, Walt expected Dad to scoff repeatedly, then lean over to whisper, filling in the gaps in the stories or to point out to him what was true and what wasn't. But Dad had enjoyed the tour thoroughly and gained a strong respect for the tour guide. No small feat, that.

Dad had been a bit of an amateur historian, diving into the bizarre and tragic bits as a sort of specialty. The dark corners and inconsistencies. "Weak spots in the fabric," he called them a few times.

Dad would occasionally allude to strange things he'd seen and heard in his ninety-two years, and of course he had Walt's utmost respect, but it was still hard to savvy with some of Dad's beliefs when Walt himself had no experiences that he considered remotely supernatural.

The best story he'd ever heard Dad tell was from his time in the Army, a topic he otherwise never broached.

He'd come home from a bar, where he'd joined a few others from his paratrooper unit who were visiting from other states. Dad didn't drink much, and almost never more than a single beer, but that night he'd tried to keep up with the others. In a way both tragic and endearing, he reminded Walt of a drunk Mr. Miyagi, offering a rare glimpse into those sorts of archetypal still waters that ran so deep and hid so much.

He told Walt about his only tattoo, which Walt hadn't known about. Then he showed it, a crudely drawn symbol in prison-blue ink on the inside of his left biceps, only an inch long.

Walt had been fascinated, having put away a few beers himself to keep Dad's disclosure flowing like he was still at the bar with his Army buddies. But becoming tipsy by the end of the story himself (coupled with Dad's slurring and meandering) meant some details or phrasing hadn't stuck well. Now, years later, it was hard to recall all the specifics despite how compelling it had been then.

The story was about a fellow soldier who was part-Irish (and therefore affectionately called "Dublin") and whose family believed strongly in the importance of their culture's ancient symbology. Namely, the Celtic runes.

Dublin had a tattoo of a rune, which he'd gotten as protection before enlisting, despite protests from his Irish-Catholic family. Walt hadn't caught what the actual rune was called, but it was clear Dad believed in its power of protection, also, claiming it had saved both their lives when an enemy soldier jumped into their foxhole during a firefight. That was why Dad had gotten his own tattoo of the same symbol.

One detail that was still clear to Walt was how Dad characterized that enemy soldier's eyes.

"Black and borderless, like a wasp's," he'd said.

Dad had grown stern just then and said that German man had found his way into combat deliberately, through one of those "weak spots" caused by all the death and carnage. He was not just a soldier, but something evil in human form. And just when he raised his rifle to shoot, Dublin had raised his own empty right hand (rune tattoo on its back), screamed "No!" and the rifle had misfired. That gave Dad his opening to shove a bayonet into the enemy's chest.

"Death drew it to us, Walt. And that rune stopped it."

Dad had ended the story in tears, and Walt himself was in shock.

After that, Dad had shaken his head vigorously as if trying to eject the memory. His eyes glossed over and he headed to the bathroom before shuffling off the bed.

Walt, shaken and struggling to process all this, had dozens of questions to ask, but he couldn't bring himself to. The next morning, Dad didn't seem to remember telling the story and neither of them mentioned it again. The fallout of that revelatory moment became like so much else had between them.

Unspoken.

Walt's breathing quickened, and he sensed a bout of crippling, oppressive grief bearing down on him like a train. He closed his eyes, as if he could simply will it away, though this never helped, white-knuckling the sides of his desk until the cheap pressboard desktop made small creaking noises. A tear escaped one of his eyes and for an instant, he understood a bit more of why Shawn Yost had given up.

But before that line of thinking could draw out any further, before Walt drew too near the cliff, he felt a light pressure on his left thigh. Walt opened his eyes and saw Cowboy's head resting on his leg, the dog's large round eyes open and full of knowing. Cowboy stared, unblinking, unflinching, and soon Walt's chest relaxed and his breathing grew more regular.

"Th-thanks, boy," he said. Cowboy lifted his head, turned, and walked out of the room.

His composure returned, Walt tapped on the keyboard to wake the computer. A Google search of *432 Asher Street* returned the sort of results he'd expected, beginning with real estate sites like Zillow and RE/MAX stating, "This property is currently not for sale," followed by four different companies offering haunted tours. From there, he scrolled past a litany of posts and citations about the house, mainly covering its construction and early history, along with some of the bigger milestones since, including the subsequent owners and the fire it survived. Farther down the page the content shifted to the more commonly known spooky stories, legends, and myths about the house. Walt clicked on a few of these, but scanning the pages revealed nothing new to him; he'd heard all these tales about the place since he was a kid. And with Dad's insight on that tour years ago, he even had a good idea which could be factual and which were clearly not.

A nagging sense of something larger happening drove him to the second page of results, then the third, which shed no additional light. He was prepared to close the browser but then clicked on the *News* tab instead, purely on impulse.

There was only one search result listed, a post on a Facebook page titled "Heart of Ohio News," which Walt had never heard of. He first checked the details of the Facebook page, which seemed to have been created a week ago and had no other posts yet. Walt clicked the link for the post, expecting an expanded view but found only a few more words than the preview description in the search results. The entire article, or maybe blurb was a more appropriate term, was two sentences. Walt read them several times.

Abandoned property in depressed town of Oak Hollow purchased after over a decade of vacancy. Historic farmhouse at 432 Asher Street to become new location of Mnemic Family Funeral Home.

Not much information, and appearing either planted or suppressed (maybe both?), but a start. A new search of *Mnemic Funeral* returned nothing helpful, though. In fact, there seemed to be no mention of the name anywhere on the Internet. As he scanned these search results, Walt noticed the word "mnemic" didn't appear anywhere. Then he noticed the top of the page said *No results for Mnemic Funeral, did you mean to search mnemonic?*

Huh, he thought. *Is it a real name? Is it even a word?*

His third search was for the word *mnemic* by itself, and aside from the dictionary definition: *relating to the ability to retain memory*, there was nothing that shed any light on his concerns. Walt went back to the tab with the brief news blurb, wondering if he had misspelled it. The blurb confirmed his spelling, which left him wondering if it could have been misspelled there. It wasn't a last name he'd ever heard before, not that that meant anything by itself. But the general lack of results was only deepening his suspicions about the place.

At a dead end trying to research the business, and finding nothing of note about the house itself, he searched for Shawn's obituary, which brought about the strangest moment of the day.

There was no mention of his death anywhere that Walt could find.

PRESTON EMBALMS

Preston returned to the house on Asher Street in the transport van just after sunrise. He wasn't sure where to take the cadaver. Surely, the house had a back door, but he figured that was farther from the stairs. Rather than guess, he approached the front door and knocked, realizing the old guy may have gone to sleep. He did not know what sorts of hours Mr. Mnemic kept or how he spent his time. Preston reminded himself to find out more about his mysterious new benefactor.

On his third round of knocking, the door opened slightly.

From somewhere inside, Mr. Mnemic said, "Come in."

Preston pushed the door open but stayed on the porch, looking in. His voice came from somewhere beyond the foyer, a room deeper in the house. "You made it back quicker than I expected. I assume everything went . . . well?"

Preston walked inside, noting there were no lights on anywhere in the rooms he could see. The premature sunlight was filtered through layers of deep gray cloud and very little of it was brazen enough to find its way through the aged glass and into the interior of the house. He worked to determine which direction Mr. Mnemic's voice was coming from before projecting his own voice toward every room at once. "Yeah. No problems."

"Good. Very good. I'm afraid I'm not quite presentable at the moment and will need to stay hidden. I hope you understand."

His voice sounded different, deeper, plus altered in a way Preston could not discern from just those few spoken lines. As if it was coming through some type of tubing or filter before making it to his ears. Preston pictured a large, inhuman creature hunched inside the next room, upper vertebrae pressing against the ceiling and head bowed low between massive shoulders; something akin to his favorite kid's book, *Where the Wild Things Are*, but rendered in three dimensions. With its hand shoved through the back of Mnemic's bespectacled head and using sleek, clawed fingers to move the mouth open and closed like a grotesque human puppet while the legs dangled an inch above the floor. This image was quick and complete in his mind.

"I just need a few minutes," Mnemic said. "Why don't you retrieve the cadaver and bring it through the front door. And if you're feeling spry enough, be a good lad and wheel it into the morgue. It's in the basement, down the stairs at the end of the hall."

Following that was a noise that reminded Preston of the time a girl in his class had brought her pet python to school in a pillow case (something rough slithering against cloth), mixed with a stretching sound like cellophane being pulled across a metal pan.

A few minutes later, Preston stood in the recently converted morgue room, the cadaver lying uncovered on the mortuary cot nearby. Like the upstairs, this room appeared to have been completely remodeled, all white tile surfaces, spotless laminate flooring, stainless steel equipment. Unlike the upstairs, it was well lit. Fluorescent tube lights, their ballasts humming low, threw down enough brightness to make Preston squint until his eyes could adjust. In one corner of the space was a porcelain table large enough to lay a body on. It stood on a single pedestal with a hydraulic lift, its ivory veneer cracked and darkened in several places, all of which gave it an antique appearance. Preston thought something lightweight and metal, on wheels, would be more practical. Stepping closer, he noticed a grooved path along all its edges, leading to a hole at one end. The last six inches of that end hung over a sink mounted to the wall.

Mr. Mnemic sidled up to his right, so close Preston could smell him. He gave off a unique combination of clean linen with something warm and earthy. Like he'd just come in from digging a damp grave and put on clothing fresh from the dryer without washing himself.

"Are you ready to begin?" Mnemic asked.

Preston nodded, cracking his knuckles, glad his wait was over.

Mr. Mnemic stepped past him, rounding the table. Preston thought he saw movement beneath the skin of Mnemic's face as he moved, like a finger sliding along the inside of his forehead, but it may have been a trick of the bright lights. Then Mr. Mnemic had a hand on his jaw and was pushing it far to one side and back to the other, as if popping it into place. He wasn't wearing a suit coat anymore, the sleeves of his shirt rolled up. His glasses were gone too. The mental image of that monstrous puppet show flashed by again.

"Did you find the clothing?" he asked, drawing his mouth into a thin line.

Preston nodded.

"Good," Mnemic said, stepping away briefly, his gait more scuttle than walk. When he came back, he rolled a tall bent-neck lamp that looked like something out of an operating room on TV. He switched it on and positioned the light directly over the porcelain table. "We don't want to leave the cadaver naked when we're finished. Help me move it to the embalming table, please."

Together, they lifted the body, Preston holding the ankles (its limbs and joints already looser than last time) while Mr. Mnemic hoisted with his arms beneath its armpits. *He must be stronger than he looks,* Preston thought. While in motion, the cadaver's head sagged too far and swung too loosely. Preston waited tensely for a scolding or a *tsk-tsk* or Mr. Mnemic to shake his head in disappointment.

"I'm glad that's all the visible damage. A broken neck can be concealed easily, but had you let yourself venture much further . . . well we'd need to get creative." He caught Preston's gaze then, the terminating brightness from the surgical lamp creating a faint shadow over his round face. Perhaps another trick of the light or Preston's lack of sleep, but his body seemed to have grown in diameter, or maybe his head looked smaller without the glasses. "Don't be sheepish. I knew you'd need a bit of release, just as I knew you'd show restraint when needed. You can relax, Preston. I all but told you to hurt him, didn't I? And now comes the truly enjoyable part. We're about to perform one of the all-time great magic tricks."

Mnemic turned to the counter beside him and grabbed a pair of scissors. He used them to cut and remove the dead man's clothing until he lay there, pale and waxy and nude.

"Are you familiar with embalming, Preston? Not the idea, but the practice of it? The history. The process. Its purpose."

"No, not really."

"Would you like to learn?"

"Yes. Yes, I would."

"How fortuitous. I imagine there are few who know as much about it as I do. And you're far from my first student. Now, we could start as far back as ancient Egypt, but there are other matters to attend to soon, so what say we skip forward a few millennia? After all, their practice was starkly different, rooted in belief and ritual, unlike modern embalming, which is purely superficial and consumeristic. That started right here, in America, around one hundred and sixty years ago.

This was during the Civil War, you see, and the bodies were piling and rotting faster than we could bury them."

As he talked, Mr. Mnemic worked on the body, wiping it clean and applying disinfectant.

"Dr. Thomas Holmes is considered the foremost pioneer of arterial embalming by many, myself included. What they aren't aware of, though, is where he got his inspiration. That first spark of an idea. Back then, science was still primitive enough that no one quite understood what made bodies decompose. For a time, cadavers were difficult to come by and that made their study fractured and inconsistent. There was no centralized or complete knowledge bank for the stages of decay. But Dr. Holmes realized something his predecessors and contemporaries alike had missed: fluid was integral to the process. He understood that the bacteria already inside the body while alive would be given free rein upon its death, enzymes hungrily breaking down everything they touched. The same process that had once converted food into energy never stopped, all that changed was the dead body's own cells became food too. Nothing is off limits and the bacteria multiply and consume until the skin slides off and the organs liquify, everything dissolving and then what's left is a pile of bones lying in soup. Autolysis, it's called now. Self-digestion.

"Holmes knew plenty about chemical preservatives too. He just needed a nudge toward putting these bits of information together. Fluid already in the body caused decomposition, but if that fluid were exchanged for preservatives, it would halt the decomposition. From there, it was a simple matter of deciding how best to exchange these fluids. Take your right hand, Preston, and place it on the side of your neck like this." He demonstrated using his index and middle fingers to palpate the thick cords of his own neck. "Can you find your pulse there?"

Preston tried, quickly finding a steady beat beneath his fingers. "Yes."

"That is your carotid artery. And nearby it, the jugular vein. These are the primary pathways for blood to travel away from your heart, to the rest of your circulatory system, then back again. This is the same information I discussed with Dr. Holmes, not that it was a revelation; the man was an anatomist. He knew they were there and what purpose they served. My intervention just opened his mind to the idea of using them for his fluid displacement. The infrastructure already existed, you see. The means to deliver his preservative mixture—Innominata, he called it on the patent form—to every corner of the cadaver with great efficiency."

In response to this information, Preston grew lightheaded, overcome by a joined chorus of conflicting reactions and thoughts. He was standing in the basement of a haunted house converted into a morgue, watching a dead body being prepared for embalming by someone who had just hinted at being over a hundred and fifty years old. It was both absurd and obvious to him that Mr. Mnemic was not quite human, even if he looked the part. Enough information had been presented to show this. But what was he, then? And how old, exactly? Could he be two hundred? A thousand years? More? And what did he really want from Preston? When he decided earlier to learn more about Mr. Mnemic, he had expected nothing so insane, so indigestible.

Then Preston thought about the desires of his inner shadow, the clicking it used to influence him. The temptation it brought and his fight to resist. Mr. Mnemic's permission to give up that fight. The satisfaction of snapping Shawn's neck. He couldn't comprehend staying here any more than he could accept going back to the life he was living yesterday morning. Everything he knew had changed within a few critical moments.

Terrified and entranced in equal measure, Preston fought simultaneous urges to flee and to marvel.

Now Mr. Mnemic was leaning over the table, still talking, and using a scalpel to cut a three-inch incision into the cadaver's neck. It didn't bleed. Preston stepped closer, choosing to stay and learn, feeling an inescapable momentum pulling him deeper into Mnemic's orbit. He was embracing the shadow over the normal life he'd fought to have for so long. Moving forward, not back. Into the unknown.

He peered over Mr. Mnemic's shoulder as he reached into the neck cavity to push aside grayish muscle and exposed tendons. Mnemic used a silver instrument with a small hook to pull loose the artery and vein. They looked rubbery in texture, and there was blood on them (and surely inside them), but it seemed so still, inanimate as the corpse itself. Could blood be lifeless? Preston had expected it to come gushing out once the neck was opened, but the lack of flow during Mnemic's procedure, coupled with his speech about embalming, caused Preston to see the body now as nothing more than a huge bizarre bottle. A container for fluid, covered in meat and molded into the shape of a human.

Mnemic spoke as he worked, directing his words at Preston without looking up, "We discerned a great deal about the process in short order, the good Dr. Holmes and me. Since then, it's become more refined and advanced, but we certainly paved the way. Poor old Thomas went insane toward the end. Storing preserved bodies in closets around his home and leaving embalmed heads on tabletops like horrible lamps. I miss those early days, though. Well, 'early' meaning when we first started arterial embalming. I don't think we have time to discuss *my* early days. Soon, other industrious gents got involved with embalming, and then it was 'off to the races,' as the saying goes. Scads of showoffs wanted to make their mark on this novel profession we'd invented, the brand-new industry of obfuscating death. It was a wonderful time. Body snatchers got rich so embalmers could practice their trade. Open caskets were introduced so they could flaunt their skill. Even the chemists jumped on board, offering contests with titles like 'Best Preserved Body' as a lewd form of marketing for their goods. The pinnacle, though, which I'll never forget as long as I may live, was watching them parade that top-hat-wearing president around after he was shot at the theatre. They beamed with their peacock pride and toted his pickled corpse from town to town. I laughed and swelled with pride of my own at the efficiency of these wheels I'd set in motion simply by planning well and being in the right place at the right time. Within a few generations, the process was moved out of the home and into places like this. Death and decay were removed even further from daily life while it all became more commercialized, exactly as I'd hoped."

Mnemic took a length of cotton string, wrapped it around both carotid and jugular, then tied the string to hold them in place outside the cavity. He sliced them each open with the scalpel, like chopping penne pasta in half. Then he reached for a clear tube and pushed its hardened tip into the artery. The tube led to a machine on the adjacent counter that looked to Preston like a blender, only bigger.

"Forgive me, Preston. Prattling on about faraway events that don't matter to you. What matters now is that it all led to this exact moment. The final phase. Beginning of the end. And I'm glad for your help. Here, put these on." He handed Preston plastic splash goggles, the kind worn in high school chemistry labs. "You wouldn't want the embalming fluid to get in your eyes. Trust me," Mnemic said with a knowing smirk.

Preston obeyed, noting Mr. Mnemic did not take any such precaution himself.

He held up a bottle of pink, translucent fluid for Preston to see. "Innominata. Holmes's original formula. If you ask me, no one has yet to craft anything superior. Though I'm sure he'd have wanted one of these machines to make it go faster." He poured the embalming fluid into the clear plastic hopper of the blender-thing, then turned a knob on its base. It hummed loudly as the fluid moved through the tube and into the severed artery. The blood came flowing then, steady and crimson, from the opened vein. It ran down the tilted embalming table's porcelain surface, deep red contrasting with clean white, collecting in the border groove like a beautiful, gruesome little river that disappeared through the drain hole near the cadaver's feet. Preston watched, hypnotized, his skin prickling with the electricity of a new level of life.

An age later, the flow diminished, becoming lighter and lighter in both volume and color until finally it stopped and the last drops trickled past. A sense of disappointment followed; Preston didn't want the bleeding to end. Mnemic spoke, as if reading his mind.

"Don't fret. There's plenty more to do." He turned off the embalming machine and, with his still-bare hands, picked up a metal instrument, which was approximately as long as a human arm and looked like a giant needle tip, brandishing it toward Preston first for a better view. "Now, we get to use this."

"What's that?"

"A trocar, it's called. It gets rid of all the other body fluids." Mnemic raised it overhead, then thrust it down into the cadaver's stomach, spearing deep, with a sound that was part punching and part slicing. He moved it up and down violently like he was raising a car on a tire jack, then swirled it clockwise several times, stirring whatever was inside. Soon, a brackish, oil-like gunk poured from its end, leaking liquified remains from the cadaver's gut onto the table and filling the air with the noxious odor of decay. It smelled almost sweet, like the thing on the table was a piñata full of old fruit.

"Here," he said, pulling the trocar free and handing it, one end dripping, to Preston. "Drain it. Drain it all."

Inside Preston, the shadow surged forward, like it had when he was alone with the body. Only this time, he didn't need to give it permission. Once the trocar touched his fingers, the next few hours became a frenzied blur during which he helped Mnemic remove the partially liquified eyeballs and replace them with cotton, cover the empty sockets with plastic caps, stretch the lids down over barbs on the caps and glue them shut, insert a mouth former, sew the jaw closed with a gun-shaped needle injector that spit wires like bullets.

As they finished, and Preston's conscious mind swam its way up from beneath the shadow's heavy dominance, they were working with the clothing he'd retrieved from the dead guy's house, cutting it up the back so it could be made close-fitting. Next, they shaved his face—Mnemic had to take over because Preston's hands were trembling and making cuts that would never heal—then used tubes of something called Cyn-Gel to rehydrate the exposed skin, followed by garden-variety makeup.

"We'll have to exercise some caution," Mnemic was saying, "when we get the casket situated upstairs. To ensure his head appears to still be attached correctly." He winked at Preston, something like pride playing around his eyes.

Preston smiled.

Mnemic took a step back from the table, scanning the final result. Preston scanned as well. He hadn't known Shawn Yost, never met him alive, but still, he could tell that regardless of all the steps taken to restore his appearance, it just wasn't quite there. They'd made his skin appear more pink and less cold, his features more filled-in, his face and attire presentable, his neck intact. Shawn Yost was neither alive nor dead. They'd changed him into something else, something in-between, similar to Preston's hair collection. Next to life, but not part of it. Like it, but also different.

Life-adjacent.

"And now, our magic trick is complete," Mnemic said. "We've restored his natural appearance to the best of our ability, albeit in unnatural ways. We started with a corpse, bottled chemicals, plastic, and wires. And we transformed it into a unique product. The current industry term is 'memory picture,' I believe. But, rather than selling this product like other morticians do, we're going to trade it for something far superior."

He walked to the opposite side of the table and placed his hands on the shoulders of his apprentice. Through Preston's T-shirt his hands felt colder and harder than those of the embalmed corpse on the table.

Mnemic held Preston fast with his gaze, and again he saw movement beneath the skin of the old man's forehead. Mnemic made to speak, but at first only an alien chittering sound came out, not unlike the clicking from his inner shadow. After a few seconds, it morphed into words.

"*Chktchktchkt . . . chktchktchkt . . . chktchktch . . . ktk . . .* and this is where my design becomes more exposed, Preston. More vulnerable. It will need protection. Protection I can't provide without help. Therefore, I need a soldier."

Mnemic's eyes blazed, the skin across his entire face rippled slowly, darkening to a deep, marbled gray with a sheen like a parking lot in the rain. "Can you . . . Will you be my foot soldier, Preston?"

For a split second, Preston wanted to scream, "No!" and run, then Mnemic made that sound again. This time, it resonated within Preston, joining forces with the clicking he'd always known.

"Chktchktchkt . . . clickclick . . . chkt . . . click . . ."

Preston nodded and everything went silent again.

Myrtle Plans

Myrtle woke in a haze, sitting in her shabby orange recliner with more tightness in her spine than usual. Disorientation hung curtain-like, surrounding her on all sides. She rubbed at her eyes, forcing consciousness into herself, bringing a bone-deep pain from her hand (the not-good one) that broke through the din. Fragments of memory followed, and she examined them, trying to form the full picture of what happened last night.

She recalled Rosita's warm breath on her bare chest, that other-worldly moment of expectation, their joyous reunion poised to break through the surface the next instant.

Then, shouting.

Panic.

Myrtle was forced to stand, to fight. She'd pulled out the last item in her bag of supplies, a ten-inch length of iron pipe, and made to swing it at her foe. But she'd grabbed it with the wrong hand and her swipes were slow and weak. There was a brief struggle, and she landed only one decent blow to her assailant's head before the weapon clattered to the floor. The boy woke and screamed. Rosita screamed. Myrtle screamed. The rest was incoherent.

She knew she had run, faster than she thought herself capable. She knew she had left the pipe and her bag behind, perhaps in the bedroom or on the stairs, perhaps on the street. She thought she'd seen a flicker of recognition in Rosita's eyes as she looked back. And she thought she'd seen the woman change as she struggled to rise from the floor, blood streaming down her (its) face. Growing wings from her/its back.

After that, her memory was blank. There was a gap, lost time. What had happened then? How had she made it home?

As her senses returned, bringing aches and throbs in several more places, Myrtle Fallsworth finally understood the reason she'd been unable to save her daughter. The cause of the invisible barrier between them. The idea had tripped around her head before, but now she had firm evidence.

She was not fighting for custody against another woman. Instead, this was a foe beyond her understanding, beyond her means. All the signs were there.

Rosita was in the clutches of a demon.

Myrtle climbed and squirmed her way upright in her recliner, but when she stood, the pain in her back flared. She had taxed her body too much last night and now there was a bed of thorns running up her frame. Every minor shift or pivot flashed red inside her old bones.

And she smiled. Because whereas most people would be defeated in the face of such pain, Myrtle Fallsworth thrived on it. Pain was her life's only constant; she'd be lost without it.

From a young age, it had been by her side, and as she ambled down the goat path toward her bucket, she ran through a mental catalog of pain.

She thought about a car crash on the way home from Sunday morning mass. Myrtle, age seven, her twin brother sitting to her right on the leather back seat as her father suffered a massive stroke, her mother screaming from the passenger side, the massive gold Cadillac striking a tree. She'd had to wear a neck brace for weeks and became known as "Myrtle the Turtle" at school. Her father had died after two bedridden months, yet the taunting moniker stuck.

Then there was her first marriage, the better of the two, but short-lived. She had given Todd her virginity, and he had responded by neglecting her, then running away with one of his students.

Her second marriage was longer, both chronologically and psychologically. It ended decades ago but still loomed large in her mind daily. The sweet and shy Percival she had met at a Christian mixer was a mere ruse, a rusty, tooth-filled trap waiting to spring.

The real Percy thrived on control, compulsively directing and manipulating every aspect of her life, down to the smallest action or detail. For six years, he abused and tortured her. First verbally, but soon enough that devolved into hitting, then cutting, and then to advanced forms of punishment and torment she could never bring herself to speak of.

He broke my hand, she thought. *I was cleaning up a puddle of his vomit on the cold kitchen floor. He stumbled through, too drunk to notice me, and stepped right on it.*

She'd felt the bones break.

And he wouldn't let me see a doctor, so the bones healed wrong. She held her bad hand up now, studying it. The damage he did was visible by the next day and it slowly morphed into this lumpy, contorted mess. Since then, arthritis had settled deep, leaving her with a constant humming pain. Most days, she could only move her pinkie, leaving it more a stump than a hand.

That was the beginning of the end, though. Because then I had to use my other hand to iron his clothes and made a burn mark on his favorite shirt.

"I'll teach you how to treat a man's clothes," he'd said, holding a knife.

"Please, Percy, it was an accident. My hand . . ." She tried to show him how painful it was, the limited motion, but her ploy for sympathy only enraged him.

He picked up the iron, still hot. "Take off your shoes, Myrtle."

"No." She knew it was a mistake even as it came out.

"Seems I need to teach you how to *speak* to a man too." He pointed the knife at her. "You know I'll use this. So you just need to decide, which is it going to be?" His eyes went from the knife, to the iron in the other hand, then back. "Which one?"

"Percy, please," she'd said, wishing for a turtle's shell to protect her. *All men are monsters,* she'd thought.

"Iron it is, then. Take off your shoes. Socks too."

Brittle, beaten down, and hoping to avoid making things worse, she obeyed. Giving him what he wanted usually de-escalated his anger in a hurry.

That time, it hadn't.

He'd pressed the iron to the bottom of each foot. Hard. Held it in place while her screams built, then fizzled into whimpers.

"Now walk," he'd ordered.

Then, for over an hour, he'd made her not just walk, but *drag* her blistered soles across their coarse Berber carpeting. The knife never left his hand.

Midway through that barbaric exchange, a part of her had died, replaced by something else, hollow and uncaring. The next day she took two of his insulin needles, filled them with the medicine and stuck both into his armpit while he was sleeping. His prescription was for the U-500 strength, and the amount she'd used was nearly five times his normal dose. For a few seconds, he tried to push her away, but then his eyes went glassy and confused, his jaw lax with spittle dripping from his bottom lip, before slipping into diabetic shock. He twitched and writhed his way out of the bed, went comatose, and then he was gone. She had called the police herself, played the distraught wife, unsure if he had simply forgotten that he'd already dosed himself or if it was a planned suicide. A few days later, they weren't even asking her questions anymore, and she switched roles to grieving widow.

From there, Myrtle had amended herself away from all the filthy men of this world, their disgusting extremities, and their foul ideas. Her only regret was the loneliness her post-marriage life saddled her with.

Alone again, each waking moment contained a deep longing for a child of her own. To laugh and play with and protect and dote upon. And just when Myrtle thought this world of men had beat her with finality, God had sent her little Rosita. Her miracle.

She had loved Rosita as best she could, dedicating her spare room not as a nursery but a glorious shrine to her fragile, beautiful infant, rocking her to sleep, giving of her own body's milk, and showering her with love and gifts and the promise of a future diametrically opposite of Myrtle's own horrid past.

She'd made a home for her daughter. For herself.

Those were Myrtle's most cherished memories. Her shelter from the terrors lurking all around. The two of them had lived in a dream-like perfection together and Myrtle had been healed. She had wanted only to go on living that way, preserved like dolls, she and her baby girl.

Together. In their home.

Until something bad happened. Something inexplicable.

Myrtle had awakened one day to find Rosita gone. Her nursery empty except for a few boxes of moldy old men's suits and despicable yellowed magazines with nude women on the covers.

She called the police to report the disappearance immediately but in an absurd twist of fate, the detective who came to speak with her (a filthy man) told her there was no record of Myrtle having a child or even giving birth.

"I don't know what to tell you, lady," he'd said, frustration swirling in each word. "I've checked birth records at every hospital in a fifty-mile radius. If you could give me a bit more to go on, then I may be able to help. But you can't even answer simple questions and I've got no proof anything you say is true. Where and when was your daughter born?"

"It. Was. Here," she'd told him, her own frustration mutating her voice to a growl. "Right in this home."

"I'm sorry, lady. It wasn't."

Then he left, and soon the police station stopped responding to her calls.

Where has my baby gone? Myrtle wondered for days on end. She cried so much she thought her eyes might detach themselves so they could dry out, like clothing hung on a line. Spent all her time and energy searching aimlessly throughout Oak Hollow and several neighboring towns, sometimes walking dozens of miles in a day and shouting until she would fall to her knees or became so hoarse she sounded like a dying frog.

Until last week, a ray of hope. She had been walking and shouting only a half-mile from her own home when a little girl heard her and came walking over. Myrtle had tried to contain her excitement long enough to make sure it was really her baby, because Rosita had somehow aged a few years in a matter of weeks. And her hair was a different color.

What kind of mother doesn't recognize her own child? Myrtle had scolded herself, then her defenses came down, and she ran toward sweet little Rosita so she could scoop her up and flee back to that sanctuary the two of them had built together.

Only, when she got close, that wretched woman had appeared, called Rosita by some other false name, and Myrtle had tripped on the curb trying to catch up to them as they got into a car and sped away.

How can this be? she had thought. *Who was that woman and how had she tricked my baby into leaving me?*

Finding the Rosita look-alike doll was a clear sign, though. A gift from heaven, confirming her righteous motherhood and proclaiming her as a warrior for her child. Last night, her attempt to reset Rosita's mind had felt like a failure. But now, in the light of day, fueled by renewed physical pain, Myrtle saw a clear path ahead.

That appalling woman, Rosita's captor, with her profane mouth and crude clothing, was not human. Transmogrifying before Myrtle's very eyes, even as she was forced to flee. Not a *she*, but an *it*, some sort of witch or foul spirit. How else could it advance Rosita's age and turn her against her own mother that way?

Myrtle now saw her true obstacle and knew that before she could triumph over it, she first needed to understand it. Its powers, desires. Its strengths.

Its weakness.

Now, all Myrtle's pain, past and current, conspired. It lifted her.

After she emptied her bucket next to the house, she searched in a dust-covered pile of books near the basement door and found one titled *The Compendium of Myths and Monsters*. A gift from an eccentric aunt, and as a child she had treasured it. The book contained over 1,000 entries with encyclopedic detail and images of creatures, spirits, deities, and other mythological beings ranging from prehistoric cave drawings to blurry twentieth-century photos. It covered seemingly all major cultures, eras, and regions of the world.

Myrtle sat in her chair, reading page by page, discerning each entry for fear of overlooking a key piece of information she could weaponize.

Soon, she found what she had been looking for.

The thing that had stolen her child from her, was a succubus.

There could be no other explanation.

"Succubus," Myrtle said, feeling a surge of inner power as she named her adversary aloud.

Rosita was the captive of this particularly nasty type of demon that seduced men using a twisted form of female sexuality. Myrtle found it both sadistic and ironic that such a creature—with its desires to consort with filthy, disgusting men—would also choose to take away the only happiness she had found. She, such a proud, God-fearing, and wholesome woman who loathed men and their coarseness more than any woman in history. This creature was clearly manifesting as a perverse and inverted version of herself. Opposite and sinister in every way. A taunting satanic mockery, like an inverted cross turned humanoid and hungry.

The anti-Myrtle.

Armed with insights from her compendium, she knew a succubus was only vulnerable at the precise moment when it was feeding on a filthy, disgusting, deplorable man. And it was then that she would have to strike.

She checked the time, realizing she had missed her window to be first in line when the thrift shop opened, but quickly decided that did not matter. For once, her day had purpose again.

She took six extra strength Tylenol to mute the pain somewhat until she needed it.

It was time to get moving.

Myrtle was surprised at how easily one can come by a hypodermic needle—with the right story, that is. She had boarded the #17 bus and completed two transfers across the state line to New Gilman, Indiana, where she walked to a veterinarian's office. She told the young girl behind the counter she had traveled in to visit relatives but had forgotten the syringes to administer her cat's insulin. The girl sold her two for one dollar each, no tax, no questions asked. Myrtle paid cash.

Stepping off the return bus now, she went in the opposite direction of her home and headed toward Vine Street to wait for the anti-Myrtle succubus to come home. Hoping it was only a matter of time before it was spreading its legs.

On the way, she stopped by the little bench on Asher Street again. This did not register consciously, but a quieter part of her realized that bench had provided a spark of inspiration last time and could do so again.

It did. And quickly.

There came a whisper. Only this time, it came from behind her instead of from her mind.

"She . . . It has a date tonight," this voice whispered.

It was a man's voice, stirring a powerful distrust in Myrtle. She stood to leave, her years of abuse always bubbling below the surface, now agitated and set loose by that one sentence into a hive of anxiety.

The voice continued. "Leave if you like. I understand why you want to, even—"

"Who—"

"—but I can help you kill it. I've done it before."

"I . . ." Myrtle had not spoken directly to a man in years. And being addressed by one she could not see made it more disconcerting. Her will melted to a puddle at the back of her throat, and despite the pain driving her focus, keeping her sharp, she was on the verge of panic. She stood, her body rigid, her good hand clutching the needles inside her pocket.

"Myrtle."

"H-how do you know my name?"

"Myrtle," it said again. "I know what you're afraid of. But you needn't be. I promise I will never, ever touch you. I will not lay a finger on you."

"You won't? That's exactly what a rapist would say."

"Well I suppose that's true. I give you my word, though. I understand that doesn't mean much yet, but if you'll hear me out, you can decide whether you'd like to stay or go."

Myrtle looked behind her and saw the owner of that voice in an open window across the porch. In that moment, her desire to be with Rosita again won out over her sense of self-preservation. But just barely.

"My name is Lloyd. Lloyd Mnemic," he said, offering a hand. "Would you like to come in and hear what I have to say?"

Myrtle ignored his extended hand with its long, knotted fingers like discolored crab legs. She nodded and walked through the open front door.

A few moments later, they were sitting on a pair of lovely antique couches made of plush white fabric framed in polished mahogany, adorned by clawed feet. Lloyd was across from her and on the desk beside them were two teacups of fine china.

"Would you like to take your coat off?" he asked.

"N-no, thank you," she said.

"Of course not, I apologize for the question. I should have known better. And I realize you may not believe me, but there is nothing more than Earl Grey in those cups. Again, you have my word."

The look in his eyes put her at ease. A knowing look, sympathetic but strong. His round, jovial face and wide-set eyes were unlike the features of any man she'd known. They were softer, more open.

She lifted the cup by its delicate handle and sipped. The tea was warm and strong. Soothing. As she drank, Myrtle balanced the mug on the back of her bad hand, concerned about dropping it.

Lloyd's eyes went to her hand, his brow furrowing in concern or confusion. "May I ask"—he pointed, his lengthy index finger a stark contrast from her gnarled mess of useless extremities—"what happened to your hand?"

Myrtle, self-conscious, set the mug down with care and quickly slid her bad hand inside the sleeve of her cardigan, where she liked to keep it most times.

"That," she said, "happened a long time ago."

"It was a man, wasn't it? A man did that to your poor hand."

He knows too much about me, she thought with alarm. Myrtle stood, making to leave in a hurry. Everything about this situation, this stranger, was wrong. There was nothing but danger here, a honey trap, and she the wayward fly that had not learned to be careful enough. She should never have walked in here.

"Please," he said, standing himself. "I only ask because I think I can help you. That's all I'm here to do in Oak Hollow. I want to help those who need it most. Forgive me for saying so, but I think you're at the top of that list."

"You know too much," she stated firmly, seeing no reason to bandy words or play mind games with him. "You shouldn't know these things about a stranger. It's not natural. I'm going."

She walked past the desk, but he was in the doorway in a flash. Too fast, she understood. She was old and frail and slow, so he could have time to grab her shoulder, pull her back into the room, perhaps. But the desk and chair had been in his way, then several feet of open floor, and yet he beat her to the doorway with ease.

Then, in another blur of motion, both of his hands were on her bad one, and she felt a sensation that could only be described as unfamiliar. It had some similarity to pins and needles, the wakening of sleeping nerves in her hand and forearm, but it was far deeper, as if the bones themselves were waking up and moving around. Re-knitting.

Myrtle screamed, more from alarm and uncertainty than pain or even from fear, because even as this unknown feeling washed through her bad hand, she knew it was healing. Lloyd was healing her. He held on firmly and within seconds, she stopped struggling and watched his face while concentration wormed through all his features.

Then he let go. Neither spoke as Myrtle examined her hand. It was still deformed, still tender to move a few of the fingers, but it was a stark improvement.

"How? How did you do that?"

"That's a trade secret, I'm afraid," Lloyd said, winking. "Though I hope it helps to prove my intent. And I'd like to talk to you about your other, bigger problem. The thing—"

"Succubus," she said, reflexively, cutting him off.

"Yes, that you're facing. You know it can be killed, and I feel you even know how to do so. You have a plan, I understand?"

"How? How could you know this?" As soon as she asked it, an epiphany came. He knew things he shouldn't know, had healed a decades-old injury. Lloyd Mnemic was not a man. Not a person. He was her guardian angel.

Their eyes met, and he nodded knowingly, pressing a finger to his temple as extra confirmation.

"I've been keeping an eye on you." He gestured her back to the chair, then sat across from her once more. He leaned toward the table, narrowing his eyes as if preparing to issue a secret. "And I know that you have overlooked a key detail."

"What detail?"

"You have considered everything until *after*. After it is done. Then what? What benefit will there be if you free your child from this beast only to watch her grow up from behind bars?"

"I've done it before."

"Well, yes. And no. You have slain a beast before, yes. And you have escaped the consequences, the laws of this place. On that, we can agree." He leaned to the side, crossed his legs, and sipped from his own cup. As his hand came back down, part of his face shifted. She saw movement beneath his skin, like a finger pressing out near his temple, then rolling across his forehead. It could have been a trick of the light or her agitated state of mind, but she did not believe that. The timing made it appear intentional. He wanted her to see. "But I would argue that you have not done *this* before. This will be quite different."

"I even have the needle," she said, pulling it from her coat pocket to show him.

"And what happens when the foul creature lies limp at your feet? You take the girl and leave?"

"Well, yes."

"This creature, 'succubus,' as you call it. It is a master of trickery, even in death. It will revert its host to human form, and they will call it murder. They will take her from you again, and this time you will be powerless to get her back."

"Oh." Myrtle felt weightless as she considered his words. Drifting. He was right, of course. She had planned nothing beyond pressing the needle's plunger as far as it could go and emptying toxic liquid into the succubus's vile blood. "What do I do?"

"Listen carefully, and do exactly as I say."

WALTER WALKS

Maybe it just hasn't been long enough? Walt thought. *How long was it before I posted Dad's obituary? A few days, at least.*

Margie said Shawn had died "the other day," so he supposed the arrangements weren't made yet. But Shawn didn't die of natural causes, and Oak Hollow has plenty of slow news days.

When his half-assed Internet sleuthing turned up nothing further, he'd stared blankly at the screen while questioning the original source of information (a parting shot from Margie the gossip queen wasn't exactly an infallible scientific fact), and the more he thought about this snowballing group of strange coincidences, the more unsettled it made him. The impression of some common thread, a malefic linkage connecting the new funeral home, Shawn's death, the caginess he sensed about all of it, like something bigger was happening. It also awakened a curiosity he'd not felt recently, a concern, a desire to know.

What the hell is going on around here?

Even the word "Family" in the place's name stood out. It seemed a common practice for funeral homes to do that, but here it felt forced. A posture. Subterfuge, as though it were jammed in there as a strategy to deceive the crowd. Misdirection. *Don't worry, we're a family place. Nothing to see here.*

There must be thousands of "family" funeral homes around the country. What made this one feel like a falsification? Was it that most family-owned mortuary businesses were a multigenerational practice? Calling it a "Family Funeral Home" here gave this sense the owners were trying too hard to blend in. To pretend they'd been here all along. They were one of us. But that was crazy, right? There could be nothing predatory about a funeral home. It was an ignorant reaction to a place that dealt in death and cadavers. Not to mention his recent experience handling Dad's service and burial.

A weighted dread came, surrounding him like he was sinking to the ocean floor. He hadn't been to a funeral service since his father's, and though there was a desire to have closure with his friend, along with the nagging thoughts about this new funeral home, Walt stiffened at the prospect of going to another wake or stepping inside a funeral parlor again. He wasn't ready to see another body in a casket, didn't think he could face that atmosphere again so soon. Even for a few minutes, it would be hard to keep himself together in there. His own grief was still too active and too unpredictable. He was already stalling like a failed mutineer on the plank, seeing sharks below.

Trapped in another toggling moment, between his desire to pay respects to Shawn and offer condolences to his family, against the fear of confronting his mounting dread to participate in the outside world, more alone than ever without Dad. Walt walked over to Cowboy's bed, squatting and fidgeting with the sleeping dog's creased helicopter ear as he contemplated what to do.

"Tell me I'm nuts, boy," he said.

Cowboy opened one eye and directed it at the sound, but didn't move otherwise.

"I should go, shouldn't I? I mean, it's important. Not just for Shawn and his family, but for me too."

The dog picked his head up then, making direct eye contact.

"You're right," Walt said. "It's one thing to stew in this house and let myself devolve into a crazy hermit with conspiracy theories. But here's a chance to slow that process down and help out a friend at the same time. And I don't even have to stay long."

At that, Cowboy stood, stuck his rear end as far back as he could, stretching his front legs. Then he walked to the kitchen for a drink.

Walt watched him lap water from the bowl, his mind wandering.

Was it better to stay confined and safe and secluded? Or to force himself to rejoin the world for a few moments and say goodbye to a friend? And, in doing so, either put his fears to rest or protect Oak Hollow from yet another threat?

He felt pulled toward some larger and older debate, like his limbic system had swollen and mutated, an animal in a trap of his own design. Suddenly, the internal conflict wasn't about whether he should leave his house. It was grander and more looming, more imposing. It was about whether he would let his own grief consume him.

Fight or flee?

Succumb or stand?

Swim harder or hold still and drown?

By dusk, Walt had failed in all attempts to take his mind off the growing certainty that a correlation existed between this new funeral home, Shawn's sudden death, and his own inability to find any information to help clarify things. Either something foul was afoot in Oak Hollow and trying to stay hidden, or his self-imposed isolation was causing a break from reality.

Walt didn't know which possibility was worse.

Eventually, he decided on a compromise. He would go to Asher Street, but not for the viewing (at least, not at first). He would go tonight when no one else should be there and scope it out. And he would take Cowboy. That way, he was just taking his dog for an evening stroll, the healthiest thing he could think to do about it all.

He told himself, *Either do this now, or you'll end up one of those people who dies alone at home and no one even knows until the neighbors smell your rotting corpse.*

He recalled this morning, Cowboy's timely intervention sparing him another bout of crippling grief and anxiety, yanking him back from the edge. Just then, the dog trotted into the room as if Walt had whistled for him.

"What are you doing up, boy? Tired of sleeping the day away?"

Cowboy stood statue-still, neck straight, his eyes peering up but his head level with Walt's bent knees, ears flat in their usual awkward pattern like there were opposing magnets in their tips.

"Want to go for a walk?"

Cowboy reacted to the question immediately, wagging his tail, tapping out a little dance with his front feet, and rearing his head sideways toward the door a few times, reminding Walt of where the leash hung.

"Okay, okay. Let's go."

Outside, Walt breathed deep, awakening a mixture of unease and relief. The sun was fading and a light breeze slid around them, rustling leaves mildly. It was quiet both up and down the street, allowing Walt to press his resolve and start down the sidewalk before he could change his mind and rush back inside.

For the first few minutes, Cowboy's excitement was uncharacteristically noticeable as he looked rapidly up, down, side to side, bouncing along with his mouth open, straight ear standing up and the creased one lying sideways across his crown. Then he settled in, keeping pace at Walt's left side.

The trek to the funeral parlor was a few blocks farther than the hardware store, which had been about the only place he walked to, but it was mercifully uneventful. And Walt's anxieties grew dormant while Cowboy began lagging a half-step behind as he lost stamina. Like all greyhounds, he could go from standing to forty mph in three strides, but they were not built for long distances. They passed no one, and Walt assumed most people were gathering indoors, maybe sitting down to a Sunday dinner.

In the center of town, there were a few cars moving down nearby streets, but the remaining distance to the old house looked free of people. The walk had cleared Walt's mind, as if all that time spent alone had dulled his senses, the weeks of isolation generating mental clutter, nurturing irrational anxieties, and reinforcing circular logic. Being outdoors allowed him to realize how ridiculous some of these worries had become, growing unchecked in dark corners like poisonous mushrooms. It seemed so clear out here that other people had real problems to contend with, putting his in perspective. His grief, though terrible, seemed more proportionate and would not measure up to that of Shawn's widow. His anxieties no longer felt crippling and also more self-imposed, manageable if he could just expect more from himself, show some discipline, make better choices.

The old house came into view, and from a few blocks out, Walt noted it looked no different from his memory, in either construction or condition. Nothing had changed about it, and he wondered again how it could be ready to operate in anything less than a few months' time.

Walt stopped in front of the neighboring building to take it in. Those big stained-glass windows like a chameleon's eyes, watching.

The metal spike atop the added turret, pointing. The marred section of brick, sloughing. The rusted fire escape, dangling like an imperiled free-solo climber. If someone were ready to run a business in there, they'd made no progress updating the exterior. He added this to the growing list of strange coincidences.

Cowboy took a last, long stride and stopped next to him, leaning against Walt's leg and panting. "Good boy," he said, patting the dog on the side of his deep, furry chest.

Suddenly, the air felt charged, like the whole street was holding its breath to see what happened next. Walt stood still, the only sound around them was Cowboy's hurried but quiet breathing. They were waiting, with no idea what for. When nothing happened for two minutes, and Cowboy's breathing slowed, Walt walked closer toward the old house, feeling Cowboy's resistance grow more active.

The house was dark, inside and out.

The last time Walt had been this close to 432 Asher Street was the night of the tour, when they'd gathered across the street for a broader view. Of all the stories Walt had heard, only one came to mind now.

The tour had mentioned it, but then Dad elaborated with details he'd tracked down personally. The house had served for one season as a makeshift hospital, housing spillover patients during a terrible epidemic. The tour guide said it was a tuberculosis outbreak, but Dad's research suggested it was more likely for victims of yellow fever. He said there were several outbreaks due to the proximity of ponds and lakes near town, and physicians at the time not understanding that mosquitos were the vector for spreading the virus. During the worst of these outbreaks in 1877, over three hundred people had died in less than forty-eight hours. Since the bodies could not be refrigerated while awaiting burial, they were stored in morgue tunnels beneath the building. As Dad told him about this, he seemed quite proud and boasted that almost no one knew about those tunnels anymore. He called them the "Dead Rooms," and that term had stuck in Walt's mind.

Dead Rooms.

And now, sitting atop them was a funeral home. Rooms for the dead atop the Dead Rooms. The dead stacked on the dead in a dying town. A shiver passed through Walt's neck, shoulders, and torso.

He mustered himself and gave the leash a light tug. They crossed the street.

Walt stepped onto the rim of the sidewalk and no farther, Cowboy stayed in the street, his body vibrating with nervous energy like it did during thunderstorms. Walt didn't have the heart to force him any closer. If they stayed much longer, Cowboy might howl in fear.

He sympathized because something about the old house scared him too. He realized then, the walk had cleared some mental cobwebs but the sense of ominous, impending events was just as strong. Leaving the house was good for him, but his instincts were still clamoring out an alarm.

He made to leave, to head home and mull over coming to pay his respects tomorrow and do a little more snooping, when he noticed a figure in the bay window of the turret on the other side of the house. Or what looked like a figure, an outline in shadow. There were no lights on inside, and the exterior lights along the street were causing glare, but he thought someone was standing just inside the glass. A person? Short and broad, with something protruding from their mouth, like a cigar, only larger.

Walt recalled another story about a man who had died in that room and now haunted it, but both the tour guide and Dad had debunked that one.

A car drove by, headlights flashing across the glass.

When it passed, the window was empty.

MNEMIC OBSERVES

At dusk, Mnemic watched from behind the antique windows of 432 Asher Street. When not otherwise engaged, he had taken to standing in the turret room to keep aware of any unwanted attention, knowing that would come soon. This room had the best view of the street outside, and while he'd gone to great lengths preparing the town—far more meticulously than he'd prepared any cadaver—and limiting his exposure, inevitably, his actions would catch notice. The authorities would have no reason to check up on him yet, still completely unaware of his arrival, but small towns like this were rife with concerned citizens and busybodies.

It was acceptable, too, so long as he could proceed through all the milestones in time. Past attempts had taught him much about the vulnerabilities in his design, but he'd enacted additional safeguards this time.

And his apprentice was positioned as the final failsafe.

As the sun retreated further, he saw a man approach, bringing with him a large, lean dog.

Mnemic sensed their fear, strong even from across the street, wafting toward him like the scent of a freshly prepared meal. The dog's terror was primal, simple. It wanted only to flee, as was its nature. Simple fear was predictable, more easily managed. If Mnemic chose to twist that, which he could do with ease, he knew exactly what would happen.

The man's was more complex, though not unfamiliar. Like them all, he feared what he did not understand. But this was tempered by rivets of rational thought and layered with other emotions, memories, experiences, all forming a unique, and therefore unpredictable, stew of behavioral triggers and impulses.

Mnemic had learned, no matter how sure he was of the outcome when he twisted a human's fears, that their response could surprise him. This did not happen often, but when it did, the fear in question bore similarities to that of the man standing outside right now. There was fear of death in that mix, the crop Mnemic had sown centuries ago, but it was different. Muddied. Coagulated with some recent experience he was still sorting. It would be harder to use.

Mnemic vowed again not to repeat past mistakes by acting hastily. He let this man go, rather than attack and draw attention before the next milestone was achieved. These same missteps had combined to thwart his last attempt.

In the place they now call Texas, a scant decade before he enacted the first step of his current design. He'd been exposed too early by members of a nearby village, ignoring any threat they might have posed, thinking himself invulnerable. They came for him in a heated mob, in a vulnerable moment, and had branded him.

They simply weren't scared enough.

He shut down his machine before it could complete the cycle, fleeing to regroup and try anew. A most frustrating outcome, though he couldn't help but be amused with the name they'd since assigned to his wreckage.

"The Devil's Sinkhole," they called it.

Humans and their simple ideas, he thought. *Everything they can't explain is angels or devils. Heaven and Hell. They fear demons and ghosts when there are far greater threats beneath their very feet. They think we want their souls, but I've found something far sweeter to take.*

The man outside walked closer, crossing the street and pulling his terrified dog behind, then stopped at the edge of the sidewalk. Mnemic moved back, further into shadow. It was unlikely this one would find the courage to come any closer, but Mnemic had come too far to take unnecessary risk. Best to avoid being observed in his current form.

Unseen, the flesh of his face rippled, the matter beneath swelling then collapsing lung-like.

This man's visit was a noteworthy, though minor, development. Nothing more. But Mnemic would not underestimate him. If anything more concerning happened, he need only contact Preston. His design was protected.

Yes, everything was proceeding apace and soon this dying town would be his.

Forever.

MONDAY

KATHERINE MOURNS

K atherine Yost was sure she used every drop of her energy when she told her children their father was dead, yet somehow, she was still moving the next morning. Still moving as they arrived at Mnemic Family Funeral Home for the service, along with her parents.

The kids each took the news in their own way, in obvious reflections of their age, personality, and relationship with their father. Ten-year-old Megan, who had been closest to Shawn, took it the hardest. She and Katherine had spent hours sitting on the couch, arms around one another, crying hysterically. But then Megan showed an unexpected level of strength and asked if she could help tell her brothers, eight-year-old Trevor and four-year-old Samuel. Trevor was devastated, too, but intuition told Katherine his reaction was more about seeing how distraught she was than about Shawn. Samuel's reaction was noticeably different; he seemed only curious for a few minutes, then almost apathetic, asking if he could go play in the backyard. An hour later, he was singing and drawing on the concrete with chalk. Katherine wondered if that made Sammy better off than the rest of them, or worse. Nothing is permanent at that age, but is that a help or a hindrance?

Katherine's mother tried to confirm all the kid's reactions were typical, what one would expect under such circumstances, but Katherine couldn't ignore that her mom had no more experience in this situation than the rest of them. And Shawn's voice kept popping in to remind that her mother wasn't from Oak Hollow, as if that mattered a whit.

Draining as that step was, she realized it was just the beginning. She'd need to tap into deeper stores within herself today.

Perform a fracking of the soul.

That's why Lloyd Mnemic's help and presence were welcomed without question. He waited to usher them toward the most difficult day of their lives.

They walked through the front door of 432 Asher Street and into the chapel, Katherine and her ruined family unit, hand in hand and wearing their best clothes and false composure. The two boys were on their tiptoes as they entered the solemn, mysterious room where dead things were shown, and Katherine nearly followed suit on impulse.

The chapel's atmosphere demanded their silence, as if more than a mere wall separated it from the surrounding rooms, instead a spiritual barrier that must be respected. Lloyd insisted they spend a moment with Shawn before anyone else arrived. The casket was positioned across the room from where they stood. The air hung heavy and graveyard-still around them. Katherine relaxed her grip on the boys' hands, wanting not to force them to see the body as her mother once had. They stayed in tight formation on approach, a tentative flock of geese in their black clothing.

The body inside matched the one in her persistent mental images, not the one she had loved, married, and shared a life and a home with. The shape was recognizable, but his hair wasn't quite right. His hands looked shrunken. His lips held too much color. Perhaps if she could see his eyes . . .

Here was her dime-store simulacrum. Her wax rendition stand-in.

Katherine and her fatherless children stood beside the casket, taking turns staring at him or the walls or at their feet. Somewhere in that lost time, Katherine summoned the voice to tell her kids everyone else would be here soon, and if they wanted to speak to Daddy alone, now was the time. Megan broke into awful sobs, heartbreaking to watch, reached in to hold not-Shawn's hand, then leaned to whisper in his ear, "I'll miss you . . . " Katherine couldn't hear the rest because she was crying too loudly herself. Her daughter placed a worn copy of Shawn's favorite Louis L'Amour novel near his hand and walked away.

On Trevor's turn, he made to emulate Megan as best he could, only his crying was near silent. He whispered, "I love you, Daddy," as he placed a Columbus Blue Jackets hockey puck from the one game they'd attended together atop Shawn's chest.

Little Sammy looked inside the casket briefly, said nothing, but wrinkled his nose. He left a picture of a race car torn from a coloring book, then said he needed to go pee and walked out of the room to find his grandfather.

When the rest arrived, through the first few moments, Katherine fought to convince herself she wasn't smelling formaldehyde, that it was only in her mind. But the wafts of phantom scent kept coming because she was standing next to a chemical-filled balloon in roughly the shape of her husband, with an angry red burn around its neck concealed by more chemicals blended into a powdery flesh tone. Every time someone approached her, the old house's floorboards creaked, sounding to her exactly like the rope swaying and stretching under Shawn's weight.

It wasn't long before she felt herself detaching, hanging in a liminal form of consciousness, like drifting off to a sleep without borders. From there, she experienced her husband's Viewing not through her own lens but a combination of all those closest to her. Watching her children, her parents, and Shawn's family each give birth to a grief with its own identity, as if she had the multifaceted eyes and emotional maturity of a housefly.

Lloyd Mnemic was a godsend. He knew exactly what they each needed to hear (even if that was nothing at all), how best to convey it, when to hold their hands, wrap an arm around their shoulders, or simply stand nearby. He focused this individual attention on them each in the moments when their need for comfort was its strongest.

Throughout the day, he was even quick to intervene when someone in the receiving line—which was almost exclusively made up of Shawn's extended family—said something insensitive or touched a nerve that was too raw. He'd reminded her to sip water, handed her a tissue, placed his assuring hand on her shoulder while standing at her side.

He interrupted Shawn's cousin, Margie, and a trio of women (none of whom Katherine recognized) from posing for a selfie with his body, ushering them politely but forcefully aside like he was shooing pigeons in a park.

As the morning passed, Megan remained distraught, and Katherine was selfishly glad to have her so they could lean on each other a bit. Trevor was visibly sad, but there were deeper feelings below that which were harder for her to read. At different points throughout the morning, she sensed tones of anger, remorse, maybe guilt. Samuel spent the day either running back and forth between the rows of chairs, or asking questions that those present had neither the heart to answer with full honesty nor the callousness to avoid.

"When will Daddy wake up?"

"Why does he look like that?"

"Where are his feet?"

"Why didn't God save him with his God powers?"

"Can I have his candy bars now?"

"Will he remember us in Heaven?"

The last barrage pierced her, and her merciful detachment broke, then she broke. Lloyd glided over, escorting her from the room and into his office. He left her there, closing the door as she fought for composure. Aiming for any useful distraction, her eyes went to the window, peering down Asher Street on a bright spring afternoon. Thinking about the town of Oak Hollow, once her home and now poisoned, and wishing she'd never set foot here.

Then Lloyd peeked back in. "I understand little Samuel is taking a nap now," he said. "He won't be asking any more questions for a bit. And the guests continue to arrive."

MYRTLE KILLS

The enormous yellow school bus lumbered and groaned its way up the street, around the corner and growing smaller (but still loud), and Myrtle emerged from her hiding place behind the bus stop. She watched the back of the bus, a cold weight inside her chest as it pulled beyond her view, pining for a chance to be closer to those small silhouettes inside and imagining their cheerful melodic voices.

Row after row of living dolls.

"The driver on the bus says, 'Move on back,'" she sang to herself. "'Move on back.'" Her little Rosita was on that bus somewhere, and the only way she kept herself from giving chase was a firm reminder that her shortest path to reunion lay inside the house across the street. She would see Rosita tonight if this all went as planned.

"'Move on back,'" she sang once more.

She looked side to side to ensure she was alone, not registering that she had too little experience at this and would likely not have noticed if someone was twenty feet away and pointing a camera at her. She patted the small leather folio in her coat pocket containing the loaded hypodermic needle.

As she walked toward the house where Rosita was being held, she reflected on how Lloyd had generously, meticulously listed instructions for her. He had thought of everything and Myrtle was grateful for his timely arrival. Without his help, she was now convinced she would have failed and found herself in prison with no means of ever seeing her child again.

My guardian angel, she thought.

Birds chirped nearby, and the sun was cresting behind the homes down the street. She had divine guidance.

It was a fine day to kill a demon.

The dewy grass rustled mutely beneath her feet as she rounded the house through the side yard. The back door was unlocked, just as Lloyd had said it would be. She entered the house to find herself in a modest and clean kitchen, dishwasher humming to her left, otherwise quiet.

If Lloyd's guesses had all been correct, and she'd no reason to think otherwise, the creature would be in its nest upstairs, sleeping and in its most vulnerable state. Having shuttled its precious cargo off to school (per Lloyd, this was only a temporary measure to keep up appearances while it continued to gain strength), it would have let its guard down and perhaps even retaken a semblance of its truer form.

The home was old, like most buildings in this part of town, and so the stairs creaked. Myrtle took her time—feeling a small comfort because she'd been here before and this time there was daylight to help her see—hoping the beast was distracted enough to give her time for action.

At the crest of the stairs, she paused, listening. She heard a noise, muffled as if coming from behind a closed door. It sounded like a creak mixed with cloth moving, coming from her right, the opposite direction from the room where Rosita had been sleeping last night.

Afraid she would be caught, panic gripping her heart as she thought about the extremeness of what she was preparing to do (*poison a she-devil with a feline diabetes needle*) and then about what was at stake (*Rosita's very life and soul*), Myrtle's mind entered a familiar blank state, a reflex she had cultivated during her years of abuse. Her eyes glazed over like she was approaching sleep. She removed the folio from inside her cardigan sweater, zipping it open as she walked toward the closed door where the sound had originated. She grasped the syringe, dropped the leather folio, and flipped the plastic protective cover off with the thumb of her good hand.

With her other hand (more useful now), she turned the brass door-knob and shoved the door open. It swung open roughly, clanging against the plaster wall of a bedroom. As Myrtle strode into that room, her gait full of authority and confidence, she found a bed in the far corner where a motionless figure lay beneath a large tan comforter.

When you see it, you cannot afford to hesitate. Not even for an instant. It's too powerful, Lloyd had said.

She held the syringe above her head, inside a clenched fist and aimed at her target. Then pounced. Swung the needle down like it were the righteous sword of an avenging angel. With the force of her downward swing, there was minimal resistance as the needle penetrated the comforter, a sharp cry of pain when it pierced. Myrtle held her thumb on the plunger and depressed it before the succubus could wrench free. Then it spun away from her and she was left panting next to the bed, holding the empty syringe.

The shape beneath the comforter groaned, moving about brusquely, trying to find its way out. Then it rolled toward her and she took a step back as it fell off the bed, landing near her feet, still rolling until the comforter fell off and she could see a face.

It wasn't a demon. Or a monster.

It also wasn't a woman.

It was a boy, in his early teens by her estimate, older than the boy she'd seen sleeping in the bunk beds with Rosita last night. He must have stayed home sick from school because as she looked around the bed, she saw clumps of used tissues, a bottle of cold medicine, a bag of cough drops.

He looked up at her as the life slipped from his eyes, face twisted in confusion and shock.

Myrtle gasped and fled the house, tears landing on the front of her sweater with each step.

WALTER SUSPECTS

Walt drove to Asher Street for the service because it was quicker, and without Cowboy he'd be too vulnerable on foot in the wide-open air. Still, he had considered walking, leaving the dog tied to a pole outside like he was visiting a saloon in the Wild West. Barring that, he wished for a greyhound's speed so he could bolt away from anything threatening. He reminded himself there were no greater threats than letting anxiety continue growing its control over him.

I'll make this quick. Talk to his wife, take a good look around the inside of the house as a reality check. Then I'm out.

When he arrived, there were no people in sight. A few cars parked on the street nearby, but he'd expected there to be a sizable crowd based on Shawn's status in Oak Hollow and the tragic nature of his death. The low turnout would have made more sense had Walt arrived early. But by now, it should be crowded.

In daylight, the poor condition of the building's exterior was more apparent. Even from a dozen feet away, Walt noticed scores of warped boards, paint peeling in easily a hundred different places. A few shutters hanging crooked. Three broken window panes upstairs. A lone Christmas wreath hung next to the easternmost upstairs window, lilting in the slight breeze. A wrought iron fire escape hung loosely from the second floor, rusted through in multiple places and looking about as safe as a toaster in the bathtub. A large patch of brick had been repaired with plaster, then painted. The color was noticeably lighter, pinkish, giving the appearance of a large scar growing new skin.

Who would open a business in a building that looks abandoned like this? Especially when part of what you're selling is dignity.

Since last night, someone had hung a carved wooden sign above the awning over the front porch, reading *Mnemic Family Funeral Home*. On any acceptable building front, that sign would have been nondescript. But here, it was like putting a sharp new bow tie on roadkill.

Walt swallowed hard at the analogy he had just conjured, feeling a bit like he had pulled back the veneer of the universe. There was something strangely aligned within it, which he couldn't place. One of Dad's weak spots? If one existed within a hundred-mile radius, this would be the logical place.

Logical, sure. Running short on logic this week, old man.

Lack of logic may cause irregular bowel movements if left untreated. Thanks, Dad.

The front door was propped open and Walter entered, immediately raising stinging memories from the last funeral service he'd attended. In a way, he knew what Shawn's kids were going through today, but at the same time, he very much did not.

It was as if he'd stepped through a portal to another place and time, leaving him disoriented and far too vulnerable. Panic clutched him. and he would have fled if he had the coherence to signal his limbs just then.

On one hand, the inside of 432 Asher Street did not match the outside. The décor was tasteful, clean, modern. An abundance of fresh flowers on several nearby tables filled the room with pleasant color and scent. Comforting instrumental music played over sleek speakers recessed into the walls and ceiling. The lighting was bright, walls freshly painted. He noticed a large flat-screen TV nearby running a slideshow, a stream of pictures displaying a gleeful Shawn with his wife, their three children, his championship bowling team.

It's nice in here, he thought. *Comforting. That's how a funeral home is supposed to feel. But why put it in this building and then start using it before the exterior is ready?*

There were less than a dozen people in attendance, all clustered in a room where the open casket rested, just above waist-high for the average person, flanked by two large potted flower arrangements. It was a rich mahogany, the overhead lighting reflecting off its glossy surface. It could have been the same model Walter had ordered, or maybe they just all looked alike. A somber silence filled the air, disturbed only by sporadic sobs from different parts of the room.

On the other hand, the setting teleported him back to Dad's funeral, the experience still raw and jagged. A different location but very much the same atmosphere.

That place probably would have felt comforting too. If not for Dad's corpse in it.

Dozens of semi-strangers and distant relatives acting as if it were a run-of-the-mill social gathering while they stood next to his father's remains. Until they approached to offer empty condolences—hollow, trite phrases about better places and time healing wounds, as if grief and losing a loved one were events with silver linings or inconveniences you could "get over."

Walter had to keep pulling his conscious mind back into the moment like it were a child's balloon in a windstorm, desperate to detach and float elsewhere. Staying present only grew harder as the viewing went on, but there was no one else to take his place next to the casket. The strategy that had finally worked was hyperfocusing on the official pieces, the planning and paperwork. The way a surgeon stops seeing their patient as a person to keep an efficient, clinical state of mind, Walt had made it through his father's viewing and burial by dissociating from what it truly was. Masking where he was and what he was doing. He was somewhere else, not next to a corpse, while everyone hugged him and told him how sorry they were. He was rerunning the litany of legal documents, transactional steps, or prefatory matters he'd discussed with the funeral director.

Mourner #37: Heaven gained another angel today, Walt.

Walter: That's so kind. Thanks for coming. Who was last to sign the Transfer of Custody form?

Mourner #164: It's all part of a bigger plan, you know?

Walter: That's good to hear. Can't forget to call the County Death Certificate Office next week.

Mourner #219: Let us know if you need anything.

Walter: Thanks, I'll do that. What was in the third line of the Coroner's Amendments?

Walter looked into the chapel now, recognized several of the people in there, Margie in particular, and assumed most of them were Shawn's family based on how they were standing as a group to one side. His own grief occupied his stomach passively, as it did most days, and to his surprise, its presence motivated him to speak with Shawn's widow rather than retract. Maybe he could offer her a truth from his experience rather than fill death's silence like everyone else leaking words toward her that helped only themselves.

He recognized her from the slideshow pictures he had just seen, though they'd never met. She wore a sleek black dress and her face was wet and puffy. A girl of about ten or eleven years old walked up and stood next to the widow. The girl held a single yellow flower with a long stem, which Walt assumed she had pulled from one of the arrangements lining the hallway.

He approached the casket.

Shawn's widow looked up, her eyes bloodshot.

Walt nodded to her, stopped himself from saying anything that turned him into a walking Hallmark card. Instead, he stood in silence and saw the cadaver. Like others he had seen, it looked like the person he knew but it also didn't. He thought of Dad and of his own mortality.

To his surprise, what Walter felt then was not fear, only a profound sadness for what he'd lost. The Oak Hollow he'd grown up in, then Dad. Now Shawn. Their funerals being so close together had conditioned him, just slightly, to seeing death in his days. He wondered how often that happened anymore, with so much about death hidden beneath a shroud and handled only by professionals.

Shawn lay there among the silk and cushions, hands arranged on his stomach. Eyes closed. Thick makeup covering most of his face, but not quite hiding the ligature marks around his neck or the bruising under his eyes. The bottom half of the casket was closed.

He wore a black suit, thin black tie.

This man he had known, respected, discussed repairs, and traded hobbies with. Now nothing more than a set of clothing and rubbery, dead skin.

A tear rolled down Walt's cheek, and he was glad he'd come.

Mrs. Yost broke the silence.

"Have we met? How did you know Shawn?"

"We haven't met, no. I'm Walt. And I-I . . . We were friends, I guess you'd say. He was a good person. I liked him. He was easy to talk to, and well . . . I don't find that often."

"Thank you for saying that, Walt. He did mention you, actually. I'm his wife, Katherine. And this is Megan." She squeezed her daughter around the shoulders, pulling her close. Her gaze slackened, turning to her sons seated in the back row of chairs with a woman Walt assumed was their grandmother. Then the widow looked toward the ceiling, staring at nothing.

Walt recognized this, a sign she was detaching from the moment. Playing a part, the best she could, for a disparate crowd. The poor woman had hours left to endure, and making it through the wake was the least of her problems to come. Walt wanted to help, say something to make it more bearable for her, but he knew that spitting recycled comfort words at her would do more for his comfort than hers.

"This must be so hard for you," he said, settling on something he remembered the funeral director saying to him. "I just wanted to stop by and offer my best to you and your family."

"Thank you for coming. I expected more people, so it means a lot that you're here."

"My dad died recently. Wait, sorry. I didn't mean to make this about me. I was just thinking, during his wake, my mind kept wandering. I . . . I think that's natural. Trying to escape or step away from it like that. One thing that helped me was to think about all the boring, impersonal stuff."

She gave him a confused look, tilting her head and narrowing her eyes.

"Mommy," Megan said, "I'm going to use the bathroom."

The widow nodded, kissed her forehead as she left.

Walt continued. "What I mean is, everything was so raw still, and my experience couldn't compare to how hard yours is, but I wanted to be present and not be at the same time. I wasn't ready to face it, but you don't really have a choice. People coming up and saying their bit. It was . . . hard. So I ended up keeping my composure by focusing on the paperwork and the official steps of everything Dad needed done, down to the last detail. I think I'd do okay on an entrance exam for mortuary school by now, if there is such a thing. Coroner's papers, enzyme tests, death certificate, transfer of custody forms, all that jargon. It was all so . . . dispassionate and oddly grounding. I still have the NJA number memorized. In a weird way, it helped me to process how I felt too. I wore it like armor that day while I started adjusting to life after loss."

He waited while she processed this, expecting the confusion to lift from her expression. It nearly did, her brow flattened, her lips drew out wider. But then it returned, amplified.

"NJA?"

"Oh, that's the one they assign before the funeral home takes over. It's like giving them permission to have the . . . never mind, it doesn't matter. I just thought—"

"I didn't do any of that. He told me he'd take care of it all and I accepted that. So he never gave me details."

"Oh, well, I'm sure that's fine. It's better to have help. I . . . I'm sorry I brought it up."

"He told me to focus on the kids, and he'd deal with everything."

"That makes sense, of course."

"It was comforting, so I went along. But to hear you talk about it, now I'm wondering if I should be more involved. I'm usually very good about details, but I haven't even seen the obituary yet. When I found him, hanging in our house, I didn't even call nine-one-one."

That was surprising to hear, but Walt had no response, flummoxed silent by his own poor decision to bring this nonsense up, making her feel worse instead of better. Why didn't he just offer condolences like a normal person?

He watched as her expression changed again, several times in the space of seconds. The confusion returned, then became something more contemplative, like she was weighing conflicting pieces of information. Next, she grew visibly upset, not in mourning but closer to anger. Nostrils flared, standing taller, her eyes darted around the room, searching.

Shawn's relatives were still clustered but had moved closer to the exit. No one had arrived since Walter. Her two boys were still in the back with Grandma, now Grandpa had joined them.

Who is she looking for?

"There he is," she said under her breath as if speaking only to herself.

A man entered the chapel from the hallway, walking toward them. His attire and pleasant demeanor suggested to Walt that he was the funeral home's owner or someone employed here.

"Mr. Mnemic?" Katherine said.

"How are you holding up, Mrs. Yost?" he responded, not acknowledging Walter.

"What is Shawn's NJA number?"

He seemed taken aback but quickly recovered. "Why would . . . I don't have it with me at the moment, but I can go check if you'd like. Perhaps you could use a break, anyway."

He raised his arm out straight, beckoning her over. The sleeve of his coat slid up and Walt glimpsed a black mark, a few inches long, near the inside of his wrist. A symbol, not unlike Dad's rune tattoo, but with fewer lines, maybe. The patch of skin around it was discolored, as if covered with makeup that didn't match well. He lowered his arm, and it was gone. On their way past, he offered Walt a dismissive, "Excuse us."

As they walked toward the hallway, she said to him, "There's nobody here. Did you send out an announcement?"

Realizing he was standing alone next to the casket, Walt turned to Shawn's body and nodded. "I'll try to keep an eye on them for you," he said, not sure if he meant it at all but compelled to offer a parting gift to his friend.

"My dad talked about you a few times," Megan said.

Walt startled, unaware she had come back. "He did?"

"Yep. He liked talking with you. And your dog."

"Is it okay if I stop by your house sometime? To check on you and your brothers after the funeral?"

"Mm-hmm, yeah. I'm gonna go over with my brothers now."

"Okay. Nice to meet you, Megan."

By then, Walt's own eyes were filling with tears. He wiped at them with the back of his hand as he made his way along the front row of chairs. As that hand slid across, though, something strange happened in his peripheral vision.

The wall behind the casket . . . rippled.

Like a pond's surface touched by a strong breeze. For a half-second, it looked like a wave of movement passed over its surface in unison with the motion of Walt's hand, so precise in timing as to excuse what he saw as an illusion caused by his hand tugging at the corner of his eye, stretching and blurring his vision. As that rolling wave cascaded diagonally across the wall, Walt's eyes took in two different images: one ahead of and also behind the wave, the second was inside the wave itself.

That second image bulged inside a stream of bent light as it traveled down and across the wall, as if an unseen hand was moving a huge magnifying glass from the top corner to the bottom behind the casket. In it, the wall was decrepit. Its condition matched the exterior of this home, a building two hundred years old, neglected and abused for decades. Not clean, unmarked drywall under a fresh coat of paint, a look that would have matched all the other walls around it. Instead, inside that rolling wave was discolored plaster marred by webs of cracks, spots of mildew, and several holes—one large enough to expose a section of naked wood behind it.

That's the way it should look in here, the Dad-voice in his mind said, sounding less facetious and more curious. *The way the whole interior should look.* He broke his gaze and fled.

Walt rushed out the front door of 432 Asher Street and heard Shawn's widow crying behind him.

KATHERINE BARGAINS

The meager crowd had left, barely enough to fill out one page of the guest book near the front door. The Yost kids were sent home with their grandparents.

Katherine was alone with Shawn's body again, as she'd been when she first found him hanging. Rather, this time, she was alone with his waxy body double. She wondered if there was sawdust inside him or if that was just for taxidermied animals. She saw his head mounted on a fireplace wall like exotic game and tried to blink it away.

She knew what she was supposed to do but couldn't bring herself to.

She wasn't ready to say goodbye.

Lloyd had pulled her into his office, shown her some paperwork and insisted again that everything was in order. Not fully reassured, but still desperate for help and aware it was too late to change anything now, she had returned to her dutiful place beside the casket. After that, only one more person arrived. Selfishly, she was glad there were so few attendees to deal with, but it was clear he had only relied on word of mouth to inform the town of Shawn's service today.

Everyone else was gone.

How could she want to flee and to stay at the same time?

Despite the murk inside her, in that moment she felt love and longing most. She missed him already. Theirs had been a good life, a good partnership, until more recently. And when times were hard, they had each other.

Now, she had to face the worst times yet, alone. She studied his face inside the casket, colorless and lifeless, and found she couldn't say goodbye. Not to this imposter. And even if she could bring herself to speak to it to him, she'd only want to ask him the question that had nagged her for days.

Why, Shawn? Why?

Without speaking, she reached for the casket's lid and pulled it down. It closed noisily, falling shut and causing an echo in the stillness of the empty old house. Above her, a TV hanging in the corner was still playing the slideshow of family photos, accompanied by a lyric-free version of a Fleetwood Mac song she and Shawn had both enjoyed. She stared at the screen as her mind worked at a tangled ball of questions.

Lloyd interrupted before she could unravel that ball any further. His voice a beacon, carrying a smile through the air.

"I believe everyone else has left, Katherine."

She turned to face him. He placed his hands on the edges of her shoulders, arms angled up because of their height difference, and they stood at arm's length.

"What do I do now?" she asked.

"I wish I could tell you the next step will be easier. But I know that you have the strength to face this too. Even if you can't feel it right now. You're not used to being in death's presence, and that's understandable. If it helps, in my experience, what death wants us to do, is pause. And take stock. Consider what is most important because we all have limited time. Everything dies, Katherine. Everything. And this is a reminder that you will die too. So embrace this pause that death is offering and seek understanding with it. I'm sure you feel overwhelmed and confused, but deep down, you already know what it is you need most. It takes courage to voice, but it's there. Can you hear it? Through the silence of death?"

"Well," she answered.

His eyes glistened as they ran across her face, seeking. "Now, tell me. What is it you need most?"

She turned away.

"I've been doing this a very long time, and there's hardly a thing on this Earth I've not been asked. What will bring you closure, Katherine?"

"It . . . it's just."

"You want to know why he did it. Don't you?"

"How did you—"

"Please, come now. I just said I've been doing this forever. Far longer than I'd care to admit. It's what anyone in your situation would want to know. I'd like to know myself. I realize I'm new in town, but hearing the well-wishers and friends today, it's clear he didn't seem ready to leave."

"I just don't get it. Why would he do that? What made him think it was necessary? That it would help? We could have figured out something. There had to be a better way." She glared toward the closed casket. "Why? Why, Shawn?"

"I understand, truly. Of course, on the surface it appeared he saw no way out, that he was making the only choice he had left. Still, when we try to put ourselves in his position, his state of mind, it seems so clear that he made a permanent decision in response to a temporary problem. So, there must be a larger 'Why?' Much more to it than just what he thought in that moment. Perhaps the question you seek to answer is not 'Why?' but 'How?'. As in 'How could you?' or 'How dare you?'. May I make a suggestion, Katherine?"

She broke her stare from the closed casket and their eyes met. Hers, red as stoplights, his shining like silver coins in a gutter. The room was a vacuum around them. Noiseless and anticipatory.

"We could just ask dear Shawn that very question."

Soon, Katherine Yost followed Mnemic down a narrow hallway. All the lights in the funeral home were behind her and she was walking into darkness, until he slipped through a doorway she hadn't noticed, then dim lamplight bubbled from it.

In that moment, she noticed a stark difference in the atmosphere. When the old house had been filled with people, it was solemn, quiet. Reflective. She herself had been in a beleaguered state of consciousness but still aware that those around her were there to lend support, to help hoist her and her family up as they said goodbye.

Now, the quiet was not borne of dignified reflection, it had turned oppressive. Like the calm before the storm.

No. More like she was about to be chased, alone in a forest and something was stalking in the brush nearby. Crouched to pounce.

Her pulse had been frantic since hearing Mnemic say something impossible, but her shock in reaction to the words he had spoken was forming an emotional dam. Everything she should be feeling was blocked behind it and backing up inside her lest her head burst from disbelief.

How could they possibly ask her dead husband why he had killed himself? Mnemic had not elaborated yet and surely, she had misunderstood. She was inferring it was a chance to *speak* with Shawn. No way that's what Mnemic meant. Maybe he had found a note near the body and waited for now to share it, trying to give her closure after the viewing.

But after he said it, he grabbed her by the forearm and led her into this hall.

She stood still for what felt like hours but was surely under a minute.

He stepped back into the hall, the weak light from the next room outlining the contours of his face, closing the distance between his eyes, and making him appear predatory.

Did he have less hair now?

"Now then," he said, "let's discuss terms, shall we?"

"Terms?" she answered, her tone revealing a weakened resolve. "For what?"

"Why, for our . . . arrangement." He moved his hand up to her shoulder, his grip tightening. His smile widened. "You realize, of course, what I'm offering to you?"

Despite the reeling in her mind this conversation was causing, Katherine sensed a strangeness about the way Mnemic was questioning her.

"Did you find a note?" she asked.

"No. I have something far better than stagnant words on paper. I'm offering you a chance to speak to your husband. One last time. So you can ask him."

Again, something odd about his speech. Was it the phrasing? So hard to think.

"Oh," she said, failing to conjure anything larger. This was all nonsense, of course. She had spent the last several hours staring at Shawn's corpse lying in a box. Before that, she had found him dangling with his feet six inches above their basement floor with a noose around his neck. Perfectly still, his face mottled purple and spittle falling from his cocked mouth. Now he lay in a box with his insides removed and his mouth sewn shut. There was no speaking to him, ever again.

Full stop.

She knew this in her head. But her heart pled differently. It needed no logic or reality.

"How?"

"I'll explain soon enough," Mnemic said. "But first, I need to ensure that we have an understanding. An agreement. This is something you want, yes?"

She opened her mouth to respond, then realized what was standing out about his manner of speaking. He was phrasing so much of this as questions or explanations, but none of it felt open. There was no upward inflection in his voice. Instead, he was injecting each sentence with a sternness that implied a lack of option.

He was issuing commands dressed as an inquiry.

He wasn't confirming her agreement, he was pressing for it.

"No," she replied. "No, I can't do that." She looked at him, suddenly appalled by this situation. Some of her delirium lifting to reveal a foundation of logic she'd long held as a personal strength. The last few days had certainly injured her mental state but not killed it. As her senses returned, she quickly felt trapped. Cornered.

"Thank you for everything, but I should leave," she said.

"Oh, but we have not concluded our business." His hand squeezed her shoulder. He looked up, straight into her eyes and she froze like a rodent in a metal cage.

"But . . ." she said, then reached into her purse, produced a cell phone, and swiped the screen to unlock it.

Mnemic's hand snaked toward her, gripping it with just one finger and thumb, taking it with no protest from Katherine.

The phone's glass screen popped and splintered beneath his thumb.

"We don't have time for distractions like that," he said, craning his face closer to hers. He smelled of dirt. "And I understand your hesitation, but we need to finish."

"M-Mr. Mnemic, this is—"

"Is what?"

"It's, well it's crazy," she said, with the last of her recovered willpower. Something in his eyes was draining it, delirium seeping back in like an ice cube dropped inside her brain.

"We have come to a decision point," he said. "An intersection between life and death. I can sense that you want this, yes? You want to speak to him. One last time."

Frail, frightened, defeated, she opened her mouth to speak until he placed a finger to her lips, its surface too cold and hard, more like an eggshell than skin.

"This is something you want. Yes?"

Slowly, Katherine nodded once.

"And you would give anything for it to happen, yes? Of course, I ask only for a bit of your time in return. Do you agree to this?"

Again, she gave a single slow nod in response.

Mnemic leaned in, his eyebrows raised, goading.

Pulling.

"Yes," she said, the word slipping out on a tiny cloud of breath.

He sighed with a shudder. In the poor lighting it appeared as if a wisp of steam escaped his mouth, like the building had dropped temperature within seconds.

"Good," he said. "That's very good." He closed his eyes, lowered his head, and took two slow breaths. Deep and deliberate and full. As if composing himself after a fire and brimstone sermon to a sea of impressionable converts.

Then his eyes opened and met hers again. They had changed, now full and black and insectile. Pupils without borders.

"This way, please," he said.

She followed on feet no longer her own.

Mnemic led her through the door at the back of the long hallway, down a flight of wooden stairs only two inches wider than her shoulders—unreliable stairs that wobbled too much in use. At the bottom was the old house's basement. Like the upstairs, it was in a restored condition that belied the building's terrible exterior. The lighting was clean and bright, as were the white walls and the tile floor.

It appeared to consist only of one large room, perhaps thirty feet across and considerably longer than it was wide, making it feel like a submarine.

As Katherine scanned, she noticed a large porcelain table in the left corner connected to the floor not by four legs but by a central pedestal, one end overhanging a sink.

That's where he prepares the bodies, she thought. *Where he prepared* Shawn's *body.*

"This way," he said, jarring her from a mental image of her husband's naked and sallow body with a vinyl tube coming from his neck, running all his black blood into the sink in a noxious stream. She could hear its steady dripping.

Mnemic led her toward the embalming station, past the table, within inches of touching it.

A single drop of blood sat on its rim.

They approached a door in the center of the far wall that looked too small and foreign, like it was the only remaining piece of the original basement, perhaps leftover from when it was a root cellar with a dirt floor and vegetables hanging from low rafters.

"He's right in there," Mnemic said, gesturing to the door.

She looked behind her and up, toward the room where the viewing had been held. The room where his body still sat inside its casket. Lid closed. He was up there, she knew. She shook her head side to side in denial.

"Oh, don't be so damn naïve," Mnemic said. "He left that stupid fragile meat before you found him hanging. But if you'll just step through this door, you can speak with him again."

Katherine was frozen, standing next to the embalming table and running through a gauntlet of related mental images. A bounty of corpses trading places on that table like the flipping numbers on a countdown clock, all shapes and sizes and conditions. She was on the verge of screaming when Mnemic snapped his fingers just in front of her field of vision.

She tamed her scream down to a brief shriek.

"Katherine, dear," he said, tapping his wrist demonstratively, "we do not have much time. He'll soon be gone. Unreachable. The connections are very short and fragile, you see. Now, if you please . . . "

She pulled on the door's metal handle, it took a surprising effort to pull open even just the few inches she needed. Its bottom rubbed against the white tiles, again implying it did not belong in this sleek, clean, modern space. As she pulled, it screeched along the floor.

Inside the door was another staircase, narrower than the last, leading down to a pure, dark abyss. She could see nothing beyond the first few steps, which appeared to be made of rock. There was a steady, distant humming sound in the void below.

She glanced back to Mnemic, a questioning expression on her face.

"One step at a time," he said.

She forced her leaden right foot onto the first step, and it felt like the ambient temperature had dropped before she could follow it with the left.

"Aren't you—"

"I am right behind you, dear, and you may want this." He handed her a small black flashlight, slightly bigger than an ink pen.

Katherine walked down the steps at a pace that was even and mindless. As the beaming lights of the basement faded behind her, she felt like she was losing bits of herself, as if disintegrating, becoming weightless, but continued to step down. Again, again and again. The flashlight could not contend with the oppressive darkness this far below ground and she could see only a foot in front of herself. Nothing beyond that but black upon black.

The stairs went down, on and on forever, and she attempted to count, reaching the number seven-hundred and sixteen before fear overwhelmed her too much to keep track. She did not know how many steps she had passed before counting, but a vague sense of tracking her footfalls told her she may have descended close to a thousand stairs. Perhaps more. A notion that was both absurd and unavoidable.

Pressure built inside her ear canals, like she was sinking deep underwater.

All the while, she was surrounded by walls made of some manner of clay, emanating waves of cold while the humming noise grew until she could feel it in her bones.

At regular intervals, there would be a trim beam archway, hewn roughly and buttressed against the narrow walls, like those found in a mineshaft, meant to keep the ceiling from falling in, she supposed. She considered counting those as well but did not want to lose track of her stairs count, though eventually she did anyway.

More sounds came as she continued to descend. All from somewhere distant and indiscernible. First, what sounded like voices speaking in a broken manner or in a language she did not recognize. Then a muted shuffling sound added in, like something large dragging along the dirt floor or maybe along the clay walls. Could it be movement along the ceiling? Then a chittering, light and repetitive, conjuring an image of giant irradiated crabs or insects from a pulpy old horror movie.

And then, when she tried to take another step forward and down, her foot bumped into something solid at ankle level. A wall. She turned left and found another wall. Turned right and thrust the small light ahead of herself.

"Yes, that's the way," Mnemic whispered in her ear.

She jumped, wholly unaware he was still with her. She could not sense him nearby, either, and told herself that was merely a trick of the low light. He must be close if she could hear his voice.

She took a few dozen steps forward. Slowly, deliberately. Could see nothing beyond her small bubble of light, and her mind shared disjointed images of creatures that dwelt in the nothing around her and would clamor for her very life had they known she was here. Things that belied description. Eyeless and tentacled. Lumbering. Feeling their way along the corridors with enormous antennae. Salivating and mindless with hunger or desire.

She turned her head backward and called, "Hello? Mr. Mnemic? I can't see. Please, can you tell me how much farther?"

There was no reply, and she waited, counting her breaths to avoid a panic attack. She was not claustrophobic (at least that she knew) but the depth and darkness were culminating in a level of disorientation that bubbled inside her like wayward stomach acid looking for a higher exit. She yawned, trying to equalize the pressure inside her head like a scuba diver. It failed.

Katherine was about to turn, deciding to go back the way she had come and flee from this place, never to see Lloyd Mnemic or smell his moldy aftershave again, when a light came on overhead, revealing that she had entered a room similar to the basement, now a thousand steps (or more?) above her, in that it felt like a hospital sub-level. Like a morgue.

White tile covered the floors, walls, even the ceiling. When she tried to look up to see where the light was coming from, it was too bright and she was forced to shield her eyes with her forearm and turn her gaze back to a more level direction. The overt brightness left flowers blooming across her vision, and as those slowly faded, she looked around the room to get her bearings.

"Welcome to the Dead Rooms," Mnemic said. He stood a few feet in front of her, his posture rigid and upright, hands clasped primly in front of his waist. And next to him was some small piece of furniture.

A table?

No, a decorative column adorned with a curling scroll embellishment on top. It was three feet tall, roughly the same height as an end table.

On top was a bright red telephone.

It was vintage, with a rotary dial base and a handset attached by a short length of curled red cord.

Katherine opened her mouth, preparing to ask a question she didn't even possess but unable to react otherwise. Before she could form a sentence, the phone rang.

Her heart stopped for a moment both brief and eternal. Then she noticed this phone had no other cord aside from the curled one between the handset and base. It was not connected to anything. It *couldn't* be connected.

She was staring open-mouthed as this phone, underground with the planet's surface a skyscraper's length overhead, was ringing.

"That'll be Shawn now," Mnemic said, his all-black eyes gleaming and gesturing toward the phone with one hand, the other held behind himself at waist level like a butler. His hair was completely gone now, and a deep groove ran the length of his bald head, cleaving it from front to back. The whole of his head shined as if covered with petroleum jelly.

"As I've mentioned, the connections are short, and they're also quite unpredictable. I think you should answer."

Katherine picked up the phone.

MYRTLE RESTS

For the second time in as many days, Myrtle Fallsworth came to in her chair with a sense of lost time. The sunlight was fading, it was late evening, and she did not remember most of the morning nor any of the afternoon.

Fleeing for home was a natural fail-safe, the loudest part of her rote memory, yet there was still an unease caused by that gap in her recollection. Where was this time going? And what had she missed?

Then it hit her with the force of a jet engine stream. This morning she had murdered a boy.

She had done everything right, hadn't she? She'd been patient and caring and understanding. She'd followed Mnemic's instructions to the very letter.

All the same, now she was a murderer, a killer of innocents, and she'd never see her little Rosita again. She would spend all her remaining days hiding or in prison. The urge to flee, to leave Oak Hollow for good, was strong, but if she did that, she'd be leaving her dreams behind. What options did that leave?

Everything had changed in an instant, just like when she killed Percy. Only this time, it had been an innocent at the end of her syringe, someone who had done her no harm, had likely done no harm to anyone ever. A child. Instead of a righteous kill, ridding the world of an evil inhuman presence like she'd intended, she had stolen God's greatest gift from a sleeping angel. She knew the look in that boy's eyes would never leave her mind. His confusion, his surprise, that uncomprehending stare, screaming "Why?" with his eyes. They would haunt her until the life left her own eyes one day. And right now, she wondered how far away that day would be.

But this wasn't like her, pivoting away from strength and toward weakness. Instead of embracing the fight to recover Rosita and regain her joy, she was now looking forward to her own death, to the end of all the pain, rather than steeling herself for another bout.

No, she thought, *I'm nothing without my pain. I won't let this beat me either.* She refused to return to a life of weakness, to backslide to a place of subservience to all those awful men.

The only option she saw was to go back to Lloyd for help. If he truly was her guardian angel, then he would know what to do. She wasn't thinking clearly, so there was probably something she had overlooked, something she had done wrong. But he could help. He had healed her hand, he could do things that defied rationality, so could he fix this? She at least needed to ask him.

Yes, that was the answer. And she still had plenty of fight in her. Only . . . she couldn't go now, too much chance of getting caught. She'd need to wait, and it was already growing dark. For now, she'd lie down and rest, feeling her heart heavy and weak, fatigue taking over her limbs. Her bad hand was throbbing, suggesting that whatever Lloyd had done to heal it might have been temporary or the first step of many.

She'd sleep for now, then go beg for Lloyd's help first thing in the morning.

WALTER DECIDES

S itting in his car, parked around the corner from Asher Street, Walt stretched to rationalize what he'd just seen. Tears had blurred his vision, or maybe it was the cascade of negative emotions messing with his senses. No matter what label he affixed to it, one thing was certain, he had not (had NOT) seen the wall ripple like there was a sheen of unreality disguising the true condition of the interior of Mnemic Family Funeral Home.

That was absurd.

But still he found it difficult to rectify the condition of the outside against that of the inside. Sure, it could have been restored but that should have taken months, and why only the interior? Even if he ignored the optical illusion, so much of what had just happened didn't make sense.

Katherine's reaction to Walt's suggestion, the confusion and betrayal on her face. Then the funeral director, Mnemic, and his sudden change in demeanor when she questioned him. The mark on his arm.

Need to remember that mark.

He grabbed a pen and scrap of paper from the console between the car's front seats, then drew the symbol. It could be a rune, like Dad's, but Walt knew nothing about them. Luckily, it was a simple image: a capital *H* with the crosspiece at a slant.

Probably nothing but a strange coincidence. And not the only one.

How come Katherine was as surprised at the low turnout as he was? Even questioning Mnemic about it as they left the room. Walt himself had only known because of Margie. What had she said? Something about the owner asking her to help spread the word. Was that all he'd done? Rang the gossip line? No formal announcement anywhere? Or an obituary, for that matter? It was as if the service was a façade or camouflage. A certain number of people were quietly invited. Enough to make it seem real at a passing glance without drawing too much attention.

Compiling all this, Walt felt his curiosity morph into a vague tingle of alarm, like pre-storm electricity charging Oak Hollow's atmosphere. He'd gone to the viewing to put his fears to rest and left with more uncertainty instead. Most troubling of all, he couldn't explain away that optical illusion. It was the merest glimpse, illusory, but he knew what he'd seen.

Maybe he'd just had his first supernatural experience, the house showing what it used to look like. Dad would have enjoyed that *(Talk to your doctor about glamours today!)*, but Walt was fighting the sense of impending disaster and the incredulity that no one else seemed to notice how strange this all was. Oak Hollow was in bad shape, but had everyone in town stopped watching out for each other altogether?

Could he have been the only person who saw what he saw in there?

He walked inside the house and placed his keys on the kitchen counter, making a sound just startling enough to cause Cowboy to raise his head one inch. The dog was lying on his bed next to the fireplace, and this lack of greeting when Walt arrived home was not abnormal. Cowboy seemed to be equal parts dog and cat, typical of greyhounds in Walt's understanding. From one moment to the next, he could be detached and aloof or stuck to your leg like Velcro. Whereas most dog breeds would near-assault their owners at the door when they came home, Cowboy only greeted Walt about half the time, when he deemed it appropriate evidently. When he did, it was endearing, his long, thin tail twirling like a helicopter and his feet tip-tapping on the hardwood floor. But somehow it was also endearing to come home and see his big white and brown-spotted shape lying in the corner like a potato and barely noticing the door had opened. To Walt, it meant the dog was supremely comfortable, that he was where he should be. This was his home.

And after the morning he'd just had, Walt needed to absorb some of Cowboy's calming, steady energy.

He stooped to pet the dog's head. Cowboy responded by rolling onto his side and holding his front leg in the air, pawing gently at Walt's arm a few times, guiding it toward his belly instead.

"Okay, okay," Walt said, "I'll pay the toll." He scratched Cowboy's chest for a minute while the dog's eyelids closed again. "You feel like doing a bit of the Scooby-Doo thing today?"

Cowboy gave no response.

"We've got a mystery on our hands, all right." Walt stood, hesitating at the foot of a major decision.

If there was something bad (maybe even paranormal) going on out there that no one else had noticed, he could either shut himself in and hope it never reached his door, or he could try to stop it. The first option meant turning his back on anything that may come after, ignoring his promise to look after Shawn's family, and failing to protect the town his dad loved.

Walt didn't feel like a protector, though. So, maybe he'd just call the authorities, relay his half-baked observations and ill-formed conspiracy theory, then turn his back, fully expecting them to take no action. That could give him some peace of mind, but on a more real level, he'd know he was taking the easy way out. No one would take him seriously or respond. He'd be handing things off to help that wouldn't come.

No, there was someone else he could talk to. Someone better suited to listen and make sense of what Walt had to say. A believer. And if that amounted to nothing, Walt figured he could live with his own actions in response.

The problem there, was getting in touch with that person. But not because Walt didn't know how, that was easy. It was a problem because it meant going through Dad's private notes, something he had avoided doing so far.

Most of those notes Dad had gathered intending to compile them into his book about Oak Hollow, insisting that he'd let Walt read the finished product, and not a single paragraph before that. Then the heart attack had stolen his time to finish it. Walt saw it as a betrayal to touch them now (they weren't ready), but he also feared what he might find if he went poking around in there.

He suspected they contained some of the unspoken things. As much as these gnawed at him, he was apprehensive to read them. For a time, he'd not understood this hesitation. Right under his feet was the means to get to know Dad better now that he was gone, but Walt couldn't even look?

Then he'd realized the cause of his avoidance.

Reading those notes would be the last conversation Walt could ever have with his father. So long as they went unread, things remained unspoken. Once he'd read them, he'd know everything Dad had wanted to say and it would be just Walt's side that stayed unsaid.

That was the end.

That was goodbye.

Cowboy came to his side, resting his ribs against Walt's leg as he stood at the top of the basement steps, as if lending strength.

Walt decided then not to turn a blind eye but to act. Protect his home.

He went downstairs.

The basement was silent as a tomb.

Herein lies the unspoken.

It had been so long since he'd come down here that the space itself felt foreign, as if it didn't belong in the house where he lived.

Walt surveyed the area which had been Dad's sanctum. He'd spent hours sitting in the quiet down here, reading and annotating, sponging up those nerdy little details he loved so much: the name of Oak Hollow's first mayor's Irish wolfhound, or the hard science about lymphocytes that was so detailed it made the plot of a Greg Bear novel believable. Whether it was a thick sword and sorcery epic, a slim volume of local history, or a campy space opera, he would scribble in the margins, dog-ear pages, add to his unnavigable stack of colorful Post-it notes.Walt didn't know what prompted Dad to finally tell him about the book he was working on, but when he did, he described it as a meta-blend of local history, his own experiences in Oak Hollow, and supernatural horror. Dad's favorite book in recent years had been Richard Chizmar's *Chasing the Boogeyman*. He'd been enthralled by how the narrative was interwoven with the author's real-life experience and true events, all framed by the specter of something inhuman and dangerous, waiting bladelike around the edges of the story, so sharp you felt the pages could cut you if you turned them in haste. That book had cast a spell on him like few others, and when he told Walt he wanted to write something similar but leaning far more into the supernatural angle, he'd said it around the biggest smile his only son had ever witnessed.

Walt had asked, "What are you going to call it?"

The biggest smile ever grew bigger still, for one instant, then softened and Dad turned his face away, breaking eye contact. A quiet, reserved, and guarded man, but this had never been the obstacle between Dad and Walt that it was with others, and seeing this reaction caused Walt to regret his question. He feared the thought poised in Dad's mouth would become unspoken.

"Well," Dad had answered after a pause, "my working title is *Hollowed Home*. But I've got a few other options in mind too."

This showed Walt how deeply personal that memoir/novel was. Walt knew Dad had always felt lonely from the loss of his older sister, who had disappeared when they were both young, leaving no trace. There had been one—and only one—time Dad mentioned it to Walt, and then he'd used similar phrasing, saying their home had felt "hollowed" after she disappeared.

With effort, Walt broke concentration now from the pile of notes and annotated books left in the center of the workbench, seeing a stack of green banker's boxes in the corner—the most likely place to find what he'd come down here for.

The first box was filled with financial statements, tax records, and other such documents. The one below it was all old family photos, filled with people Walt didn't recognize and yellowed with age. He moved these boxes to the side and opened the one on the bottom, finding baseball cards, sports memorabilia, and some other collectibles and knickknacks. Pressed against one of the cardboard sides, pinned in place by a Lucite box containing a signed baseball, was the item he was looking for.

A book. A unique book.

Its cover depicted a portly middle-aged man with a thin ponytail, wearing a tuxedo and skinny black bow tie, hunching over a crystal ball, his hands hovering a few inches from it as a bright light shone up toward his face. The guide from their tour, credited on the cover as Finnegan the Fortune Teller.

Powerful Secrets of the Ancient World, it read in an overstylized font that stretched a few letters until they were barely readable. Walt flipped through the pages, noting chapter titles like "How to Read Palms," "Card Spread and Card Reading," "Chinese Zodiac," and finally, "Rune Casting."

There were diagrams of at least a dozen runes, each with an accompanying paragraph. And on the second page of that chapter, listed third from the top, was the symbol he had seen on Mnemic's wrist.

It was a rune, and apparently it was called "Hagaluz."

Next to it was a short paragraph.

Hagaluz/Hail/Disruption
Ancient man had to deal
intimately with nature.
Hail storms devastated
his land and crops.
This Rune can indicate
forces beyond your control.
Misfortune.

As he read and reread it, Walt felt the hair on his forearms stand.

forces beyond your control.
Misfortune.

Why would a funeral director have that tattooed on his wrist? Walt could chase that down later.

He flipped a few pages past the remaining runes and saw "About the Author" on the inside of the back cover. Walt read what should present as credentials, but were only a few exotic places Finnegan had traveled to and a vague mention of playing guitar in a rock band, then a phone number for Midnight Mysteries Tours.

As an amateur historian, spending hours poring over details in books that would make most readers' eyes go crossed, Dad was perpetually looking for new ways to explore the events and stories of Oak Hollow, Gables County, and Ohio.

While growing up, Walt had found this a strange contrast in a man who had shelves filled with the works of authors like Philip K. Dick (PKD to Dad), Terry Brooks, Arthur C. Clarke, Anne McCafferty, and of course Isaac Asimov. Plus, the full series of Tom Swift books, with their matching yellow hardcovers. This on top of being an ardent subscriber to *F&SF* magazine back from near its inception. Obscure historical facts and bizarre, sweeping fantasy didn't seem to pair.

But now, with more wisdom in his neurons and experience in his veins, Walt understood Dad's passions for local history and weird or fantastic fiction were extensions of the same interests. Dad liked to explore the deepest parts of stories he loved, along with the breadth of worlds both real and fantasized, past and future, close and distant. The man had been a sponge for detail, driven primarily by the smaller points, the minutiae where life was held. In conversation, he'd skip past remarks about the weather and ask someone how their marriage was. Dad didn't settle for what was on the surface, he wanted to tap the core of whatever held his interest.

"Guess what?" he'd said to Walt one evening, just after dinner. His voice was dressed in restrained excitement.

"What?" Walt had asked. "Did the Reds finally add to their bullpen?"

"Better," Dad had answered. "Much better. There's a new tour starting next week. And it ends at the Koenig House."

Together, they'd been on over a dozen such tours all over Gables County and its neighbors. Chillicothe had several to offer, and they'd even been as far as Mansfield to the old State Penitentiary, the Variety Theater in Cleveland, and Waverly Hills in Louisville.

"What's this one called?" Walt had asked, unimpressed.

"Midnight Mysteries!" Dad answered, practically shouting.

"Oh, is that—"

"And it's not just another ghost tour. It sounds like it goes way deeper than that. Plus, from what I can tell, the guide has really done his homework."

That last line was high praise indeed, coming from Dad.

He'd signed them up for opening night, and when the tour ended, they'd stayed to talk to the guide for over an hour. Dad bought this book, which Finnegan had signed on the spot using a metallic silver Sharpie.

Walt looked at the picture of Finnegan on the cover once more, noting its unintentionally goofy quality and having second thoughts. *What the hell am I doing? This is none of my business and I'm definitely not the type to mix in.* Then he thought about Katherine Yost and about Shawn's kids. His half-assed promise to check up on them. He thought about the town Shawn and his dad had loved so well, about Dad's unfinished memoir/suspense novel scattered and unorganized on the table next to him. Then he remembered the rippling of the wall and the vibes he got from the viewing and from Mnemic himself.

He took one more glance at the back of the book in his hand, reading its text.

Leave your knowledge of fortune-telling at the door and witness the marvels of the most ancient methods of divination! You'll learn the real secrets of symbol interpretation and know what the sages knew. All the answers you seek are waiting.

"At least he's living his hobbies," Walt said to himself as he dialed the phone number for Midnight Mysteries Tours.

KATHERINE ASKS

At first there was only silence on the line and Mnemic grinning at her, his head marked by that horrible groove, insectile eyes bulging.

She tried to speak, and the words caught in her throat like fishhooks. Still silence, but now enough time had passed she was feeling foolish for thinking that anything else was even possible.

Of course there's no one there, she thought, scolding herself. *He's clearly preying on you at your most vulnerable. Any fool could have told you that.*

Dear God, she *was* vulnerable right now. How had she not seen it before?

She moved the phone's receiver away from her ear, overtaken by terror as she faced the danger of this situation underground with an inhuman monster goading her. Mnemic could be capable of anything and there was no escape.

She held the receiver out, a lame weapon. A twig against a battleship. "You stay away from me."

Mnemic stepped back, nodding toward the receiver. She looked at it, too, then. And heard a small, detached voice coming out.

It was too quiet to make out the words at first, and Mnemic said, in a sharp, clicky voice, "Pat*ck*ience, of course."

Katherine pulled the phone back to her ear.

"Hello?" she said, aware of the absurdity of using the most standard greeting in the human language for a phone call bizarre beyond imagining.

A man's voice spoke back.

"K-Kit?"

It punctured her, that voice. She gasped, pulling the world into her lungs. A warmth trickled down the inside of her leg. Her heart shuddered in her chest, a car with a bad motor going uphill.

It couldn't be him.

It couldn't be.

Could not.

Shawn was dead. Dead.

He had died, like everything dies. He had been alive and fine, and they had a fight, and then he was dead. She had seen him, dead.

Twice.

First, in their home. And the second time, after he was embalmed, for God's sake. He had hanged himself from that beam until there was no breath left in him, no life. Then he was upstairs in this terrible old house, all his blood drained and replaced by a gumbo of preservatives with unpronounceable names. Mouth sewn closed. Eyes glued shut. Lying in that casket.

Viewed. Viewed dead. Very, extra dead.

So it simply couldn't be.

It could not be him.

Could not.

But . . .

"Kit?"

But.

It was him.

It was.

Somehow, it was Shawn's voice in that phone.

Not dead. Talking. Speaking his pet name to her.

Only Shawn ever called her Kit. Short for Kitten, derived from Katherine, to Kate, then Kat. At first, she had hated it, but it was the only nickname that had lasted more than a few days and so it grew on her. But she didn't recall telling Mnemic about it, so he shouldn't have known.

Should he? she asked herself. She had forgotten where she was and that she wasn't alone when Mnemic spoke again, his tone mocking, half the syllables morphing into uncanny clicks like his voice box was lined with hard plastic.

"Somet*ck*imes it t*ck*akes a few moment*ck*s to get the hang of it*ck*, you see. Things are quit*ck*e ... different*ck* for him t*ck*oday. I'm sure you underst*ck*and."

Again, she tried to speak Shawn's name, but again, the word evaporated inside her like a dream lost to the waking world.

"Kit?" the voice came again. It sounded like Shawn, but there was also something different in it. Something amiss. His voice in a different throat. Her heart raced, and the words welled up behind her tongue.

"He-here."

"Where am I?" it asked.

"Shawn." A flat whisper she'd meant as a question.

"Where am I?"

Then it was like his name had broken the surface and the trapped speech came rushing out.

"How? But . . . how can this be? Is that really you?" she asked, not waiting for responses. "No. No, it can't be you. I left you upstairs. You're dead."

Mnemic feigned alarm and shook his head. "Best*ck* not ment*ck*ion that part*ck*," he said.

"Why?" she mouthed, but he only grinned, showing pointed teeth.

"What?" the voice asked. "I'm what?" It sounded strained now, like speaking came at great effort, and that emphasized the change from Shawn's voice as it existed in her memory.

"I suggest*ck* you get t*ck*o the point*ck*," Mnemic said, gliding behind her and letting it out in a taunting hiss. "He won't*ck* be able t*ck*o . . . hang around long."

"Kit . . . where am I?" His voice sounded thinner, smaller. Stretched.

"Shawn, I-I have to know something."

"Where am I?" Smaller still, but also growing hoarse. And she could hear something else in the background. Like the pops of a campfire. "It's dark."

That hit her in the chest, an icy stabbing.

"It'll be okay," she said, then immediately realized how ridiculous a statement it was.

"Dark," he repeated. "Cold."

Mnemic had walked in front of her again and was tapping his wrist in that showy way, gesturing for her to hurry.

"Shawn, listen I have to— There's something I—" She paused and took a deep breath, trying to compose herself as the voice from the phone continued repeating those two words with a childlike pleading.

"Dark. Cold. Dark. Cold."

"—have to know. I need to understand—"

"Cold. Dark. Cold. Dark."

"—why, Shawn? Why did you do it?"

"Cold. Do what?"

"Why did you kill yourself, Shawn?"

"Why did . . . Did what?" the voice said, louder.

"You're dead. I . . . I found you hanging in the basement."

"No."

That single word of denial ignited her smoldering frustration. "What do you mean, no? Your body is upstairs in a box."

"Can't be."

"Don't tell me it can't. People paraded through here today, Shawn. Holding my hands and hugging me and saying empty things that don't matter and handing me flowers and comparing my grief to theirs and promising to call or send food. Food? Like food will fill something in me. Because you're dead. You're dead and I found you hanging. In our house. You killed yourself in our home. Where our kids sleep. Why?"

"No. Not."

Frustration boiled into anger then, as she realized this unnatural series of events had led to nothing more than another argument with him. "Yes. You did, you are, and goddamnit, you left yourself there for me to find. And now I have to figure out how to go on and live and raise those poor kids without their father in this terrible world."

"No."

"So you just—" she said, talking right over it, or him or whatever was on the other end of this phone that wasn't even connected to anything. "—just fucking tell me! Why?"

"I . . ." it said, surrender weaved through the tone of that one word. "Didn't want to. I . . . I stopped."

"What? That makes no sense, Shawn."

Hot tears stung her eyes anew, and Mnemic started laughing deep in his throat with his mouth closed.

There was a *click* from the phone, then only silence. She dropped it. Dangling from the red curled cord, it swung in an arc away from her and then back, a cruel, mocking pendulum.

She cried.

A soft, green light pulsed around the chamber. Somewhere in the distance, the humming continued.

And Mnemic laughed in tune.

TUESDAY

MYRTLE CONFRONTS

Myrtle rang the doorbell of 432 Asher Street before first light. As she did, she also pounded on the door with her good hand, unsure if the bell was working at all. Her bad hand sang with fresh pain, nearly as strong as normal, so maybe she'd ask him to help with that again too.

In her peripheral view was the section of the porch where the bench had been. She looked toward that, noting it was now gone.

That's strange, she thought.

Then Lloyd was opening the door, having arrived within seconds, surprising her. She'd been concerned about catching him off guard at this odd hour, perhaps even waking him up. But he answered the door quickly, wearing another tailored, three-piece suit, his hair styled and precise as ever, his eyes alert. And Myrtle remembered he was an angel, not some weak, flawed being like herself.

"Ah, Ms. Fallsworth," he said, with the same toothy smile and mild tone. "I'm so glad to see you."

The sun was playing coy, peeking over the horizon like a mischievous child spying between fenced yards. There was a sconce next to the door, but it was turned off or broken. Myrtle made to speak, caught off guard by his immediate response to her knocking. He'd opened the door so fast it made her wonder if he had been waiting just inside, expecting her to come now.

But of course he knew she was coming. Her guardian angel knew everything about her. He knew things she didn't know herself.

"You . . . you're here . . . waiting?" She hadn't meant it as a question, but it changed on its own once it left her mind.

"I had expected to see you today, and this business I've chosen requires me to keep odd hours. I assume you've done what we discussed?" He paused, studying her face, then added, "Wait, did something go wrong?"

"It all went wrong!" she shouted. Then she was overtaken by the weight of her failure, leaning forward to catch herself against the doorframe before she could drop to the ground in defeat.

"Oh my. Oh my," he said, his voice painted with genuine concern. "I should have known you'd only be here at this hour if something were wrong. Come in, please. I'm sure we can fix this."

"He's dead. I killed him."

"You killed someone?" he asked, adding a flare of accusation.

"I . . . I think so."

"You're not sure?"

"No. He looked dead. I did what you said. I went to the house. I went upstairs and found her bed and used the needle. Only it wasn't her. It wasn't her in that bed! It was a boy. An innocent boy and I killed him."

"Did anyone see you?"

"I . . . No. I don't think so. Maybe."

"Well which is it?" His voice had changed, tone harshening.

"I'm not sure. I don't know what to do. What do I do?" She knelt on the floor, her face buried in her hands.

"Myrtle, I gave you very specific instructions."

She looked up at him through tear-streaked eyes. "You . . . have to help me. You're my guardian angel. Aren't you?"

Mnemic laughed.

Myrtle rubbed her eyes, seeing his face more clearly. Like his voice, it had changed, and that change was more than just a different expression. More stern, more waxy. His eyes gleamed, appearing closer together than they had before. When he spoke, his voice held an edge that reminded her of Percy when he was drunk. There was a violence hiding just behind his teeth now. The primary effect of these changes was to reduce Myrtle to the same whimpering, battered woman she used to be. She was helpless.

"I'm no guardian and I'm no angel," he said, holding eye contact. "I told you what to do, woman."

"I did that. I did exactly what you said. I did, I swear. Help me, please. Lloyd?"

"How can I do that? You're a child killer now. And let's do away with the pretense, shall we? My name is Mnemic."

Myrtle gasped, placing a hand over her mouth and backing away from the desk. Without realizing it, she was approaching the door to the basement, a desire to escape overwhelming her logic.

Mnemic smiled, his teeth unnaturally sharp and narrow. As she watched, his pupils spread, overtaking the whole of his eyes until they were full black. His hair fell out in clumps, disappearing smokelike before it could reach the floor. The skin at the outer corners of his brow bubbled, stretched, then split. Two hardened, black lumps emerged, pushing outward. Horns?

She should have known. Should never have trusted a man. Or something disguising itself as one. Her stomach sank, the pain that previously fueled her singing now in mockery throughout her old, withering body. Myrtle had wanted only to rescue her daughter, even if she had to kill a monster along the way. But now she saw that her fate was attached to a worse monster.

"You're no angel," Myrtle said. "You're the Devil?!"

"No," he responded. "There's no such thing. The Devil doesn't exist. But me? I'm right here."

She spun away and ran down the basement steps.

Mnemic gently closed the door behind her, locked it, and walked away.

WALTER CALLS

By midmorning, Walt was sick of waiting. There were hours left until he could meet with Finnegan, but sitting here was only compounding his worries.

Nothing could keep his attention, all his thoughts bent on what had happened at Mnemic's yesterday. After checking his watch for at least the hundredth time, he decided to call and check in on Shawn's family. If everything was fine there, it would calm his nerves a bit. And if it wasn't . . . then at least he'd know there was no time to waste.

He scrolled through the contact list on his phone, finding *Shawn Yost–Home* to be the very last entry alphabetically. When they'd exchanged numbers, Walt had no expectation to use it, let alone under these circumstances. But he was glad he had it now.

After two rings, a harried-sounding man with a gruff voice picked up the phone.

"Hello? Hello?"

"Is this the Yost house?"

"Yes, are you with the police?"

"No," Walt said, and his stomach sunk. A clear sign things may be worse than he'd hoped.

"Then I'm sorry, but we're waiting for a call, goodb—"

"I knew Shawn."

"Please, this is not a good time."

"I . . . I'm a friend. Maybe I can help if you tell me what's going on?"

"Katherine is missing."

"Missing? She didn't—"

"No one has seen her since the viewing. The kids are all at our house, she was supposed to come there. She never showed, so I came here to look."

"Oh no. Is there anything I can do?"

"The burial is later this morning, and we don't know what to do. The police still haven't even called back. Now, please. Unless you know something about that, I really need to go," the man on the other end said, then hung up.

Walt stood aghast, realizing things were far worse than he'd expected. First Shawn, now Katherine missing?

He looked out a nearby window, thinking he'd seen movement near the side of his garage, but there was nothing there.

PRESTON DISAPPEARS

"**F**oot soldier," Preston repeated, grinding a clump of Shawn Yost's hair between his molars as he slid around the garage, staying out of sight. His time in the morgue had been transformative, transcendent, but this was where he was most experienced: waiting, watching.

Lurking.

Watch him closely, but don't be noticed, Mr. Mnemic had said.

Preston spent hours watching the old man's house, beginning shortly after sundown. At first, he moved from window to window, including the second story, for better views or better cover as needed. He hadn't even wanted to leave when the old man went to bed. Instead, he crouched in the shadows and chewed. Did push-ups and wind sprints to keep himself sharp, like any good soldier preparing for combat. Building his collection had made him quite skilled at the shadow ops stuff, but he'd never been in an actual fight and he dare not disappoint his new mentor.

A few minutes ago, though, his eyes were growing heavy and as he drifted toward sleep, he saw himself dropping from an open window into the old man's bathroom. Pulling the sink stopper out and sliding the first two fingers of his left hand inside the black, mucky drain. Then a distant dog bark brought him back, and he snapped to in time to see the old guy making a phone call. Preston caught enough of the conversation to learn what Mr. Mnemic needed, feeling like a guerilla warrior, and now it was time to report back.

"You've done well, Preston," Mnemic said, as he placed a slender hand on Preston's shoulder, ushering him from the front hallway of 432 Asher Street back to the office with the large executive desk at the center. "You've done very well."

"It was easy, sir."

"As I expected."

"But, I wasn't really sure what you wanted me to look for. What you needed to find out."

"Well, you needn't have worried about that. Your instincts led you to the pertinent details, as I knew they would. All we needed to know for now, was whether he acted or kept to his own tiny affairs. And his choice is clear now. I can only assume he saw through my glamour, but I'm not surprised. His fear was not as . . . malleable as the others."

"I don't—" Preston said, but was overridden as Mr. Mnemic continued.

"What remains to be seen now, is what sort of action he will take. And I think it's wise to keep my distance, still, rather than overplay my hand. He may yet pose a threat, but I doubt it very much."

"What are you going to do?"

"We."

"What?"

Mnemic leaned toward him, plying his fingers fanlike across the sheened surface of the wooden desk. "You're asking what are we going to do. Are you not, my foot soldier? This will be an opportunity for you, Preston. To prove yourself. I believe we have an understanding. I help you with your annoying little . . . tic, give you an opportunity to satisfy the inner shadow, the dark drive behind the noises inside your head. In return, you help me accomplish a few minor tasks. Are we aligned?"

"Yes." It excited him. *What kind of tasks?*

"Every milestone so far has been met as expected. But as I've mentioned, this is where my design is most vulnerable. And unfortunately, I can only exercise so much control from within this house." At that, he gestured to the symbol on his wrist.

"Right, you can only go so far from the Dead Rooms."

"Yes. This brand has me crippled, but I'm far from helpless. All it does is limit the range of my influence. And that means I need you to be where I cannot. Why I needed you to retrieve Shawn's body and then the other young man's."

"Did you already . . . embalm him?"

"No. We'll prepare that new body shortly. But right now, I need you to take on more responsibility. You've seen and heard much of what I intend to do. Do you still want to be my apprentice? My solider?"

"Yes," Preston said. "Definitely."

"Good. There is still much to do. I'm asking for your faith, and that's no small thing. I have the power to help you, and you have the means to help me. And if you do, Preston, if you help me, then I can assure you, not only do I have the power to help you, but I have power to share."

"Oh, I . . . I believe you."

"That's kind of you to say, Preston, but I can hear and see that you're just trying to give me the right answer. I never expected you to be convinced by a few measly words. Words are nothing. Control is everything. So I've planned a small demonstration. And if, after that, you are still hesitant, then we can part ways amicably. Agreed?"

Mnemic stood quickly, walked around the desk, and knelt in front of Preston. "Hold still," he said, then raised his hand, fingers straight and level with the floor. "Hold very still."

Preston felt a charge in the air around him, heard the thudding beat of his own heart. Mnemic leaned in, close enough that Preston could smell him—the same stale, earthy scent, as if he'd been interring corpses by hand. His hair looked thinner than before, and a strange line ran down the middle of his head like a perfect scar.

"I must warn you," he continued, "this will not feel pleasant. It will hurt quite a bit. But if you can withstand it for a few moments, you'll see a great benefit."

With their eyes locked in a circuit, Mnemic reached out and grasped Preston's wrist, pulling the arm toward himself. At his touch, Preston felt a jolt of energy transferring to him, like some part of Mnemic was filling a void within himself. His breath hitched, and he held it, pressure building in his face and lungs. Mnemic turned Preston's hand until his palm faced the ceiling, then spread it wide by pushing his own down on top of Preston's, finger to finger.

"Yes. Keep it just like that," Mnemic said, then he repeated the motion for the other hand, leaving Preston positioned like he was about to undergo a double palm reading. "You must hold still, and I mention that again not only because it's important, but also to emphasize that it will take some effort." He broke eye contact, moving his gaze down to Preston's hands as he pulled his own back several inches, opening a gap between them.

Mnemic tightened both of his own hands into fists, then reopened them. When his fingers were fully straightened, a small, bloodless hole opened in each fingertip, in unison, the skin retracting itself from their centers like a camera aperture. Ten thin, black strands emerged, growing and resembling slim, animated electric cords. At first, Preston thought they could be blood vessels that were darkening as they oxidized, but they kept growing and their surface (*skin?*) wrinkled and glistened until they resembled oversized, ink-black earthworms.

"Wh-whu . . . gh." Preston's speech was blunted by the shock of what he was seeing. He fought against the urge to pull his hands away, to protect himself from those terrible vines extending from Mnemic's bony fingers. It was all he could do not to bowl the smaller, older man over and flee through the open door behind him into the night. He tensed his legs instead, every muscle fiber from his hips to his toes locking into place. He was a missile in a silo, poised to launch through the ceiling. Willed himself to remember how badly he would need relief later if he refused Mr. Mnemic's offer to help, and what he'd be forced to do to get that relief. Despite himself, Preston's whole body trembled.

"I said *hold still*," Mnemic commanded, regrasping one of Preston's wrists as the wrinkled, black shoots coiled and wound snakelike closer and closer until they made contact. Festooned with panic, Preston didn't register that both of Mnemic's hands were still connected to both of his, yet something was holding his wrist at the same time.

The tendrils wound closer still. When they touched him, probing against his fingers, Preston shuddered, his upper lip pulling into a sneer of disgust. They were clammy and warm and soft, these alien-looking appendages touching him. Then they snapped into a rigid line, piercing into him, and he gasped, sensed the blood draining from his face.

Mnemic said, "Put your other palm back up, boy."

Somehow Preston obeyed, and those fingers were penetrated too. The skin on his fingers was stretching, he could feel it, like his hands were shrinking from inside. Mnemic was draining his life, like some bizarre finger-vampire. He looked up at the ceiling, willing himself not to move, not to faint, not to scream. Not to—

"Almost done," Mnemic said. "Stay with me, Preston. Look. Look."

He nodded toward their conjoined hands, and when Preston looked down, he saw the tendrils retracting, shrinking, and the pain lessened in a flash. There was a series of tiny noises as they pulled out of his fingertips, a near-inaudible *pop* from each of the ten coils. He felt an odd, healing catharsis, like he had just vomited poison or expelled a sickness from his body. The holes Mr. Mnemic's tendrils had made in his skin closed immediately, as if never there.

Mnemic smiled broadly, and Preston gasped.

"There," Mnemic said. "That should help you avoid detection. What do you think?"

Preston held his hands up toward the light, bringing them close to his eyes, inspecting. First one, then the other, and back to the first. The pain faded more, but now the skin of his hands felt stretched. What he saw was more shocking than Mr. Mnemic's inhuman operation had been.

Preston no longer had fingerprints, they were just . . . gone. All ten of his fingertips were perfectly smooth. Everything Mnemic had said was true. He could lead Preston not only to a life free of the clicking sound, free of consequence, but to a seat of power.

"How? How did you—"

"As I've mentioned, I have many talents. Among those is a complete mastery of human flesh. I can manipulate it in any variety of ways. And Preston, I assure you, that was a mere parlor trick compared to what else I can do to it. Perhaps if you remain as loyal and effective as you've been thus far, you'll find an opportunity to see more . . . grand examples." With those last few words, he cast his eyes suggestively toward the door in the back of the office. Preston's eyes followed, and when they landed on the door, he noticed a shiny metal hasp and padlock, wondering if it kept people away from whatever lay beyond that door or held something in.

What's down there? In the Dead Rooms.

A fatigue crept into his hands, like he had just finished working out with large dumbbells, and he rubbed his thumbs along the pads of his other fingers. Their new smoothness was alien, reminding him of lost teeth in childhood, and how with each time he would run his tongue incessantly around the new hole for days. Those holes had always made it feel like he was tonguing someone else's mouth. And these were now someone else's fingers, weren't they? They belonged not to Preston Clark, the unwanted-child-turned-would-be-psychopath, but to someone else entirely. These were the fingers of a ghost. A wraith. He'd become someone untraceable and exceptionally dangerous. And then he realized the true gift Mr. Mnemic had just given him.

Freedom.

He was free to indulge himself, to obey the inner shadow instead of fighting it. Free from temptation, from consequence. Free to act.

Free from identity.

Free to kill.

Mnemic smiled, stood, and walked back to the other side of the desk. "Great benefit, just as I said. Wouldn't you agree?"

"Will they stay like this?"

"Yes. Unless I choose to restore them, which I can do just as easily. So it's advisable that you not give me cause to take it away. Don't fail me, Preston." A note of insistence came to Mnemic's voice as he spoke, highlighting a contrast from his previous, more guiding timbre. He wasn't trying to convince Preston anymore, not trying to earn his trust gently. Now he was providing strict guidelines, rules. Setting guardrails. "If you do what I ask, I can give you so much more than that."

"What do you need me to do?"

"That's an excellent question," Mnemic answered, his voice resuming its previous warmth and geniality. His posture changed as well, returning to the slight forward lean that Preston had noticed when they first met. The line along his skull faded like a time-lapse shot of a wound healing. "The answer may seem long-winded, but I assure you that everything I'm about to explain is pertinent. For you to understand your mission, I first need to explain what I'm trying to accomplish. Starting with why I came to Oak Hollow. Why here, why now, what I see in this tiny, dying community. That way, you can go about your new duties with a sense of purpose."

He paused, straightening his tie as he resumed his seated position behind the desk.

"For a very, very long time, I have been mining a particular resource, something precious. Due to a unique set of circumstances that I have spent centuries arranging, Oak Hollow has the potential to provide that resource in a sufficient quantity. That resource, is time. A singular breed of time, though. Let's call it . . . *dwindling time*. The final moments, those which contain the utmost desire and concentration. The distillation of an entire lifetime, condensed to its purest, most potent form."

Preston gave a confused look. "Centuries? How . . . how old are you?"

Mnemic's eyes sparkled with knowledge, but he dodged the question. "I can tell my explanation is falling short. Let's try another way. You've now seen a dead body. But have you ever seen someone die? Watched them go."

"No," Preston said.

"I see. What I'm referring to are the final moments when a person knows they are about to leave this world, when their time is dwindling to its final drops. It becomes infused with an unearthly energy that allows them to revisit things from long ago, digging up memories that were buried for decades, refining their focus toward the most minute and forgotten details. And the closer they get to the end, the more refined this resource becomes. When their life is 'flashing before their eyes,' as the saying goes, a tremendous amount of unique energy is expelled, stretching that finite, dwindling time halfway to infinity, allowing them to be in hundreds of times and places at once. Time-bending energy, space-altering energy. Do you understand the power that holds? I mean to harness that power, and though stealing time from humans is something I can do with ease, they tend to notice, and I prefer not to be noticed. Also, dwindling time is hard to come by naturally. Therefore, I have carefully arranged a means to acquire this resource while avoiding detection long enough to enact my full design. To achieve my final goal."

"What goal is that?"

"You'll find that out when you're ready. I must keep some things secret until you've proven your faith to me. Give me that and we'll go far together. My machine is almost ready, Preston. I just need a few more bodies to complete it and a bit more of the dwindling time to power it. In two days, my design will be complete. So go out there and prove that you believe me."

Preston swallowed hard, clenching his fists in trepidation and thrill.

"Prove your faith, Preston."

MYRTLE FLEES

In yet another senseless panic, Myrtle missed the last of the steps leading to the basement, stumbling and falling onto her side on the cold tile floor in pitch dark.

She could not tell where she was or how big the surrounding space was. She stood, blindly waving both hands in front of her and moving in a hesitant circle in search of a wall. Or better, a light switch.

Finding neither, she walked forward, a hint of logic returning to tell her the room was certainly finite and moving in a single direction would eventually bring her to its edge. After a moment, she banged her left hand against a hard surface. But when she reached for it again, it was gone.

Not a wall, she thought, moving her hand back a third time but aiming lower, where it had first collided. It worked and this time, she grasped porcelain with both hands. A sink? A counter? Or some kind of table?

She waved her hand over the top of it in a vain hope for some light source. Flashlight, candle, anything.

What she found felt like a row of tools, several of them covered with a thick liquid that clung to her hands. And one of them made a light cut on her palm. She cried out in the dark. Panic returned in full force.

Just then, a light came on. Myrtle saw blood and shiny silver metal. Again, she turned and fled. And again, in an unthinking moment of pure panic she ran through the closest doorway to descend a set of stairs into the unknown.

After a countless eternity of stepping down time and again, her feet swelling, ankles singing with fatigue, her hands moving over the bumpy cave-like walls on either side of the narrow stairway in pure dark, she heard a humming noise. It was continuous, yet patchy. Not stopping, but with frequent ebbs and flows in volume and pitch.

Aside from the clinging dampness in the air and the feel of clammy rock along her palms, that sound was the only sensory input available. It sounded like a large machine in the distance. Perhaps a struggling old furnace or an antiquated drainage pump. She went toward it, soon finding herself in a dimly lit cavern of unknowable size but grateful for the meager light up ahead.

She could not go back, there was nothing but pain and sorrow behind her. Whatever new terror lay ahead could certainly not over-shadow those she was leaving. Could it?

The humming grew louder in symphony with the rising light and then she was proven wrong. Desperately wrong.

The light was coming from a mass of purplish material with an uneven surface. She knew this from a distance, and as she moved forward, more clarity brought a horror she could never have prepared for.

It was moving in dozens of places at once, irregular light from multiple sources highlighted contours along its surface. There was a familiar quality she could not place yet, and she moved tentatively closer. She stopped within ten feet, squinting and willing her eyes to interpret what they were receiving.

This shape was massive, she could tell that much. Perhaps the size of a modest house. Two dozen feet tall, twice that in diameter. And shift-ing constantly in a thousand places at once, but with no uniformity.

Unlike a pulsing or rippling movement, this was more spastic and unorganized. Her eyes slowly adjusted to the lighting and a particular, furtive movement on the edge of that shape closest to her caused her to realize two awful truths at once.

First, the humming she had followed was not coming from any type of mammoth machinery, it was the joining of human voices, groaning and mumbling independently, then cobbled into a nightmarish unison.

Second, the movement that caught her attention was a set of fingers.

Combined, these truths meant she was staring at an enormous mound of body parts that were conjoined like a putrid Frankenstein-snowball.

She dropped to her knees as the dark reaches of her imagination spilled forth, as if Mnemic had lured her here, then reached inside her mind and unzipped a portion she'd never dared tap into herself.

In this setting, deprived of reliable input or awareness, she could not comprehend how this thing could be, what had caused it to assemble, how this piecemeal abomination of human parts was alive and moving and together.

And moaning. Crying. Pleading without words.

Attached to an arm far too large to be its original mate, the fingers she was staring at clasped together in a fist, reopened, reached toward her. She rose, stumbled backward, pitched sideways. Vomited.

The Frankenstein-mountain continued its chorus of pain and tragedy even while Mnemic's voice interrupted it. She scanned it and saw no less than twenty eyeless faces, contorting and shrieking and moaning in concert.

"What do you think?"

Mnemic appeared beside her, hands clasped together at his chest, looking up in admiration at the heaping mound of conjoined limbs and twisted faces.

"Your victim will make a nice addition. After the service, of course. We must appease the family before he can achieve this new purpose."

"What . . . " she said, finding no words and tasting bile. The poor lighting made it difficult to tell, but she thought her vision was swooning. Or it could have been the effect of the asynchronous movement of all those arms and legs and mouths and feet making her feel dizzy.

Mnemic was out of sight but continued talking, "I call it my Infernal Machine. Oh, I know that's a bit of a misnomer because the term has gained a specific interpretation among your species lately. But frankly, I don't care. I find it fitting. And to be quite honest, its final purpose is close enough to be apt. Not that anyone will debate these points in the end, mind you."

"I . . . don't understand," she said, bumping her good hand into a wall and voluntarily sliding down it to avoid falling. Her legs had given out again, taking with them any option to escape.

"And you're not meant to," he said. "I just wanted you to see it." He stepped within the ring of faint light that was coming from nowhere and everywhere at once.

"How did you . . . "

"Oh, surely you don't expect t*ck*o comprehend? You're here simply t*ck*o be shown that*ck* what I am doing is *beyond* you, lit*ck*tle cog," he said. "I've waited eons to get*ck* here. And I have not*ck* the pat*ck*ience to show anythiiing fuuurtheeerrr."

Myrtle watched in horror as his mouth elongated into some inhuman proboscis.

A long divot cleaved the crown of his head in a dark line; his scalp and face lost all color, turning the tint of wet concrete. Above the outer corners of his eyes, what she'd mistaken for horns grew out into thick antennae, half the length of his arms, and whirling about as if sensing the air between them.

Myrtle collapsed, her lungs emptying themselves without her order. Her blood ran cold, all warmth rushing down and out through her feet onto the rocky floor of the Dead Rooms. He wasn't a man. Wasn't an angel or the Devil. What was he?

Mnemic's transformation continued. His arms were next, and as they grew longer his sleeves ripped and hung loose while the skin stretched and tore into bloodless strips revealing inhuman musculature more resemblant of clay than living tissue. Then his legs distended much the same, joined by a second pair that sprouted from above his hips. Soon he towered over her and reached a black-shelled claw to grasp her neck as she tried to stand, to run. Her feet circled vainly while the thrumming of that horrid mountain of rearranged flesh droned between them.

Myrtle fainted, seeing a flash of little Rosita's face as she went.

WALTER MEETS

The greasy spoon Finnegan had picked was called Riley's Diner. Dusk had gathered and as he approached the door, he noted several letters burned out on the exterior sign, leaving it to read *R-ley-Di-e-* in the dimming evening light.

A look around the restaurant confirmed Walt's suspicion of it being a dated relic with bright red pleather upholstery, banded silver surfaces, low-hanging lights, and Chuck Berry playing through speakers in the ceiling. It held a certain charm, and he developed a new suspicion that the food would be great.

There were few customers, and it was easy to spot Finnegan in a corner booth. He noticed Walt enter and stood to wave him over, wearing a black trench coat and combat boots, which prompted Walt to think that despite being in his mid-forties, he was dressed like this was the last stop before meeting his high school RPG club.

As Walt walked over, Finnegan reached out for a handshake that flung the last few inches of his dyed-black ponytail forward.

"Walter?"

"Yes, thank you for meeting with me so quickly."

They sat. Finnegan picked up his mug of coffee and took a sip.

"Oh yeah, of course. I was off work today anyway."

"Work? Are you still doing the tours?"

"No," Finnegan said with a sigh. "Had to close that up recently. Couldn't get anyone to sign up for them anymore. People in town don't have the money for stuff like that these days. And nobody from out of town stays here long enough for them. So I went back to my day job at the library a few months ago, at least until I can get my true crime podcast up and running. You hungry, man?" He motioned to the open seat on the opposite side of the booth.

A waitress arrived to take their orders and Walt mentally noted she wasn't wearing roller skates, marking his first incorrect assumption about the place. Finnegan ordered something called the "All-day Breakfast Feast," and Walt asked for a turkey club. He wasn't hungry but wanted to be polite.

After she left, Finnegan gave him a questioning look. "Have we met before?"

"Yes, on one of your tours."

"Oh, okay. That doesn't narrow it down much but your face is familiar."

"It was a few years ago, maybe one of your first, so I'm sure you've seen more than enough other faces to lose track of mine. But my dad really enjoyed it. He was invested in local history, especially the macabre stuff, so he signed up as soon as he could. He stayed behind to talk to you for a while after, I think." Walt straightened in his seat, suddenly feeling like he was representing Dad.

"Hmm," Finnegan mumbled, sipping coffee. "I think I remember him. Kind of skinny? His name Walter too?"

"Yeah."

"Okay, yeah. I remember him. He asked a lot of really good questions. Knew his stuff." He paused, tilting his head, pondering something in his memory, perhaps. "Now that I think of it, he was the only person on a tour who knew more about some locations than I did.

When I researched, I talked to plenty of people. Most of them wanted to talk about historical figures and events and had good details—all of which I needed, of course—but for my purposes, I needed to get more into the shadows. I wanted the after-dark tales because I was planning an after-dark tour. Can you imagine how long I would've lasted if my best bit was all about the few years when the county seat was located in Oak Hollow? Or how the windows on the main floor of city hall were accidentally installed upside down? That's barely good enough for a matchbook cover, let alone a haunted walking tour."

They both laughed. Walter felt more at ease after that.

"But your Dad, Walter Senior, he gave me one of the best facts about 432 Asher that I'd ever heard. I wanted to use it the very next night, but I had to look into it a bit further. Believe it or not, I'm aware that people may not always take me seriously. And maybe I don't always take myself seriously. But, my stories? I take those very seriously. There's no room for error, so I triple fact-check everything."

"Was it about the underground tunnels?"

"Yes! That's exactly what it was. 'The Dead Rooms,' he called them. Something about him, the way he told it. I believed him right away, he convinced me just with his own sincerity."

Walt smiled. Despite his initial discomfort, now fading, there was a clear validation in hearing Finnegan compliment Dad. "Yeah, that sounds like him. He had a knack for convincing people." Saying this reminded Walt that it was a quality he himself lacked and was very aware of in certain situations. He was downright envious of it when Dad was alive, and now without him, it was just another form of loss. He'd been able to count on Dad's charm so many times that he felt lessened without it. Even now, sitting in Riley's Diner and talking to this strange man about strange things.

"He sure did, Walter Junior. I just wish I'd been able to find some kind of proof or documentation. I believed him, but I'd done overnight investigations there and never found them. If they do exist, they're well hidden. I mean, you understand, right? If I just picked up every cool spooky story I heard and started waving it around to sell tickets, for one, I'd be no different from any other haunted tour guide. I might as well dress in Victorian garb and show up in a hearse. Worse, all it takes is one person outing me on a story that isn't airtight and what does that do for my credibility? If it was something absurd, then I'd probably mention it just to contrast against the ones I can prove. But that one made perfect sense, and I just couldn't find the proof. Which is weird all by itself. It was common practice at one point to keep the bodies cool when they just couldn't bury them fast enough. It's easy to find documentation of the morgue tunnels below Candler Memorial Hospital in Savannah. Hell, at Waverly Hills in Kentucky, they take the tour groups inside theirs."

Walt absorbed all this while his focus strayed once again to memories of his father, feeling himself shrink a bit, closing the gaps around his grief mold, pushing snugly against the inside of his midsection.

"You look like him, Junior. A lot like him, now that it's coming back to me. I didn't remember you so much, sorry, but I remember talking to him after the tour. You know, we even exchanged a few emails after that. How's he doing?"

"He died. A few months ago."

"Oh, damn. I'm sorry . . . I didn't mean to—"

"It's fine," Walt said, again taken to the visual of a black orb inside himself. *My grief isn't shrinking, I'm growing around it.*

"He seemed like a great person. I mean, I know I don't need to tell you that, but you should hear it, I think. He was smart and really interested in that old house. I admired him, and I don't say that often."

Walt smiled again. "That's what I wanted to talk about, believe it or not. The house."

"432 Asher?"

"Yes, in a roundabout way. There's some stuff going on, or— Well I think there's some stuff going on. Weird stuff. And that house seems to be at the center of it all."

"I like weird stuff. What kind of weird stuff are we talking about, Junior? Increased HOA dues? Bloody pentagrams surrounded by salt on the floorboards? Lights in the sky? Bigfoot caught on camera?"

"No, ha. Nothing that obvious. It's hard to explain, but the important part is that it all seems to come back to that house. You know that it's a funeral home now, right?"

"Yeah, I saw a sign in the window on my very last tour, actually. That was the last straw, in a way. I was losing money and figured if that place had a new owner, it took away some of the mystique. It was the biggest draw on the tour, after all. The last stop."

Walter squirmed, knowing the conversation was about to change tone, and that he could end up regretting this whole venture.

"Okay, so—hopefully I don't lose you on this sequence of events—the town is in bad shape these days, right? No jobs, people moving away, rising crime rates. Everyone is scared and on edge. The powers that be don't have plans to put out fires, let alone turn things around, so everyone is just getting tense and pointing fingers or leaving for greener pastures. Then the first sign of any new commerce is a funeral home, coincidentally in the house that everyone believes is haunted."

"I don't believe that."

"Oh, right. Anyway, by itself I don't think that seems bad. Odd, sure, but just a coincidence. And this next bit, I'll admit, is purely subjective, but to hear people talk about this new business coming here, they're making it out to be our saving grace. Granted, that's probably just desperation or some outlet of hope, but the town's whole economy is on the ropes and they think a funeral home is a sign of things getting better. Then it seems to have opened for business in record time. Not an impossible time, I suppose, but damn close. That house was not in good shape, right?

"I haven't been by in a few days, but it had been vacant for twelve years, by my count."

"Then within a matter of days, it's ready for formal gatherings? Ceremonies for the dead? Could they even have cleared all the red tape and legal requirements?"

"I take your point."

"That happened so fast, followed immediately by a tragic death. And a poignant one, at that."

"You're talking about the guy who hanged himself last week? Did you know him?"

"Shawn. I did. We weren't real close, but I'd say we were friends. Again, that one event, one small bit of information, taken by itself doesn't look like much, just a tragic death in a small town. But the thing about Shawn was that he loved Oak Hollow and he, more than anyone else I know, believed it would turn itself around soon. He had this infectious enthusiasm about it, his home. Would talk about how deep his roots were, how good the place had been to his family for generations. But then, I suppose he wouldn't be the first person who put up a brave face to hide that he was wasting away inside. Maybe all that boasting and cheerleading about the town was to convince himself that it was worth staying here. Still, it's the most public and unexpected death I can recall in . . . well as long as I've lived here. So maybe that just means we're due for a little tragedy, I don't know. I guess the more I sit here and try to lay this all out, the less it seems to form a picture of anything larger. Maybe I'm wasting your time and mine."

"There's more, though. I can hear it in your voice. Might as well finish throwing it all in the air and see where it lands, Junior. You said it all connects to the house?"

"Shawn lived pretty close to that house. I know you say it's not haunted, but here comes the weirdest stuff."

Finnegan leaned forward.

Walt told him about the viewing and the contrast between the interior and exterior of the house. He described the encounter with Katherine and her confusion when he'd mentioned some of the specifics of Dad's funeral prep. Then he recounted her interaction with the man she called Mr. Mnemic.

"He left the room in a bit of a hurry," Walt said. "Almost seemed like he was dodging me, but I can't see any reason he'd want to—"

Finnegan held up a hand, motioning him to stop. "I gotta say, Junior, I consider myself an open-minded guy, and it's not that I don't believe you when you say weird stuff is happening. But so far, it all seems like things that can be explained away. And far from an emergency."

"I saved the worst for last."

"What's that?"

"The widow hasn't been seen since the viewing."

"When was that?

"Yesterday."

"And how do you know she's missing?"

"I called Shawn's house this morning. I promised to check up on his family and it was the only way I knew to get in touch with them. A man answered, her father, I would guess. He told me they were waiting for the police to call back, then he hung up."

"Well, I think you and I both know they're not going to come anytime soon."

"Agreed. But I can't just wait for them to show up, so I figured it could help to talk to you because you know about the house and the town. Plus, you have experience with researching weird stuff, fact-finding. So while I was waiting to meet with you, I looked into the business itself. I guess I figured if I could find something funky going on there, it could help raise the alarm bells and speed things up. It's easy to see that funeral homes are more regulated than some other types of business. If I wanted to open a secondhand shop or some other new retail store, that is more straightforward. But the government doesn't let just anyone hang up a sign, then move dead bodies around and start embalming or cremating them. There's licensing involved, connections with the coroner's office, oversight from the county. And I would assume some type of inspection process is required first. I couldn't find a trace that any of that happened. Could be that it's not public record, but still. At a minimum, it really must have happened fast, or someone knew this Mnemic guy was coming a lot further out than it seems they did. Shouldn't I be able to verify that all the bureaucratic boxes were checked before he started having visitations for suicide victims? Do you have any idea how to verify stuff like that?"

"I'm sure the county records office could help. But it might be easier to just go talk to the guy, Walt. He's new in town, trying to make connections and build a rep. Why not just go see what he has to say and where the conversation goes? Listen, Junior, I don't know you. I didn't know your old man all that well, either, but if you're much like him, I'm confident in your ability to be rational and make good decisions. So I'll level with you because that's what you asked me to do. I think you're jumping at shadows. The house is there every time you turn your head because you've made yourself hyper-aware of it. Like the blue car phenomenon or whatever it's called."

"You really think so?"

"Don't discount the power of suggestion. Once something gets in your head, it stays there, especially when you try to force it out. Quick, whatever you do, don't picture a polar bear."

"Yeah, okay. I see what you mean."

"It's a trick I used all the time on the tours. Get that idea in their head that something sinister is afoot and people double down on the whole haunted house vibe. So I get it. And I'd be lying if I said I'd never been down some very similar paths myself. But so far all you've got are your own isolated musings and a bit of Google time. The missing widow is concerning, but for all we know she just went on a bender or a vision quest because she can't handle it all. Don't start being a rube, Junior. Walt Senior wouldn't like that much. Coming to me was a good idea. But I really think we can put this whole thing to bed by just talking to this Mnemic guy."

"We? Did you say 'we'?"

"Well . . . yeah. Is that an issue?"

"You want to come with me? Why?"

"It's not obvious? I'm bored, Junior. I'm so bored."

MYRTLE CRAWLS

Trapped in an exhausting pattern of lost time and cognitive failures, Myrtle again came to with precious little awareness or memory of where she was or how she got there. Her skull felt filled with potting soil instead of brain matter, moist and weighty and not fit for anything beyond occupying the space and releasing nutrients to keep her functioning. There was a pressing, tomblike silence on all sides as she drifted through levels of semiconsciousness. She opened her eyes (or thought she did), seeing nothing except a darkness so deep as to sap her awareness further.

Ever since she'd killed Percy and freed herself from a life of man made slavery, she'd been so clearheaded. A spectacular mother, driven by purpose. Strong. Resilient.

But now? She was reverting to that weak-willed state of obedience and hiding. She hated the thought of becoming that naïve, battered version of Myrtle again.

As she pondered what to do next, how to regain her sense of place for starters, the utter lack of sensory input suggested that she may have died. Would that be so bad if it were true? What if this place was purgatory, and she was in God's waiting room about to be judged? If that were the case, she feared the outcome.

With noticeable effort, she moved her arm, waving it in a tight circle, sending her good hand forward into the impenetrable darkness like a scout. It found nothing. She moved her jaw, made a whimpering sound, testing if her ears were functioning. The tiny noise sounded out of scale, amplified and too large, and she realized it was echoing off nearby surfaces. Assuming she was still alive, the space around her could not be much wider than arm's length. She shifted her weight, rising to her knees and wincing at the pressure on her tender old joints.

"H-hello?" she said, louder than the last sound. *Hello?* the echo answered, twisting her voice in mockery.

As if unlocking something, the sound coming back into her muddy brain brought with it whispers of memory. Her terrible mistake, her crime. Mnemic and his devilish tricks, sneering in joy at what he'd driven her to do. That impossible pile of massacred bodies and human remains, still moving, still feeling, calling out in agony. What had he called it? And right before she'd blacked out, he had been … changing, becoming something else. Surely, those things couldn't have been real. Could they? Maybe she'd hit her head, concussed and hallucinating, confusing real sights and sounds with nightmarish visions from her subconscious.

Uncertain if the place she was in now was even tall enough to stand, she shuffled forward on her hands and knees. It was torture, but as always, the pain lifted her.

For an immeasurable time, Myrtle crawled in the dark.

WEDNESDAY

WALTER WITNESSES

Finnegan, the fortune teller, arrived at Walt's house early the next morning, driving a navy blue Buick that looked at least fifteen years old. There was a long, meandering crack running from the top corner of the windshield to the opposite bottom corner, and Walt clocked several rusty spots on the passenger side before opening the door and leaning in. He expected the interior to smell like feet or cigarette smoke, perhaps both, but was wrong about Finnegan yet again.

As if mind reading (Wasn't that part of his schtick?), Finnegan called out Walt's observations before he could even consider voicing a reaction to the car.

"Ignore the rust, it's the one thing I can't afford to get fixed right now, but I've got a plan. And the windshield just happened a few days ago. Got an appointment with Safelite for tomorrow, actually. Turns out this is their busy season, right between the plows making potholes and the municipalities not bothering to fill them."

"Wasn't going to say anything, actually," Walt replied.

"Not judging on first impressions, just like your old man, huh? I admire that, Junior. I really do. Ready to go?"

"Yeah. Let's take my car. Don't want that crack getting any worse for now."

"Good idea."

"Well, quick question first."

"Shoot."

"Mind if I bring my dog?"

They walked to Walt's car, a gray Kia he had purchased shortly after Dad's death.

Walt wanted to like Finnegan because Dad had. So far, it was happening, but he didn't picture spending any time with him after this was over.

Cowboy settled into the back seat quickly, used to riding in the car and probably expecting they were going to a park. Finnegan put his hand on the gear shift, but Walt spoke, stopping him short.

"Before we go, do you think we should come up with a plan at all?"

Finnegan looked at him, puzzled. "What do you mean?"

"Well, is it a good idea to just show up there asking those types of questions?"

"Sure, why wouldn't it be? Unless they have something to hide. Which I doubt."

"For one, what I'm trying to find out could easily land wrong if it's asked abruptly, with no lead-up. It'll feel like an attack. Or, at best, like I'm some Michael Moore wannabe or second-rate nightcrawler journalist."

"I guess you may have a point there, Junior," Finnegan said. Then he bunched his face up, exaggerating features for comedic effect. "Is it true you've been handling dead bodies in here without permission? That's very naughty. You're supposed to ask first and get proper clearance and licenses and blah blah. Also, why does it seem like you rolled into Oak Hollow and now everyone is dying or disappearing, Mr. Mnemic? If that is your real name."

Walt laughed, further rethinking his initial impressions about Finnegan yesterday. "You could give me a bit more credit."

"Yeah? How so?"

"I would have asked his full name first. For the record."

That time they both laughed, and Walt felt more at ease than he had for days. Like there was nothing nefarious or otherworldly happening in Oak Hollow. Tragic, sure, but normal in its own way. Walter pulled out of the driveway.

"Okay," Finnegan said. "So maybe we start by expressing an interest in the house. It's not untrue because I'd love to see what it looks like in there now. Plus, we could both play that part well."

"That could work. We're not there to ask about any weird coincidences or snoop around for shady business tactics. We're just there to see the house and learn more about its history."

"Yep, and I have to think he'd be congenial to a couple of townies like us if he wants to ingratiate himself to all the rubes. He's trying to build a brand here and portray the right image for a place like Oak Hollow. So we can coax a tour out of him, scope around inside a bit. And while we're doing that, we learn about him and his business too. Keep an eye out for anything that seems out of place or whatever. And if we see or hear something that's worth investigating . . . " As Finnegan continued laying out these steps, Walt heard the excitement building in his voice, like a big truck cresting a steep hill. He was full of momentum and energy.

"It's funny," Walt said. "If you'd have told me all this a few days ago, like you just described it, I'd think you were nuts. But with it all swimming around in my head unchecked, it's really built up some steam."

"I'm a natural skeptic, but I would love it if a tenth of what you're worried about was true. It would sure as hell make a great kickoff for my podcast."

"Yeah, you mentioned that," Walt said. "You haven't started yet?"

"No, but I've been gearing up for a while. Just waiting for the right story. The one that will catapult me to the top of the charts. Maybe this will be it, who knows?" He grew quiet then, contemplating for a few minutes. "Well, of course the most likely outcome of this visit is us confirming that you're forcing together pieces that don't fit. Put your fears to rest, and then we can go get a beer or something."

"That's the best idea you've had yet, Finn." Walt, unused to handing out nicknames, fought against gasping in through his teeth when that slipped out, afraid the guy would react poorly. Instead, Finnegan took it in stride (or didn't even notice).

As he drove, Walt brought up the mark he'd seen on the funeral director's wrist.

"I was reading in your book about the runes."

"Oh, sure. I studied those quite a bit."

"Did my dad mention them? When you were emailing each other?"

"Hmm. I know he was interested in them, but I can't remember any specific conversation about them. Why do you ask?"

"It's probably nothing, but since we're chasing down strange coincidences today, he had a tattoo of one."

"He didn't mention that to me."

"I barely knew about it. He only showed it to me once; it was on the inside of his arm. He told me the story about why he got it, but not what it was called or what it meant. He got it as protection because he knew someone in the Army who had one."

"What does this have to do with our little adventure today?"

"This guy we're going to talk to, Mnemic, I think he has one too. Like I said, probably nothing, but they meant something to my dad. You've studied them, and it just seems odd that another one is showing up. So, I'm wondering what that means, if anything."

"Of course it means something. These are powerful symbols of the ancient world, and they're not often used lightly. Tell me more."

Walt pulled the sketch from his pocket. "I read what your book said about it, but that raised more questions than it answered. It's called Hagalaz, right?"

"Close. Hagaluz, actually. With a *U*. Gaelic doesn't translate to English well, so maybe that's just my preference."

"So, what do you think it means?"

"I'll be able to answer that better after we talk to him. But my experience and instinct are telling me . . . it means nothing good, Junior."

Minutes later, Walt parked across the street from 432 Asher and they walked to the porch. Finnegan strode like he was approaching his own home, long coat trailing behind him.

"Ready?" he asked Walt, but didn't wait for a response and made three quick, firm knocks on the wood.

KNOCK, KNOCK, KNOCK.

The door opened, and the man Walt had seen the other day stood inside it. He was dressed in another suit, similar but a shade or two darker, no tie this time, and his face had a sleepiness that caused Walt to drop his guard a bit. It made him seem like a harmless old man, unprepared for company. He took a half-step back, rethinking whether this was a good idea or if they were just stirring up trouble.

"Yes, hello?" the man said, smiling.

"Hi," Finnegan answered. "Are you"—he looked left, reading the wooden sign near the door—"the owner here?"

"I am. Lloyd Mnemic. And you are?"

"Toby Finnegan and this is Walt."

"Morning," Walt said, realizing he hadn't heard Finnegan's first name until right then.

"Good morning," Lloyd said. Something passed across his eyes, barely noticeable. Recognition? Or annoyance, maybe? "Is there something I can help you with?"

"Well," Finnegan started, "this may sound strange, but we were hoping to talk to you about this house. I would have called first but couldn't find a number listed. We're both interested in its history, and it's been a while since we've been able to speak to anyone with inside information. In fact, I used to run a tour company, and this was the last stop on our most popular tour."

"Oh, is that right? 'Used to'?"

"Until about a week ago, yes. There just wasn't enough interest to sustain it, and as you're probably aware, the economy around here has been circling the drain for a while."

"What sort of tours?"

"Most would call them 'haunted' tours. Or 'ghost' tours, but those aren't words I would use because they send the wrong message. We talked about ghost stories, sure, but at their heart they were historical tours. Spooky history more than anything else, but history first."

"I see. Well that explains why this house would be the grand finale. Plenty of spooky stories about this old place."

"Exactly."

"Do come in, and I'll tell you anything you want to know." Walt was warming to Lloyd. The more he saw, the more relaxed he was getting. Coming here was already having the effect they'd anticipated, confirming that he was misunderstanding events and jumping to conclusions. Out here, in the morning light, based solely on a few seconds of observation when he was busy, Lloyd wasn't the conman Walter was building him up to be. In contrast, he was a kindly (if overwhelmed) business owner, new in town, and spending all his energy on helping grieving families. The rest was purely coincidence.

Maybe funeral homes could be given a grace period under certain circumstances, like an unexpected death a few doors down while they were still getting the paperwork and legal checklists in order. Katherine Yost could have taken a few days to compose herself and push through the early grieving stages so she could come back in a state that allowed her to nurture her children, putting her own oxygen mask on first. And surely, Lloyd had not meant to rush away from Walt at the wake; he just had an urgent matter and stepped away to attend to it in private. Funeral directors probably needed a lot of privacy, right?

He led them inside, past the chapel where Shawn's body had been displayed, which now held a new casket, its lid closed. Then into an office toward the back of the house. Lloyd offered them both something to drink, but they declined, and when they were seated—Lloyd behind the large desk, Finnegan and Walt in ornate antique chairs across from him—he said, "So then, Toby and Walt, what exactly are you looking to find out?"

Walt answered first. "I don't mean to pry, I'm wondering why you would choose this building. When you first located here, had you heard any of the rumors?" As he finished speaking, Walt noticed a door at the back of the room. He assumed it led to the house's basement.

"Oh yes, they're ghastly, aren't they? Is it odd if I tell you that just made me want to come here even more?"

Finnegan smiled at that and responded with, "It would have reeled me right in, so I understand that impulse."

"To answer your question, Walt, it's certainly no great mystery. It was the same reason that anyone has ever acquired a property since the inception of real estate. I bought it for the location."

"What appealed to you about the location?"

"The proximity, for one. It's within a five-mile radius of more than half the homes in Oak Hollow, close to several burial grounds and churches as well. In this business, one has to consider the effort required in transport, you see. The less distance we need to move a decedent, the easier everything that I need to do with them becomes."

"So is it just you doing everything?" Finnegan asked.

Lloyd switched to him, addressing them individually, showing a level of personal engagement that undoubtedly served him well in his profession. "I have some help, of course. But mostly, I'm a one-man show here."

"Since you mentioned the location being important, I have to ask. Is it true there are tunnels beneath the house? And if so, were you aware of them before you chose it?"

Lloyd furrowed his brow, confused. "Tunnels? No, I'm not aware of any tunnels. Under here?" He pointed toward the floor.

"The rumor I've heard," Finnegan said, "was that someone dug tunnels to store bodies at cooler temperatures during bad outbreaks of yellow fever. Either that, or tuberculosis."

"I have heard of such things, but I can assure you there are no tunnels like that here. I believe that was only done farther south, in warmer climates. Up here it would have only been difficult to dig graves quickly enough in the winter, when the soil was frozen. And if it was cold enough for the soil to freeze, well then, I don't suppose bodies being stored too warmly would be much of a concern."

It made sense to Walt. Finnegan responded, "That was my main theory. I wanted it to be true, but something didn't seem to fit."

Walt couldn't help but be offended, though, and he cast his gaze toward the door at the back of the room. One of Lloyd's eyebrows raised, in tune with the realization on Walt's part. There was a new hasp and padlock keeping it closed, the metal bright and untarnished.

Dad had been positive about those tunnels, and it wasn't like him to stake a flag that way without doing his due diligence.

Phonyalis can turn fatal if left untreated, Dad's voice warned him. Something was off here.

Dad must have found some piece of information that convinced him it was true. That, added to the vibes when Lloyd locked eyes with him, was enough to raise Walt's guard again, and he was suddenly eager to leave. He thought of the rippling in his vision as he left Shawn's viewing and squirmed in the chair like a kid outside the principal's office. They hadn't found out anything about how Lloyd was allowed to host Shawn's wake so quickly, if indeed all the proper steps had been taken with the county, or other regulations, connections with the coroner. They also hadn't been able to find out anything about Lloyd himself. If they left now, it would be empty-handed. Still, he wanted to go.

Quickly.

So he stood and made to shake Lloyd's hand.

"We appreciate your time, Mr. Mnemic. We'll get out of your way now," he said.

Lloyd pulled away, holding both hands up near his shoulders and shaking his head.

"Quite sorry," he said, "I have a service in a few hours, and I was doing some preparation. I haven't thoroughly washed my hands. Would hate to bring you in contact with any embalming residue or other . . . unsavory substances."

Walt and Finnegan exchanged looks as they walked toward the front door, and Finnegan mimed a "What?" expression. He seemed surprised by Walt ending the conversation when he did. Walt figured Finnegan was hoping to ask more questions, disappointed they'd learned so little and now he was making them cut things short, but the urge to get out was too strong.

Before they reached the door, though, Finnegan spoke to Lloyd again.

"Can I ask one more question, Mr. Mnemic?"

"Of course, Toby."

"Have you heard from Katherine Yost since her husband's wake?"

Lloyd narrowed his eyes a trace, and the wrinkles around them pronounced. "No, I can't say that I have. Why do you ask?"

A silent tension wormed through the air around Walt, like static electricity threatening a shock. He silently begged Finnegan not to keep pushing.

"Were you all finished with her? Everything signed and arranged?" Finnegan asked, his tone converting to that of an Internet sleuth on a Netflix true crime documentary or a talk show host in a moment of "gotcha journalism."

The smile left Lloyd's face. "Now, with all due respect, I don't think that's any of your—"

"Are you aware no one has heard from her since then?"

"Is that true?"

Is it? Walt asked himself. Just because I couldn't track her down doesn't mean no one has heard from her. It doesn't even mean anything is wrong, necessarily. He was suddenly quite aware that he'd come here half-cocked with a person he didn't know well, with an ill-conceived and muddy objective, and now that person was dog-legging the conversation in a direction he wasn't comfortable taking it. If they'd had more time to plan or discuss their approach, Walt would surely have cautioned against something this accusatory. But here they were, standing in the man's parlor, jumping to conclusions. What did Finnegan hope to gain with these implications? Walt was in over his head, wishing desperately for Cowboy's presence to latch onto something calming.

Finnegan continued, undeterred, with all the bluster and brava-do of a keyboard warrior vying for his fifteen minutes. Walt stood shocked, wholly unaware this side of Finnegan existed.

"It is. She seems to have vanished from the face of the earth. And I'm wondering if you may be the last person to see her alive."

Lloyd's expression changed from questioning to offended, almost in slow motion, like an avalanche was progressing beneath his skin and he couldn't fight it. "Listen, now. I'm trying to be gracious but I do have urgent matters to attend to. I have nothing to prove nor anything to hide. If you'd like to come back another time so we can discuss—"

"Shouldn't you have buried him yesterday? Or the day before?" Finnegan interrupted.

Walt silently begged him to quit. This wasn't the time to drum up drama for his would-be podcast.

"Really now, this is too much," Lloyd said. "I'm afraid I must ask you to leave. I don't see how it's any of your business, and I don't have time to convince you."

"I believe she's either contacted you, or you know where she went."

"Who do you think you are? Coming here and accusing me, you stupid glory hound."

"Why won't you just answer my question, Mr. Mnemic? Where is she?"

"What did you just say to me?"

"I asked if you knew the whereabouts of Katherine Yost. And I must say, it seems like you're dodging—"

Finnegan's last accusation was cut short, violently. Mnemic was on him in a flash, moving with speed unbefitting a man of his age and posture. In a blur, he had one hand around Finnegan's throat, causing him to gasp. When his mouth opened, Mnemic shoved his other hand inside it, deep. Then Finnegan was gagging and Walt fell back against the wall, aghast and not comprehending what he was seeing.

"Enough," Mnemic said. "I've dealt with your kind before, and I won't waste the time now. Clearly you're here for one thing only. But I won't give it."

As he spoke, he pivoted and twisted his arm and wrist joints, shoving Finnegan's head down. Finnegan, a few inches taller than Mnemic and outweighing him by at least fifty pounds, now appeared the smaller of the two. He dropped to his knees and made a pained mewling sound around Mnemic's fingers, which had to be touching the back of his esophagus because the whole of Mnemic's hand was inside Finnegan's mouth, up to his wrist.

"I'll tell you one damn thing, worm," Mnemic said. "She has most certainly disappeared from the 'face of the earth,' and that's all you'll ever know about her."

Then, as Walt held his own mouth open in silent astonishment, Mnemic clenched his hand—still inside Finnegan's mouth—and wrenched it back out, pulling something free with it. Something that looked like a noodle covered in glossy red paint, and whatever it was, it was still attached inside Finnegan's head.

Walt was transfixed, not breathing, frozen. And as he kept pulling on that pulpy red mass, Finnegan was screaming and Mnemic kept talking in fragments. As he did, he worked at the thing coming from Finnegan's mouth like a fisherman removing a hook. For a brief moment he paused and looked at the mark on his own wrist.

"You think you can stop me? It's far too late for that. Not like last time."

To emphasize his words, he yanked away with full force, putting a foot on Finnegan's bent knee for leverage. Finnegan kicked away, fell backward, and went limp along the hallway floor. The thing in

Mnemic's hand came loose with a wet flapping noise and Walt felt a hot moisture splatter across his face, his forearms. He looked down and saw droplets of blood sprayed across his front.

Walt, wide-eyed, looked at the visceral matter in Mnemic's hand, simultaneously realizing what it was and denying the possibility of what he was seeing. Mnemic was still spitting words at Finnegan's motionless body, as if unaware Walt was watching. Walt wasn't hearing those words or wasn't processing them, his entire focus directed at the thing now dangling from Mnemic's left hand. It looked like a handful of spaghetti, all woven together and ending in a single length of noodle. Or like a network of roads all feeding to a single escape point. It was covered in bright, fresh blood, dripping from two dozen places at once.

It was preposterous, impossible, grotesque, and fascinating all at once. And with no way to know or be sure, Walt had every assurance of what Mnemic was holding. What he had done to Finnegan, who was now either dead or surely would be in seconds. Saving him was impossible, a notion as absolute as Walt's knowledge of the object dangling from Mnemic's fingers.

Somehow, this man (*no, he's not, there's no way he can be that*) had reached inside Finnegan's face, grabbed hold of a blood vessel, and removed the entire network of veins and arteries by pulling it out through his mouth, still intact.

Mnemic turned to look at Walt, no sign of exertion on his face whatsoever. In fact, he looked disappointed.

Walt ran.

OAK HOLLOW GRIEVES

Two days after his mysterious death, a viewing was held at Mnemic Family Funeral Home for sixteen-year-old Austin Braithwaite, whose body was discovered at home, in bed. The authorities had yet to release any details, aside from there being clear signs of a struggle within his bedroom, and anyone with information about the adjacent vehicle fire was being asked to come forward.

As Mnemic had anticipated, Austin's age, combined with the tragic abruptness of his death and his stature in town as the captain of Oak Hollow High's football team, the Raiders, resulted in an enormous turnout without so much as a single online post or advertisement. The line of mourners wound through several rooms at 432 Asher Street, out the front door, and along the porch. From there, at its peak length, it led three full blocks down Asher Street and partway down the connecting Grant Street, forming a grim parade of concerned and reddened faces.

The turnout would catalyze the next step of the design, but it would also bring unwanted attention. It was the beginning of the end.

Inside the house at 432 Asher Street could be seen a continuous loop of photos depicting the happiest moments of Austin's life. When watched at length, they told the clear story of a bright-eyed, adventurous, and good-natured boy growing from a curly-haired baby with the standard-issue pinchable cheeks, to both a confident and capable student and well-rounded athletic teenager. There were pictures of Austin smiling gap-toothed at his First Holy Communion and of Austin smiling straight-toothed at a Cincinnati Reds game. The first time he caught a fish. Driving lessons and summer camps. School dances and T-ball games. Birthdays and Christmas mornings and Easter egg hunts and fireworks shows and holiday parades and family vacations. Austin, invariably tall no matter what age he was shown at, smiled in every one. Not pictured were the recent shouting matches with his stepdad, Kristine Macy turning him down for homecoming last year, anxiety on test days, the time he'd closed the car door on his foot, four stitches above his left eyebrow, his dead pet hamster, his mild egg allergy, the day he'd run away from home but forgotten his shoes and turned back after a hundred steps, or the night a deranged woman had injected him with a fatal dose of poison while he slept.

At first, his mother, Tabitha Braithwaite, could not approach the body on her own. Her legs gave out, so she was propped up by two nearby mourners. Then her second husband, Nate—Austin's step-dad—pushed her forward like they were grappling in front of an oncoming train. Finally, she threw her upper body atop the casket as if it were a life raft and stayed there until a crowd formed behind her.

Throughout the service, Tabitha was never more than an arm's length from the casket, which was shorter than Shawn Yost's had been. It was hunter green, with a camouflage pattern covering the interior lining, because Austin's favorite pastime in recent years was deer hunting, usually with Nate, but he'd also been a few times with friends and their dads.

Within the casket, Austin's stillness was complete. The deep hue of the exterior made his skin paler by comparison. His small hands filled with fluid that was not blood, but meant to mimic its visual effect. His straight brown hair parted in a way he'd never attempted himself.

As the assembly progressed past the body, family and close friends lingered around the room in near-silence. Every few minutes, a bout of loud crying would start in a corner and then cascade throughout the room like a contagion passing from host to host.

Tabitha was consistently either sitting or being propped up by the gentle hands of Lloyd Mnemic. When he was not attending to the grieving mother, Mnemic could be seen ushering overcome mourners into the hallway, disappearing for several minutes at a time, then returning alone. This occurred frequently as the procession of Oak Hollow's residents continued throughout the afternoon and into the evening. In his absence, Tabitha was attended to by her twin sister, Tamara, who had flown in from Seattle.

The viewing was scheduled from 11 a.m.-2 p.m. eastern time, but as the sun set, there was still a line out the front door.

And Mnemic's red phone rang deep into the night.

WALTER LEAVES

An immeasurable time passed before Walt felt like he could breathe again. Not *catch* his breath, that was unreasonable, but there came a point where part of his mind returned from shock and recalled the ability to pull air into his lungs and then send it back out. He used the first full, conscious breath to speak in hopes it would confirm he wasn't insane.

"He pulled it out," Walt said, then corrected himself. "Pulled *them* out. All of them. That's what he did. That's what I saw. I saw that man … that monster reach inside Finnegan's mouth and pull all the blood vessels out." Then he repeated, "All of them."

He was driving southwest, and since breathing wasn't something he could wrap his mind around as he fled, leaving 432 Asher Street and Oak Hollow far behind, he had no plan or destination. Steering the Kia onto I-71 and heading this direction was a default, like he was a stream of water following the pull of gravity toward the sea thousands of miles away.

Breath brought oxygen, which brought a sliver of levelheadedness. He walked back through the series of events that brought him to this point, which found him fleeing for his life like a helpless, squealing piglet.

What day was it he'd gone outside for the mail and first heard about Mnemic Family Funeral Home? Saturday. That seemed both right and infinitely wrong at once. In four days, he'd gone from avoiding his gossipy neighbors to witnessing that bizarre and brutal murder. Why hadn't Mnemic killed him too? The look on his face had conveyed that he may not have even registered Walt was still in the room. Like he'd become enraged to a level where he lost himself and all sense of place. What had set him off like that? Walt had to assume Mnemic had gone to great lengths to portray this alter ego of the empathetic, professional undertaker.

He had asked about Katherine Yost. And there it was. They'd caught him. Did that mean he killed her? Who else had he killed? Regardless of what had happened to her and how involved Mnemic was, he would have been far better off rushing them out the door than violently attacking Finnegan. No, that wasn't something he'd planned to do. Finnegan had touched a nerve. Set him off somehow. Mnemic did not strike Walt as the type to be caught off guard so easily or to do something as rash and blatantly criminal. Why risk everything just to kill Finnegan, with a witness? He'd said something about not having time. If he was in a hurry, that didn't help things for Oak Hollow or its people.

Walt looked in the rearview mirror and saw Cowboy lying on his side, sleeping like this was any other car ride. Seeing the dog inhaling and exhaling big, even breaths brought a sense of serenity, as it usually did.

The dashboard clock informed Walt he'd been driving for at least five hours. The gas gauge next to it informed him he wouldn't make it much farther. He'd need to stop soon, but wanted to keep going, feeling no farther away from what had just happened, as if danger lurked just out of view. He suddenly felt like he was abandoning his home and with it, his identity, or at least some of his deepest values. He was leaving it all behind out of fear, the place he'd grown up, where he'd lived and worked for decades, where he'd been formed. While he still felt that dichotomous love-hate view of the place, he was as much a part of Oak Hollow as Shawn Yost and his family had been. Plus, it represented a significant part of his dad's heart and identity, so he was abandoning that too. In his mind, then, was a scattershot memory of the notes and tidbits Dad had gathered intending to write a memoir of Oak Hollow and his life there. A weight sunk in his chest, thinking about how badly Dad had wanted Oak Hollow to heal and find itself again.

Walt realized he was facing a new choice, heavier and harsher than the others so far this week. Perhaps one of the most significant of his life. He could save himself, leave Oak Hollow at the mercy of whatever the fuck Mnemic was, and whatever he had planned for it. Or he could turn back and do something about it. Face down some ungodly evil and fight for the soul of Oak Hollow. The soul of his home, his father's home.

He needed a plan. Look what had happened the last time he went to 432 Asher Street unprepared. He hadn't even expected a confrontation and had barely escaped with his life. Rushing right back, he'd have no chance. But what could he possibly do to prepare? He did not know what he was up against, except that Mnemic was not human.

"How can I stop him if I don't even know what he is, Cowboy?"

The answer was suddenly obvious. So obvious it was moronic Walt hadn't already done it. It should have been his first coherent thought. He should have done it immediately, as he was running away from Asher Street.

There were others better suited to deal with this. He'd call the police, tell them everything he knew, everything he'd seen, and let them deal with it. Finnegan was already dead, he had to be. If Walt had seen what he thought he had seen (which was already becoming foggy in his mind), there was no way he could have survived, but Walt could have at least given him a chance. His cowardice and indecision had already made things worse, so it was only right that he report things to the proper authorities before anyone else got hurt. He had plenty of information to provide, and it should be no more complicated than handing that information to someone who could act on it. Then he could move on with life, knowing he'd done the right thing in the end.

The only problem with doing it that way was deciding how much detail to give. If he told them everything, he would appear insane and could risk his own freedom. If he told them half the truth, focusing on the details that kept plausibility in play, they may still think he was crazy but should at least investigate it. And if someone in an official capacity stopped by Mnemic Family Funeral Home asking questions today, they would have to find evidence of Finnegan's brutal murder. Or failing that (if Mnemic could cover his tracks quickly enough), they should find something off about the place or the things that were happening there or with Mnemic himself.

Sitting in the car and waffling back and forth like this wasn't helping anyone or changing anything. Of course there were reasons he was hesitant to call, but they didn't matter. People could be dying right now. Or worse. Mnemic was surely sliding his claws deeper into Oak Hollow.

Ultimately, from the long list of reasons he couldn't just run away and do nothing, Walt called because of his quasi-promise to Shawn.

Walt pulled into a gas station, filled the tank, and let Cowboy wander off leash in a small patch of grass. When he got back in the car, he breathed deeply and dialed 911.

A woman answered on the first ring, speaking in a frank and efficient manner, and asked pointed questions as Walt explained what he had learned and suspected about 432 Asher Street and Lloyd Mnemic.

He then told her about Finnegan's murder a few hours ago, carefully walking a line between detail and vagueness that he hoped would keep himself out of the spotlight. She promised an officer was already on the way before Walt hung up, cutting off another question she was asking and wondering if anything he'd seen or heard about the time needed to trace a call was accurate.

"Well, boy," he said to Cowboy, "now what?" The dog, sitting across the back seat like a white-furred sphinx, looked at him without blinking, then shifted to follow a bird that landed on a nearby garbage can. Walt considered looking for a motel, assuming if he waited until tomorrow to drive back to town, he'd be in a better state of mind.

He sat behind the wheel for a long time, balancing between a sense of longing for the comforts of home, and the dread of heading back toward whatever the fuck was happening there. He pulled the car out, made a right turn—back the direction he had come from—and drove for several minutes. Without warning, his heart rate shot higher, panic gripping his chest and causing his hands to shake on the steering wheel. He couldn't go back. He couldn't handle it yet. No, he needed some more time. If no distance would ever be far enough, then maybe a night or two away would provide him the space to clear his head. He made to pull the Kia around, planning a sharp U-turn so he could search for a motel nearby.

Before he could complete the turn, a black minivan came screaming out of the night and smashed into the broad side of Walt's car.

PRESTON OBEYS

On second thought, Preston went back into his apartment and grabbed the Porti-Boy too. Whoever had named the small embalming machine must have a dark sense of humor, but then you can't spell funeral without F-U-N. They were probably also a fan of comic books.

It may be a risk to use the machine, but the inner shadow was positively singing at the potential of having it in the transport van tonight. And it just made damn good sense to bring the trocar's side-kick. Didn't it?

Have no fear, citizens! Trocar and Porti-Boy are here!

With the van loaded, Preston reflected on everything Mr. Mnemic had told him yesterday, but so little of it had any clarity. Mr. Mnemic had shared so much, and too fast, and all of it was incredible or down right crazy. Too slippery for Preston to get a grasp on, so he found himself hung up on the clear realities that Mnemic was not human, hundreds of years old (at least), and had some elaborate plan that involved making people more afraid of death than they'd ever been, so he could manipulate their fear and steal their final minutes of life to power something he called his "machine."

What resonated most clearly was Mr. Mnemic's parting words. That's what mattered, and so that's what he paid attention to now.

Prove your faith.

And Preston would obey. All he needed to do was let the shadow out again.

He stood and looked out from his bedroom window, checking his blank fingertips, feeling his new non-identity like a shield as dusk came, and watching the dark growing up from the ground like an army at his back.

There were, of course, a dozen more ways he could be caught even without fingertips (a single hair left behind would do it), but it was impossible to ignore the capacity for guile he now held. Mr. Mnemic had hinted at further alterations being possible, and while Preston was left to speculate what he could do and how far, the only desire that came to mind was a new face. If Mr. Mnemic could do that, he'd be unstoppable.

Plus, as he gave in to the shadow more and more, he sensed its primordial knowledge. The art of stalking prey, the laws of the jungle, these were as deep in the shadow as the shadow was in Preston. Beyond just welcoming it now, he trusted in it.

He welcomed the violent flash-images that had previously terrified him. That night out there, waiting sheeplike outside his thin apartment walls, would be his canvas.

The trocar glimmered in his hands, catching strands of moonlight. To the new, shadowy version of Preston, it was as long as a sword and as hefty as a truncheon.

When it was fully dark, he emerged from his basement apartment into the night, a scorpion come aground, still clutching his trocar—his stinger—and considering a new name for himself. Now that he was reborn, perhaps his old birth name no longer fit. He could choose his own title. Better yet, if he were to succeed long enough to build a reputation, to be feared and dreaded by the masses, he could earn a new name. Instead of assigning one to himself, maybe the media would dub him something unique, something befitting his actions, his ingenuity. His art.

It may be something chic and elusive, like "The Wraith" because he was untraceable. Or he could offer subtle suggestions, leaving hints to guide the mob mentality a bit and await their decision. Alternately, he could follow his gut and let their interpretations of his clues find the right idiom for his work. Which was the best option?

What if he started leaving a calling card? He foresaw himself rooting in drains to keep collecting his hair samples, leaving the drains open and violated. Maybe they'd call him "The Plumber." For a moment, he considered whether that was desirable or just funny. No, that one was no good. It conjured images of a fat man in coveralls with a rusty wrench in his hand and his ass crack exposed. Whatever he was called, the most important part was that it was original. Just like himself.

And then it came to him. They'd call him "The Embalmer." When he'd first picked up the trocar, his mind's eye offered vivid scenery in which he used it either to stab or bludgeon. But as he continued to evolve into a creature more deadly and stealthy than his former self, he was also evolving mentally. Thinking more clearly, more inventively. Like an artist. And, as an artist, he would not simply use his weapon of choice like some mediocre tool. No, he would craft with it on multiple planes. As an artist, it was part of him, an extension; they would move together, him and the trocar, in a symmetry both beautiful and natural, and create.

The information Mr. Mnemic had given wasn't much, but this was the part where Preston's years of subterfuge emptying people's shower drains combined with the shadow's primal instincts would come in handy.

There were a few folks on the street who could help him keep an eye out. He knew what kind of vehicle the guy had, and he knew about how far of a head start he'd gotten. Only a few roads out of Oak Hollow lead anywhere worth going, so Preston did a bit of a mental process of elimination. There were five highways that Walt could be on. Three of them wound through an endless sea of corn and soybean fields, cow pastures, farmhouses, or woods. The closest thing to civilization in any of those would be a Family Dollar store or a Speedway gas station.

Odds were he hadn't gone north because that didn't leave as many options if he wanted to keep going. A quick stop at the bridge where Preston used to stay confirmed that.

With his embalming tools and an empty casket loaded in the transport van, Preston headed southeast to find Walter Sterling and change him into a life-adjacent cadaver.

Once more, Preston's instinct, voiced by his inner shadow, was right. He knew what kind of car to look for and that it needed gas. His contact under the bridge hadn't seen the Kia, which left a strong chance that his subject was headed southeast. Preston had stuck to Route 35 and inspected each gas station he passed. The old man hadn't made it very far, just a few hundred miles. Preston had to fill his own tank once before catching up, and he was pleasantly surprised at how well Mr. Mnemic's transport van handled at high speeds. Almost as if there were other forces keeping him on the road around sharp turns, or maybe that the vehicle itself was helping him make up time.

He was making such great time, cruising in a vehicle made to transport corpses, that he nearly missed the Kia at first, which had stopped at a gas station a tenth of a mile off the main drag, just on the edge of his visibility in the fading light. The last few hours were a blur, Preston coming back to full awareness when he'd spotted the car and entered a state of traveling chase like a natural predator that sees nothing but the path of its prey and tears forward until it reaches its goal. Had he stopped the van? Or had the van stopped him?

When he pulled into the Chevron station, he parked at the far end, putting enough distance between himself and his prey to not cause suspicion. He'd watched the old man fill up, let his dog out, and get back in. Preston could have taken him then, but he thought it would be better to wait until he'd left the parking lot. He was surprised when the old man pulled right, like he was heading back toward Oak Hollow, but then when Preston saw the turn signal and figured he was turning around, he saw an opportunity to pounce and seized it. And though it may not have registered in full consciousness, had someone asked about it, he would have told them the van pounced with him.

Given direct thought, he would have sworn all four tires left the ground at once.

MYRTLE LIVES

The light ahead could only mean one thing: Myrtle was dead. Of that, she was certain. And now that it had happened, she felt relief. Where she was still confused, though, was *when* it had happened. So she kept crawling, moving toward the light, hoping once she reached it (or maybe just by drawing near it like a flighty little moth), facts would become more clear. Death was supposed to bring the ultimate clarity, wasn't it?

Had she died when Mnemic trapped her in his endless tunnels, his Dead Rooms? Or was it earlier? She wanted that to be true because the further back her death had occurred, the less of these inexplicable and terrifying recent events were real.

What if the day she woke up to find Rosita missing had been her first day in purgatory? And everything since was a test? If so, she'd clearly failed, and that meant this was Hell. It also meant Rosita was still out there somewhere, living her gentle life in another world, motherless. That possibility was too terrible to consider.

The last moment Myrtle could recall that she wanted to be real was finding the Rosita doll. How long ago had that been? Maybe she'd rushed out of the store without paying and straight into traffic, got splattered across the road, and everything since was her divesting herself of all the emotional baggage and trauma from a tragic and misguided life. Or perhaps she'd made it home with that newfound treasure and passed away silently in her chair while the whole of her collection watched over her with their loving little eyes, their cherubic faces glowing in soft moonlight.

This blissful mental traipsing did not last long because as she continued to crawl, the pain in her joints, in her bad hand, in her back and neck, and inside her head, these all rudely reminded her she was still alive, somehow; that everything she'd been through (however impossible) was all painfully real. But if the hurt meant she was still alive, what was the light? Where was it coming from?

Was it real?

She'd been underground long enough that it was now hard to tell the time of day, or even if it was the same day. She also had no way of knowing how far she'd traveled down here or how much she'd been conscious. Surely, she couldn't have gone far; she was not fast under ideal conditions and down here, on her hands and knees and wracked with pain, it would take her an hour to go a hundred feet.

Her decades-long transformation into Myrtle the Turtle was complete.

Could she have been crawling like this for five hours? Twenty? More than that and she would be keeled over with dehydration. Despite the agonizingly slow progress, she had not stopped exerting herself since waking up in the dark.

But as she slipped closer and closer to the light—even if it was natural light and not death's border—all that mattered to her was Rosita. And Myrtle would not stop moving until her daughter was back, was safe.

It didn't matter how much she herself was hurting. It also didn't matter what she'd done to arrive at this point. Myrtle had made mistakes, many of them. Terrible, unforgivable mistakes.

But she was still moving, and she could still save Rosita.

First, she'd have to stop Lloyd Mnemic. Whatever he was, he was planning something terrible, and no one in Oak Hollow was safe from him.

She needed to find her way out of here. If she got out, she could try to stop him. And if she somehow stopped him, that could give her a slim chance of atoning for the innocent life she had taken.

If she had to, she'd plunge her bare hands into Mnemic's heart and hope that cleansed the blood from them.

Part of her wanted to die, a mercy. But she also knew she wasn't ready for that. Not yet.

The light ahead meant life, not death, so Myrtle crawled toward it.

The light ahead meant redemption, not disgrace, so Myrtle crawled toward it.

It grew in both size and intensity, and she squinted against it. Then she heard a small sound and paused. It sounded both familiar and foreign at the same time. A sound she knew, which did not belong down here. A bright and cheerful sound.

Birdsong.

The light was coming from the surface world. The real world. The light was outside. The cleansing sun.

She crawled faster, allowing the song of her pain to lift her straight toward the fading evening sun.

WALTER WAKES

Walt rose toward consciousness as if he'd fallen asleep in a glass elevator making its way to the roof of a darkened building, developing clarity. As he did, the pain running rampant along the left hemisphere of his body brought him out faster, like someone had replaced his bone marrow with sparklers and lit them for the Fourth of July. It was worst in his shoulder, a sickening heat with no source radiating into his neck, but it was also present in his hip joint, and he wondered if some of his ribs were broken. His mouth was open, and he couldn't close it fully. Was there something in there?

He strained to open his eyes, and disoriented as he was, it was harder than it should have been. Both the strain required to do it and the blurring when he succeeded conveyed that they may be covered with car wax or something like it. He focused and unfocused, willing the shadowy forms around him to converge into something more knowable.

He was on his back, looking up at a peaked ceiling made of rotting wooden crossbeams and caving-in shingles. There were several large holes up there sharing chunks of soft moonlight. His limbs felt like they were coated with plaster, rigid and too heavy. A few attempts to move either arm or either leg failed, so he pressed his chin against his chest and squinted to see if anything was still attached down there. It was all connected, all right, but there was a thick canvas strap across his chest, another near his knees, and they were cinched tight.

Before he could process more, someone spoke from the direction above Walt's head. He craned his neck as far as it would go, but they were too far out of sight.

". . . a chapel. Well, it was at one time. Now it's just falling apart. Damn it, did you open your eyes already? The glue was still drying." Then a hand covered in a vinyl medical glove invaded his mouth and pulled something out, which felt like a length of thread.

"Where . . . where am I?" Walt asked, his voice clunky and small. Images flashed from memory: turning the car, a fierce collision. "C-Cowboy?" There was no sign of the dog from Walt's limited vantage, but that didn't tell him anything. He could be close by in this strange room or just outside it, waiting. Or he could have gotten alarmed by countless new sights and sounds, then ran for miles, now hiding in a self-made burrow in the rainy woods somewhere. Greyhounds were characteristically anxious, making them unpredictable when scared, and while Walt hadn't seen Cowboy in too many unfamiliar situations, he at least knew the poor dog spooked easily. If there were loud noises anywhere nearby while Walt was unconscious, he would probably go into a mindless fluster and risk getting himself hurt or killed out there on his own.

"Cowboy?" Walt said again.

"What?" the unseen person responded. "Ha. No, no, I've never been into that Western crap. But I guess you're about that age. And if you're trying to appeal to my ego, that's not going to help. I only want one thing right now. And that's flushing you out like an old transmission and watching the light leave your eyes."

"You what?" Walt replied, the words coming without thought. His mind was a blizzard, cold and frantic and blurring, but two things were quite clear: he needed to find his dog before something bad happened, and he himself was in immediate danger. They were equally large problems. He thought about Cowboy once more, likely huddled and shivering in a den of wet leaves by some unknown road out there. Or worse. Then he took a deep breath to stave off a wave of panic that would surely doom them both, and a distant voice told him his only option was to talk his way out.

"Who are you?" Walt asked.

"My name's Preston—" the other man answered, cutting himself off as if he'd caught himself responding when he shouldn't.

The answer didn't matter—at least not until this was over—Walt realized as soon as it had left his mouth, but then strangely, in a drop of adrenaline-fueled clarity, he recalled reading an article about a school receptionist who had talked a would-be mass shooter into surrendering just by asking him questions. She'd saved countless lives with a straightforward, in-the-moment strategy. The details were gone, but the focus of the article had been on the brain science behind why her diversion had worked so well, and it had something to do with how questions redirect thought patterns. Questions were his weapon. His only chance. Cowboy's only chance, too, maybe. And thankfully, they shared a border with his instinctual reaction to whatever the fuck was happening. So he asked another before the first had been answered.

"Why are you doing this?"

Preston *(?)* moved into Walt's peripheral vision, his back turned as he fidgeted, as if moving objects around on a surface like a chef preparing their utensils and spices.

"I've got my orders."

"From Mnemic?" *Of course that freak didn't just let me get away, knowing what I know.*

"Yeah. But if I'm being real honest, I want to do this anyway. If it wasn't you, it would be someone else. You're not even my first."

"First what? What are you doing?" Walt pulled at the straps holding him down, finding only slight wiggling possible. Then he scolded himself. *Don't do that, change the focus. Don't have him explain* how *he's going to kill you. Get deeper. Get in his head.*

"I already said that. I'm going to flush you out. No more blood. I wouldn't worry, though. I don't think it will hurt for long. You see, the fluid goes straight into your carotid, so it'll be inside your heart in seconds. I'm no doctor or anything, and I guess you'll have a bit of time before your brain shuts down, but come on. I mean, how long can it take for chemicals like this to turn you off? And then all your blood ends up in this big bladder. Theoretically, if you were already dead—like most people when they get embalmed—then I'd probably have to get some of your other liquefied parts out too. You know, depending on how long you were dead and under what conditions your body had been stored. Your eyes, or your balls, maybe your spleen or your fucking gall bladder. I'm still learning that stuff. Lucky for us, we don't have to bother with that tonight. We also don't have to worry about filling your empty eye sockets with cotton or sewing your mouth shut or the other stuff Mr. Mnemic showed me. Although, maybe I'll do some of that too. The shadow eats that stuff up."

He stopped busying himself with the instruments on the nearby table and circled the cot Walt was strapped to. After walking its full circumference twice, he stepped into the cone of light coming from above and made full eye contact. Walt didn't recognize him, a young man in his mid-twenties, very fit, strong. Something lived inside his eyes that Walt had never seen before. Something dark and hungry. A primal understanding came to Walt: these predator's eyes had been waiting for a moment like this; they'd spent years hiding behind dead, glassy stares and among forced normality. But now they were free, as was the bloody urge behind them. "If nothing else, I'll stitch your anus shut," he said, in a voice one would use to indicate a favor. "To prevent leakage."

Hearing that, Walt surrendered to his terror, much as he assumed Cowboy had when this maniac had crashed into them. Then all he could do was beg.

"Please, please. You don't have to do this. Preston, please. I don't know anything, okay? If you just let me go, I don't even know who you are at all and I—"

"That's not my name. Not anymore. See?" he held his hands near Walt's face, palms out.

Walt did not understand what that meant. *Oh shit,* he thought. *He's insane. Truly insane, not in an amusing or harmless way. This is an actual psychopath. There are no more rules in here.*

"Call me . . . The Embalmer. Because that's who I am now. That's what I do." Preston turned his palms back toward his own face, giving them a look of admiration. "He remade me. I'm sort of his . . . apprentice. And his foot soldier. And you, Walt, I guess you haven't seen that many Mafia movies because Mr. Mnemic says you know too much, and only one thing ever happens to the guy who knows too much. You're a classic loose end. You seeing my face doesn't matter because he can change that. But you've seen *his* face, and that does matter. Not literally, not his *real* face, but you know he's not like us. You know he's going to do great and terrible things in Oak Hollow, and I can't let you stop him."

Preston walked out of sight once again and was gone for several minutes.

In that time, Walt's mind slowly entered a state of hyperfocus—some survival instinct he'd never needed to use before was taking over. He ignored the threats, ignored the imminent danger, and heard his dad inside his own mind. Dad was with him, telling him what to do. And Dad was perfectly calm. Whereas he was usually irreverent and lighthearted, this version of Dad's voice in Walt's head was alarmingly serious.

You can get out of here, Dad said. *The question thing was a good idea, son. Find an insecurity. Find a crack. Find a weakness and shove your goddamn fingers in there. Get in his head. Who is this guy? What is he trying to get out of this? He wants to kill you, but why? He seems like he's not been doing this long, called himself an "apprentice." Does that mean he's being trained by Mnemic?*

"You just do whatever he tells you, then?" It was pedestrian, but he had to start somewhere.

"Mr. Mnemic? Yeah. I mean, I owe him. Big time. But I told you, I want to do this. Really, really badly."

This time, when the guy spoke Mnemic's name, Walt noted a tone of reverence. Was that his opening? It could at least be a way to keep him talking, buy time. Maybe get him angry? Angry and sloppy.

"Why do you owe him?" Walt asked, hoping his voice conveyed genuine interest rather than naked terror. To himself, it sounded detached and foreign. None of this could be real.

"He saved me," Preston said matter-of-factly, as if he was surprised Walt needed to be told. He now had a large, black duffle bag and was unzipping and unpacking it.

"Saved you from what?" That time, Walt barely heard himself above his own heart pounding in his ears.

"From people like you. Who don't understand that it's still a kill-or-be-killed world. We're still living in the caves, everything else is just an illusion. And some of us are better equipped for that brutal reality. Some of us were programmed for it from the very beginning.

But along the way the wolves became afraid of the sheep, just because there are more of you than of us. Mnemic changed that. He set me free. No more hiding. No more pretending to fit in. It's eat or be eaten. And I'm tired of being hungry. Now it's time to prove my faith."

"What is he? What's he going to do?"

"Well, you'll have to excuse the cliché, but he's something you'll never understand. I'm not going to bother explaining it to you, and you'll just have to trust me when I tell you that there's nothing that can stop him now. He's done this too many times to fail again."

Fail again? Walt thought, filing that away. A drop of frigid sweat ran into his eye and he blinked it away furiously.

"As for what he's going to do," Preston continued, "He's creating his own private oasis. He told me he's tired of taking scraps from the tables of others. He's sick of slinking underground and stealing rotten meat from caskets. So he's going to turn Oak Hollow into his own self-contained banquet. A kingdom all his own. A never-ending feast for all his needs."

"Oh, and what's your role in this little kingdom?"

"I . . ." Preston stopped, a confused look on his face suggesting he had no answer. Maybe he'd never considered what would happen to himself in the endgame. What role he would play at Mnemic's side, if any. "Enough. I see what you're trying to do. It's time." He stooped over, removing an object from his bag that looked to Walt like an oversized blender. Then he set two bottles of reddish-orange liquid next to it. "I'd like to introduce you to my friend. Porti-Boy, this is Walt. Walt, Porti-Boy. Ready?"

"Preston. I—"

"No, not Preston. He's gone. He's long gone.""Bh . . . Wh . . . I-I don't think he . . . he is," Walt said, straining to form a sentence and force it through locked vocal chords, a stone through a straw. His brain was encased in plastic, his chest on the verge of eruption, but still he resisted. It was a long shot, but he figured every true psychopath wrestled with their nature at some level. "I-I-I th-think Preston is . . . is still in there, and . . . and Mnemic is just trying t-to . . . to confuse him."

"He set me free," Preston said.

Was there a tinge of uncertainty in that? "Is . . . isn't there a p-part of you that . . . th-that still wants to be . . . good? Li . . . live a normal life? It's not . . . not like that, not like he s-s-says. You don't . . . you don't . . . have to do this. You can be like everyone. Everyone e-else."

"No. No, I can't. I've tried. You don't know what it's like. Every day, every minute was a fight. The shadow . . . it craves death. It craves that moment between life and death. And there's this . . . this clicking in my head. It drives me to violence. It wants to use its power to make living things dead and to make dead things living. I fought it and fought it, for years. For as long as I can remember. But it's too strong. Once the clicking starts, it just gets worse and worse until I give in. I'm not even that old, but I'm burned out. I can't fight it like this forever."

It's working, Junior. It's working.

Walt's voice grew stronger. "There are people who can . . . can help you, Preston. You don't have to fight alone. And you can win."

That was it. He'd done it. Talked sense into a psycho.

Don't break out the champagne just yet.

Preston stared blankly ahead, as if considering this. He tilted his head to one side, like a fox curious about a strange sound. Then he shook his head and locked eyes with Walt.

"No. It's starting again. I can hear the clicking right now. No one can help me with that. But Mr. Mnemic is right. And he needs my help, so it's a fair trade. He has to stay near the Dead Rooms. Can't leave the house because of that mark on his arm, so I'm his foot soldier."

With that last declaration, Walt saw a change in Preston's face, as if some brightness surged and then left. His eyes glistened, then softened, then he blinked, and Walt was no longer looking at Preston. He was face-to-face with The Embalmer again, and out of time. The Embalmer turned away, grabbed something off the table. There was a deep clinking sound and then he walked toward the cot where Walt was strapped in, helpless.

Walt didn't recognize the thing in his hand, but it looked like a massive steel needle or like a piece of silver plumbing pipe with a sharp point.

"Now," The Embalmer said. "I can tell you won't let me hook you up to the Porti-Boy, so I'll just use this trocar to drain your stomach first." He pulled up Walt's shirt, then raised the pipe-thing above his head, spearlike.

Before he could bring it down into Walt's exposed abdomen, they both heard a sound. Preston dropped both hands to his side as the sound came a second time. "What the hell is that?"

Walt knew what it was, and his heart soared. It resembled a howl, but more high-pitched. It was close, too, and steady. As it continued, it grew more high-pitched still, almost siren-like. People familiar with the greyhound breed called it "rooing." Huskies and a few other breeds sounded similar, but there was a unique quality to the song of a greyhound, more soulful. They were usually stoic, enigmatic, almost unreadable emotionally. You could rarely tell what a greyhound was feeling unless you knew both the breed and the specific dog well. If they stood statue-still, as most often would, there was an equal chance they were bored or content or in the throes of mortal terror. They didn't lick or wag their tails or bound around nearly as much as other dogs. But one outward sign of a greyhound's feelings was their song. They were hearing Cowboy's, which meant he was close, and he only rooed when he was scared.

The Embalmer walked away, no doubt looking for the source of the sound, or making sure the dilapidated old chapel was still secure enough. He left the pipe-thing (*trocar, he called it*) lying on the gurney next to Walt's hand. Close enough for him to grab it.

Holy shit, Walt thought, floored that his would-be killer was so careless, he grabbed it with the tips of his fingers, shimmying it up for a better grasp. He had enough leverage to press it up, moving his wrist against the metal clamp of the strap across his chest, loosening it by a half inch. That gave him more leverage, and he hurried to slacken it further, praying he could create enough slack to move one arm.

Soon, The Embalmer walked back into the room, muttering to himself. He looked around, puzzled, then stepped next to the gurney.

"Where did I leave that—"

Walt cried out, jabbing the sharp end of the trocar upward into The Embalmer's side, hoping it would penetrate beneath the ribs. Luckily, it was sharp, backed by the frantic strength of desperation, and he'd hit his mark. The tip sank out of sight, six or more inches of steel disappearing into Preston's gut. Based on the thing's diameter, Walt hoped he'd hit at least one major organ. If not the stomach, then a lung. Blood poured from its hollow end, black in the moonlight.

"Gaah," Preston shouted, his breath catching in his throat as he fell forward and landed on his knees, grasping at the trocar and pulling it free. When it came out, more blood followed in a rush, soaking his gray shirt in seconds.

Walt, with only one hand loose, fumbled with the chest strap until he could wiggle both hands out. The rooing came again, urging him to move faster. He slid one foot out of the lower strap, which went limp, allowing him to bring the other foot out easily.

Dropping off the gurney to his feet, Walt felt all the pain from the car crash again and figured his short burst of adrenaline was fading already. He looked down at the man he had impaled, writhing on the floor as his blood spilled into a widening pool, and was surprised when he felt not rage or the urge to finish the job, but pity as he watched the final moments of a misguided life, cut short.

Preston was gasping, fishlike, his eyes alive and wide, searching.

"Don't fuck with my dog," Walt said, then walked outside to find Cowboy.

THURSDAY

MNEMIC LAUGHS

As Preston was taking care of the last loose end some miles away, back in Oak Hollow the house at 432 Asher Street was quiet once more. Yesterday had seen the procession of nearly one third of Oak Hollow's full population, over three thousand mourners. They had filed through for hours, a never-ending ant line, then most had gone about their lives unaware of what Mnemic had taken from them.

Some had never left.

Mnemic had led fourteen souls into the Dead Rooms, where he harvested their dwindling time and fed it into his Infernal Machine. He had everything he needed to follow through on the final steps of his grand design, and it was time.

The authorities outside of Oak Hollow were surely stirring in their beds, catching wisps of the foul air wafting off the town's bloated corpse. But there was still enough time for it all to come together.

Time.

A resource he had in abundance but other beings took for granted. And after millennia guiding and observing rogue scientists, anatomists, vivisectionists, and others considered mad by their own kind, Mnemic had finally found the means to acquire enough power to carve out his own corner of the universe. When his machine exploded, Oak Hollow would be free from its moors in this reality. It would become isolated in time and space, and he could exact his will upon it for eternity.

An impenetrable kingdom of the dead, where he could feast on their bodies for all time.

Mnemic laughed as the sun came up on Oak Hollow's last day.

Then he went down into the Dead Rooms and activated his machine.

WALTER INKS

"**C**owboy!" Walt called, hoping the dog was still nearby and not careening into traffic like an overgrown squirrel. He'd already been searching long enough that the sky was beginning to brighten slightly and was losing both faith and steam. Preston had brought them to a cemetery and there was no way to tell how far it was from where he had crashed into Walt's car. They must be hours from Oak Hollow and he couldn't do anything until he found his dog. Plus, he had no car now.

Seeing as he'd just killed someone in self-defense, Walt considered placing another call to the authorities, then decided it was more important to get back there himself. And fast.

"Cowboy!" he called again. Still no signs. "Here, boy." Walt carefully tempered his voice to avoid sounding urgent or upset because that would just scare the dog and drive him farther away. He knew he'd never catch a greyhound. He needed to coax the dog out, not scare him worse.

Remembering something he'd seen one of the adoption group's volunteers do, Walt dropped to one knee in a pratfall, plopping down on an elbow, too, for good measure. It was not as exaggerated as he'd wanted, but he doubted Cowboy would scrutinize. The technique would either work or it wouldn't. "Ow! Oh, ow. I'm hit," he said, pawing at his chest like an over-actor in a spaghetti Western and infusing his voice with a sense of pleading.

Within seconds came a soft rustle in the nearby trees, then Cowboy emerged like a brown-spotted lanky ghost in the foggy air. Cowboy approached Walt, who stayed on his side, groaning long enough to ensure the dog would stay. Cowboy pushed his cold nose down against Walt's cheek and he stifled a laugh.

"Ha. There. Hi, boy." Walt reached up and wrapped his arms around the dog's deep chest, hugging. There were a few small scrapes and cuts on Cowboy's legs and a short one on his snout, but none were actively bleeding.

With Walt fully upright now, Cowboy met his eyes, his right ear at attention while the left flopped across to touch its base. To Walt's surprise, he wagged his tail.

"Huh," Walt said. "You only do that when I feed you. Must really be glad to see me." He mussed Cowboy's ears, and the dog moved his head into the touch. "I'm glad to see you too. You're safe now. Let's get you home."

Cowboy's only response was one more side-to-side wag of his tail, then he went statue-still except for steady, deep breaths.

Walt surveyed the area. Preston wouldn't have brought him here by hand. There would be a vehicle nearby.

Walt walked back toward the decrepit little chapel, Cowboy keeping stride, and saw a black minivan parked twenty feet away. The doors were unlocked, key in the ignition. He turned it and saw the gas tank was nearly full.

Walt lifted Cowboy into the driver's side. Knowing funeral homes only use hearses for show, he looked in back and confirmed the van was a specialized vehicle for transporting bodies. *How many dead people have lay in the back of this thing?*

Walt drove along the gravel, scolding himself for again having no plan or forethought.

What was to stop Mnemic from ripping out all of his own blood vessels? Or melting his face off, drinking his bone marrow, or whatever the fuck else that monster could do to a defenseless moron like Walter Sterling, Jr.?

Need to get a weapon first, Walt thought. There was an old handgun somewhere in Dad's workshop. It was a relic from his time in the Army, but maybe it would still fire. Still, it wouldn't make much difference against Mnemic, he figured.

A flash-memory of Mnemic's eyes hit Walt's forebrain, calling up Dad's slurred description of the enemy soldier he'd killed all those years back.

Black and borderless, like a wasp's, he'd said.

Like Mnemic's, Walt thought.

Only a few days ago, Walt would swear he'd never had a supernatural experience, but clearly that had changed. Was there some connection between Mnemic and the thing Dad had once faced? Even some similarity could matter because it had been the rune tattoo that supposedly saved Dad and Dublin in that foxhole. Plus, Finnegan had spoken about the power of those ancient symbols. Mnemic had one too. That couldn't be a coincidence.

What if he'd been branded?

Hagaluz, it was called. And it meant nothing good.

The connection was possible. When reality steps away for a breather, what does that leave besides possibility? Anything was possible in that old house right now. Anything at all.

There it was, then. Not a plan, but at least a measure of protection. The gun would satisfy the normal, rational side of protecting himself.

So what was the harm in protecting that maniacal, irrational side of all this?

Plus, he needed to take Cowboy home. So he'd check Dad's notes while he was there.

And then . . .

It was midafternoon by the time Cowboy was lying in his usual spot on a plush bed in the corner of the living room.

Walt went downstairs to Dad's workshop and took stacks of papers out of two cardboard banker's boxes, then spread them across the surface of the table, urging himself to focus and not panic.

He looked down at the sheaves of random papers, sweeping his gaze back and forth, up and down. He took in a landscape of words, formats, and images that ranged from newspaper clippings to typed papers, carbon copies, loose-leaf paper with handwriting in a rainbow of colors and styles, faded old receipts, and Post-it notes. It was a mess.

Stop looking so hard. You'll see it when you stop looking.

Walt relaxed his vision, was about to reach for a different box or start over.

And then it worked.

Amidst the scattered notes was a booklet bound with a black plastic spiral. It struck Walt as a document someone may hand out to an audience at a trade event or maybe a corporate presentation. He picked it up, guessing it to be about fifteen or twenty pages, and the adjacent scraps and leaves of paper slid off to its sides. It had a clear plastic cover, under which was a photocopy of a black-and-white picture of his dad and mom (probably one of the last taken of them together), in their

Sunday best, standing next to a car as if they were about to leave for church.

Below the picture were the words *The Power of Symbolism in My Life*, and below that, in smaller font, *A Memoir, by Walter Sterling, Sr.*

Walt opened it and read.

The first few pages were meant as an introduction, it appeared. *Humans crave divination. But we cannot find this in overt displays. Instead, it is only found in forms of veiled imagery. Such matter speaks to our hearts far more than to our heads, which is both a blessing and a curse. For the head may seek to understand, but it is the heart through which we interpret.*

Hmm. Look at Dad with the writer's touch. Why didn't he ever tell me? Maybe he was too self-conscious about it?

He read on, skimming tracts about early languages, tarot cards, and some religious symbolism. Turning the page again, Walt found exactly what he was looking for.

While symbols hold the potential for immense power, those crafted in ancient times may represent the very roots of power: cuneiform, hieroglyphs of man's first societies, and in particular, Celtic runes.

Walt smiled, entertaining an idea of how to use this revelation.

Soon, he was pulling up a YouTube tutorial on stick and poke DIY tattoos and gathering the supplies it displayed.

He rushed outside shortly after, heading toward Mnemic Family Funeral Home.

OAK HOLLOW SINKS

While Walt undertook the surprise tasks of reading passages in his dad's memoir/study of ancient symbols and taking a lottery ticket shot at using that information to protect himself, Oak Hollow was succumbing to a devastating and subversive smolder that most residents failed to notice.

It originated deep underground and only rose to the surface in isolated spots around town. There was an accompanying sound, an unholy mix of tearing, humming, and grinding. It sang out in a steady, blended tone but registered at a frequency outside the range of human hearing. To dogs, it was hellish, and so there was a grand symphony of barks and yelps and howls from one corner of town to the other, but the contributing voices were spread out enough that no one quite noticed this. Every dog contributed, except a few deaf old mutts who stayed silent. Several house cats joined in to pick up their slack.

The front end of the True Value, along with portions of two other buildings situated close to 432 Asher Street, sagged noticeably down into the earth. It was closed for the evening and empty.

Strange, unnatural-looking clouds formed on the edges of town and grew slowly toward its center like a closing purple iris. The massive bronze statue of James Abram Garfield in front of city hall tilted to one side, then fell over as shifting bedrock—akin to the moving of tectonic plates—took place, unseen and unheard.

Throughout town, spiderweb cracks appeared in concrete foundations. Stair-like fissures worked through mortar joints in brick walls. Dead trees fell in waves. Fences and flagpoles canted. The backstop on the ball field behind Stewart Elementary dropped forward, raising clouds of fine dirt from the empty base paths.

A volley of sirens rose as emergency services scrambled in response to several sudden fires, injuries from falling debris or trees, and the collapse of an abandoned BSL warehouse close to the edge of town. And while several folks who occupied official capacities within the town and county were alerted, none made any connection between this series of events. It was odd, the concentration of bigger-than-small natural disasters, but a far cry from the sort of situation that warranted calling in the National Guard or FEMA.

There was also nothing significant enough to be visible from an airplane cruising altitude. But from a more zoomed-in satellite view, a rough-hewn and circular pattern formed at a four-mile radius, as if a drainage ditch had been dug in one fell swoop.

At its center was Mnemic Family Funeral Home.

The town was sinking, and very few people noticed anything amiss.

MYRTLE MARCHES

Myrtle had passed out immediately upon leaving the tunnel, finding her way out through a large black pipe that ended in a wooded drainage ditch next to Markert Street, a few blocks from the center of town.

She woke now, unaware of how much time had passed (hours, days?), starving, delirious, and starkly aware that the town was sinking around her. She felt it like one would feel a boat making a sharp turn while underway. When she stood, her old bones creaked in protest. The ground appeared level, but she had to pitch forward to keep from tumbling onto her butt. Gravity was stronger than it should be. Something was happening. Something was very, very wrong, and she knew it was related to that awful Lloyd Mnemic and his horrendous machine.

By way of a miracle, though, while she had been crawling in those dark tunnels underground, she had found more than just her way out. She'd found herself too. As if she'd sloughed some chitinous shell from around her brain and it could function now in a way it hadn't for decades. She wondered if this is what it felt like for someone with schizophrenia to find a medication that fixed their brain chemistry, or maybe the level of clarity one achieves right before death. In a way, it felt like she had reached a mental pinnacle, a new realm of understanding where her mild dementia and delusions about her life and the world around her were paintings on a wall, existing outside herself and observable, rather than distorting her perceptions like cataracts. It was already slipping away, this newfound lucidity of self and purpose, but she intended to use it while she could to do something good.

Before the end.

Somewhere back there, amidst all the wallowing and waffling, the second-guessing and self-loathing, the terror and regret and fatigue, Myrtle resigned to use this second chance as best she could. Not for herself and not for the town. Oak Hollow had never been her home. She certainly would not act now for any men either. Nor for the other denizens of this world that had brought her nothing but misery and pain. Not even for her dolls or her sad little house or the few things she loved and cherished while treading through the muck and mire and sludge that was her life on this Earth. Still, she would do it. For her real home. Her safe space.

For Rosita.

In her temporary clarity, Myrtle understood that Rosita was more an idea than a living, breathing child. But what if that idea had come from somewhere larger than herself? A cosmic memory or some type of omen? What if, in another place or time, another world, things had gone differently, and she had made some right choices? Choices that made Rosita real or a version of her. And they were together there, living in a home that was clean and pure and safe. Together.

Rosita may not be flesh and blood in this tragic world, but she still represented the innocence and pure soul of a child, the thing Myrtle had most longed for since her own was shattered. That was worth fighting for.

What could Mnemic do to her that was worse than things she'd already faced?

In the bright light of a new day, above ground, with her fighting spirit and untamable pain-powered will intact, Myrtle assembled her plan to stand against Mnemic and his machine. One thing he had said was trapped in her mind like a moth inside a lantern, thrashing itself against the glass to get out before it burned to ash.

He'd said he wanted her to see it, his "Infernal Machine." She'd heard that term before and now remembered where. Percy had been obsessed with Napoleon, often making her read to him from his books. The Infernal Machine was some sort of hidden bomb that was supposed to go off and kill Napoleon. But what did that have to do with Mnemic's mountain of detached-but-still-living human body parts? And what was he going to do to Oak Hollow with it?

It's a bomb. But why would he set off a bomb in Oak Hollow? Either to kill a lot of people or to destroy the town. Probably both. That much was clear, even if what he could gain from it was not.

These uncertainties were making her head hurt, bringing back a portion of the fatigue that had caused her to pass out in a ditch. She'd lived for a reason; there was a purpose she still had to fulfill. And no matter what that machine was intended for, one thing she could be sure of was that he planned to use it. And soon.

Myrtle would stop him, or she would die trying. Her life had meant nothing, and there was so little time left for her to change that. Maybe her death could mean something.

Myrtle brushed the dead leaves and twigs from her housedress, noting several bloody scrapes on her knees and along her shins above her medical stockings. There was steady pain in both hands (worse in the bad one), but she leaned into it, using it to bring focus. She walked as fast as her brittle, abused legs could carry her, heading toward Asher Street. There would be other people there, maybe a crowd, and that meant she could be arrested, but compared to a few days ago, that seemed a trifle. She may not even survive long enough for them to take her. Deep down, where the truth lived, she knew she was marching to her death, but that was one comforting certainty floating like a buoy in a sea of doubt.

Her eyes told her the ground ahead was level, but impossibly, she knew she was walking downhill. As if something were pushing from behind and threatening her balance. She steadied herself on a nearby tree, then stooped and picked up a large branch to use as a cane. She looked back and the effect of the illusion was amplified. Behind her, the ground was clearly slanted up, but when she looked ahead, everything looked flat. An image came to mind, a view of herself from far away walking toward the center of a meteor as it hurled through space.

She shook her head to clear the disorientation and trudged on.

When she arrived at the site of Mnemic Family Funeral Home, Myrtle stood aghast wondering how she'd gotten herself turned around. She knew this part of town well; her church and the pharmacy where she picked up all her medications were nearby. All the familiar sights were there, in place, with one exception.

The house at 432 Asher Street had disappeared.

In its place was a vacant lot festooned with hip-high weeds. Rubbing her eyes to reset reality, she paced slowly around the perimeter. Yesterday there had been a funeral service for the boy she'd murdered, and today there wasn't a single brick or scrap of wood left.

Was she too late?

Then she heard a noise, familiar and haunting. The sound of the machine, Mnemic's machine, that forsaken, pulsing mountain of remains, coming from beneath her feet. Hearing it above ground meant it was considerably louder than before. She approached the center of the lot, surprised as her outstretched good hand met with resistance in midair.

It's still here, but he's hiding it. He makes us see what he wants, instead of what's real. But it only worked on the inside before, so his power's growing. He's keeping everyone from coming inside. But there must still be a way in.

She felt along the invisible wall in front of her, gauging against memory in search of a door. She was closest to the back of the house, the opposite side from the large porch.

Soon, her hand collided with something metallic and she grasped it. A door knob, hidden by some magic or illusion, but there all the same. She turned it, pulled the door toward herself and the glamour, or whatever it was, fell like the building had been obscured by one of those fumigation tents and it dropped to the ground.

The house looked exactly the same.

The humming continued.

Myrtle entered the back room of 432 Asher Street, marching toward certain death.

WALTER STRIPS

The house at 432 Asher Street looked the same to Walt with one exception. It was just as neglected and rundown, still unique by comparison to its surroundings, a rotting tooth in the gums of Oak Hollow.

Except, now it was glowing.

Not from the position of the sun, a trick of the light, or some fast-forming cataract compounding his vision. It was more like looking at a larger-than-life version of one of those injection-molded Christmas statues if lit by a giant green flood bulb. The light was coming from inside. Unnaturally incandescent, a nauseating jade shine emanating through the very bricks and mortar while brighter-hued emerald beams projected through the windows.

Walt fought to relate some experience or align this to reality. *Buildings don't glow. They can't. You're having a stroke, old man. Or maybe some of that embalming fluid went into your mouth.* Except none of the nearby buildings were doing it. This was an acutely contained phenomenon.

Domestic aurora borealis.

Along with the light, there was a thrumming noise that emanated up from the ground and soaked into his body, like the vibrations of a nearby train in motion. The sight of the glowing house and the sensation of moving while standing still were enough to make his gorge rise.

Walt held a hand flat against his chest, pressing his shirt to the still-tender skin. There was pain, but it was duller now and he felt like a bizarre, enfeebled Care Bear.

Dad's notes had been difficult to navigate and still incomplete in their detail. But between what he'd learned there, along with clues taken from Finnegan, Preston, and Mnemic himself, Walt had a fledgling confidence that he would be protected when it mattered most. For a moment only, but maybe enough to make a difference. Until Mnemic pulled Walt's kidneys out and smacked them together like a gory Three Stooges gag. Or maybe he'd cross his arms like in *I Dream of Jeanie*, blink, and Walt's skin would all be inside out.

Walter was stern-faced as he approached the porch steps of 432 Asher Street, his mind flashing back to Shawn's wake.

The door was unlocked, wouldn't even close fully. The wooden frame was dry-rotted and crumbling where the lock would extend out and secure the door, so it couldn't be locked without some significant repairs. This confirmed one small fact for Walt, at least. He knew when he stepped inside, he'd see the true state of the building, not the version Mnemic had projected.

The interior was rough.

There was no electricity, and the house had only been inhabited by squatters and animals for years. A musty smell hung in the air: vacancy and rampant mold. Scanning, Walt noted every window was cracked, shattered, or missing the glass altogether.

It was like showing up at a carnival lot the day after they'd all left town.

Goading himself forward before he lost the nerve, Walt pressed on, walking down the main hallway to the back room where Mnemic had staged his office, dry leaves and other debris crunching underfoot. To his surprise, the desk was still there and the antique chairs.

Mnemic must have brought some things with him, then. The caskets were probably real too. And maybe the chairs in the chapel. All to avoid detection longer. But Finnegan detected something before Mnemic was ready, and . . .

Well that meant he could be triggered. And despite his inhuman abilities to steal time, manipulate human bodies, and project illusions, Mnemic was confined to this building. Which meant he had some limitations, perhaps even a weakness.

Walt walked to the door behind the desk. Padlocked shut, as expected. The wood was rotten, though, and he dislodged the hasp with a few sharp pulls on the knob and opened it.

Walt looked down the steps into the dark, a sinking feeling in his chest. He pressed a hand there, the other on the railing. Green light filled the space like smoke.

At the bottom he found a wall switch, flipped it. Fluorescent light diluted the green and soaked the basement, which had been renovated into a functioning morgue.

Walt saw a porcelain table stationed next to a sink. A cabinet with several closed drawers and glass doors presenting bottles of fluids with hazardous warning labels. Arranged on the counter was a series of ghastly instruments. Among them was a trocar, larger than the one he'd used on Preston.

Walt pulled Dad's antique pistol from his waistband, held it to his hip.

The space felt strange. Hollow, as if sound wouldn't carry correctly, giving Walt an eerie sense that he had stepped into another dimension where everyday laws and scientific properties didn't apply.

He saw a wooden door that looked displaced among all the new materials and hospital-clean surfaces. It was dark, warped, hanging off-kilter, and with jagged edges above the start of a dirt floor.

Turning back toward the steps, Walt heard Mnemic's voice.

"You."

Walt's blood froze, his veins hoping to remain in place, unlike Finnegan's. He turned with the reluctant speed of a child scanning a darkened bedroom for the boogeyman.

Will I see his true form now?

He felt childlike in more ways than one: small, defenseless, incapable. The air around him weighed with implied threat, as if the hand of a monster was placed gently on his shoulder.

But Mnemic looked the same as ever, although his eyes were wild with rage and his posture had straightened. Across the width of the basement morgue, he could have been taller than Walt now. As he spoke, his tone conveyed both surprised annoyance and a form of muted restraint.

"You shouldn't be here," he said. "Though, I suppose it's not a surprise. I take it my apprentice is dead?"

"I know what you're doing," Walt said, lying while refusing to be drawn in so easily. He raised the pistol, unsure if it would fire. His focus bifurcated between Mnemic's face and the would-be shield lurking beneath his own clothing. He wielded the silence like a weapon, more faith in it than the gun, waiting for Mnemic's next move.

They stared at each other, gunslingers at the ready but neither knowing the other's true weapon. Walt's heart hammered in his ears and sweat sheened his forehead.

Mnemic's body language relaxed, though the rage didn't leave his eyes.

"A shame," Mnemic said. "Preston had potential. And you . . . you're quite the unknown entity, aren't you? There's something blocking me, but there's also some odd connection in there. You don't interact with death like the rest. Don't fear it the same way. All they want is to shove their dead behind a closed door, throw a few coins across the table, and keep their hands clean. So much easier and safer to watch death from afar. Reduce their fate to tall tales. Eat enough vegetables and it won't happen to you. They presume it must be let in first. Death comes on its own time, in its own way. It can invade even the safest home."

He swept his arms in a wide parabola outward, denoting the house, the town itself, perhaps the entire Earth.

"What they all want to forget is that death is always beside them. It walks slowly, but it never stops. Death is patient and silent. It needs no permission. Every breath brings it closer, and death does not need to hurry. Because it always wins. Everything dies, Mr. Sterling. Everything."

"I know what you're doing," Walt repeated. "It won't work—"

"You know nothing," Mnemic said, cutting him off. "It has already worked."

"The police are on their way." Another lie. The gun shook in his hand.

"There's nothing they could do. It's been activated. There's no shutting it off now."

"Shutting what off?" Walt asked, betraying his position of posturing more knowledge than he held.

"Enough," Mnemic said. In a flash of sudden violent movement, he was halfway across the morgue, hands reaching out. Walt pulled the pistol's trigger, and it did fire, but the shot went wide.

Mnemic closed in, emerging more fully into the light, and Walt had time to note that his suit was rippling like the wall had upstairs. Not the boogeyman in its true form yet, but the illusion was falling away.

Then Mnemic was on him, throwing him ten feet across the room like a sack of garbage.

Walt landed in a heap, pain flaring across much of his body, his head smacking tile. The gun flew out of reach. He saw stars, felt a trickle from his nose, fought to stay conscious. He rolled to his back, panting and shocked. When his vision cleared, he looked up and saw Mnemic's hand, palm flat, inches from his face. Walt grabbed the wrist, pushing. The skin on Mnemic's palm bubbled, then a honeycomb of bloodless holes opened in its center, small black tendrils stretched toward him.

This is it, Junior, Dad's voice came. *Moment of truth.*

Mnemic had dropped all pretense now, his red-rimmed eyes locked on Walt's, his face a distorted mask of hate and fury that barely passed as human. "You don't know what death is. I'll show you. You'll see its face." His pupils spread like spilled ink, overtaking the whole of his corneas and turning his gaze black and soulless as a shark's.

The tendrils crept closer.

Walt released Mnemic's wrist, grasped the front of his own shirt with both hands, and ripped it open. The buttons scattered like buckshot as the tendrils reached his bare chest. Mnemic's face slackened, determination replaced with shock. Then pain. The tendrils writhed wormlike against Walt's skin, then grew hot, sizzling like they were in a skillet.

Mnemic shouted in agony, let go, retracted, and dropped to his knees. Dark gray smoke billowed from his closed fist.

Beneath a smeared layer of petroleum jelly on Walt's chest was a tattoo of the rune Mannaz, done in prison-ink style.

Dad's notes had led him to that symbol, the one he had tattooed inside his arm. The same one his Army buddy, Dublin, had once used to save their lives. It looked like the letter *X* with two longer lines drawn down from its sides.

According to Dad's notes, Mannaz was a symbol for "self." It could mean either the individual self or the collective self of mankind and held strong associations with family and society. One other meaning it held was "home."

The skin around the tattoo was beet red, and Walt stood over Mnemic with his chest thrust forward and his shirt open like a Superman reject.

The rippling of Mnemic's clothes intensified, and he slunk back, clearly unsure what to do next. His skin followed, roiling and shifting like it was melting, then rearranging.

He's weakened, Walt thought. *Now, do something now! But what? What the hell do I do?*

Not wanting to lose what little advantage he may have, Walt swung his foot forward, aiming to kick Mnemic like punting a football.

But Mnemic caught his foot, twisting the ankle fiercely. Walt fell, his moment of advantage ended, amounting to nothing more than swatting at a bear and enraging it.

Mnemic stood, his face contorting, mouth stretching forward like a misshapen insect's mandibles. Then he rose until he was hunching against the low ceiling. Thick, segmented antennae sprouted from his forehead while a deep crease cleaved his skull down the center. His eyes enlarged, his nose fell off entirely revealing the twin triangular holes of a skull. His body inflated, rounding like a balloon.

The boogeyman in his true form, Walt thought as he stared at the monstrosity, still changing. At least he'd get to see Dad again soon.

"That*ck*'s the connect*ck*ion I sensed," Mnemic said, the timbre of his voice stretching and rasping as his body grew out of proportion to his head, making it look shrunken in comparison. Clothing and skin mingled as their colors swirled, then settled into a pattern of gray, black, and white spots like a bizarre camouflage. Its texture was somehow both hairy and shell-like. A pair of huge, insectile legs broke free from his sides, curling until their single-clawed tips aimed at the floor.

His voice continued morphing, taking on an eerie buzzing quality as it passed through the mandibles. "I've met*ck* your blood before. Seen that*ck* mark before. And you're probably hoping you'll meet him again. No. There's no Heaven. Just*ck* different t*ck*ime, and that*ck*'s where he is. St*ck*uffed in a dark pocket*ck*. Alone. When I'm done with you, I'm going aft*ck*er him. I'll find him, and you'll—"

Something cut him off mid-sentence. Walt pushed himself back across the floor, his hand slipping in a puddle of blood that may or may not have been his own.

Mnemic spun away, and Walt noticed a triangular chunk of its shell was missing halfway up its back. There was a figure standing behind it. A woman, older than Walt by a good margin, perhaps in her eighties. She looked frail, spent, but pleased with herself. She held a scalpel in each hand and had used them to slice at the Mnemic-beetle's shell, their blades covered in dark, runny ichor.

"Should've killed you in the t*ck*unnels, Myrtle" the Mnemic-beetle screeched. "Your t*ck*ime was sour, anyway. Useless." Then they both screamed and thrashed at each other, and it looked like the woman had the upper hand. She arced both scalpels down together and took one of the extra insect limbs off at its midpoint. It dropped to the floor, twitching and oozing black bile.

But in the next instant it was over, as the remaining limb, plus its two semi-human hands pummeled her ruthlessly. Then the Mnemic-beetle thrust the point of its remaining extra limb deep into the meat of her leg. She stopped fighting.

Mnemic withdrew its appendage. She slumped to the floor, blood running from the open wound in a spreading pool beside her.

Walt, fighting incoherent terror, rushed at Mnemic, wielding another trocar like a sword. He hadn't planned to pick it up, but it was closest and felt familiar in his grasp. It was larger than the last one. He aimed it for the center of Mnemic's back, where the woman (*Myrtle?*) had opened a triangular shape in its tough-looking shell. His aim was true, and the trocar speared deep, causing the creature to thrash violently and grasp backward at it with every limb. It fell and rolled halfway onto its back, looking for a second like an oversized dead roach, flailing and screaming in terrible, monstrous tones that rattled the other instruments on the nearby counter. Mixed in its shrieks were sounds that could have been words in several languages Walt didn't know. It pulled the trocar loose, spilling a river of its onyx-colored blood. Then it righted itself, spun, cast one black-eyed glance toward Walt, and skittered through the far door.

Silence filled the morgue.

Walt ran to the woman curled on the floor near the embalming table. Her breath was uneven, hitching, but she was still alive.

"Let me help you," he said to her. "Can you . . . can you move? Or stand?"

She shook her head, wincing as she pulled her hand from her thigh to inspect the wound.

"I'll call nine-one-one. We'll get an ambulance. Just hold on."

"No," she said. "No point. It's my time." She paused, looking pensively at the ceiling. "He didn't steal it all."

"We . . . we can get help. You just need to—"

"What's your name?"

"Walt. It's Walt." He looked into her eyes, observing a level of lucidity, clarity, he doubted most people possessed on their best days.

"Listen, Walt. I'm not going to make it. But I know how to use these last moments. It . . . Mnemic, may be gone, but his, *its* . . . machine is still down there. I've seen it."

"I don't know what you're talking about."

"Have to . . . stop it."

"Stop what? How?"

"No idea. But I have to do it quickly. Set them all free."

"Set who free? Does he have people trapped?" Walt's voice was high-pitched in desperation, but despite his insistence, it was like talking to someone from a distance—there was a delay making what she said harder to interpret.

"No, not trapped. Re-formed. I can hear it. Getting louder. And this light." Then, as if suddenly realizing he was standing next to her, she grasped his shoulders and made direct eye contact. "Can you hear it?"

"Yes."

"That's them. His machine making the town sink. Their bodies, somehow they are still people in there."

"Myrtle, I'm not following. Tell me more, or I can't help!"

"No, you can't help. I have to set them free." She faced the floor then, detaching from the conversation and talking to herself. Walt listened, realizing that his questions were only making this take longer.

If there was anything he could learn from her, he'd need to let her finish.

"He called it a machine, but it's not like you'd think. But it wasn't— It was— He stole their bodies, their parts. Mashed them all together into something awful, but they are still alive, still moving. In pain. He can control our bodies, you see? He fixed my hand. And I think he steals our time to power it too. I don't know what it does, but I have to save her."

Walt pointed to his chest, the tattoo, because the part about controlling our bodies stood out from the rest of her nonsense. "This stopped him. He tried to touch me, to hurt me. I saw him do it to someone. But this protected me."

"A symbol?"

"I think it interrupts his power, somehow."

"What is it called? What does it stand for?"

"Mannaz. It can mean a bunch of things, but . . . but I wanted it to mean self and family and home. Everything I was protecting."

"Show me how you draw it. I want to get it right."

Walt looked around for something to write with and settled for smearing the shape of Mannaz onto the white tile with a fingertip dipped in his own blood.

The blood etched itself into the tile like acid. The two tiles it stretched across cracked and broke apart as if struck by a great force.

"Yeah," Myrtle said. "That's the one."

"This is nuts," Walt said. The symbol breaking those tiles struck his rationality deep, like a finger touching his brain. His psyche reeled, finally processing obscene data like a paper shredder grinding away at a hunk of rock. After everything he'd seen this week, the sky was the fucking limit. So whatever she said was happening down in those tunnels? Sure. Why the fuck not?

Forcing himself to contend with these things being real gave Walt a sense of something dark loosening itself in the back of his consciousness, as if the veil between life and death had been punctured inside him and many things both dark and terrible were spilling out. Even if things worked out from here in the best possible way, life would never return to normal.

The abyss had stared back this week, hard.

This realization caused a sense of defeat to drop on him like a black cloud. He shook himself like a wet dog flinging water, hoping for serenity or clarity that would not come. Did not exist.

Myrtle still held one scalpel. They shared a realization, locking their mental wavelengths.

"I have to do it," she said.

"I can help. Whatever you're planning, let me help. You're too hurt."

"No, it's mine. You're still alive but I'm already dead. You need to leave. I've done things that need atoning for, and this is how. Go. Find shelter in case it doesn't work. Leave the town and maybe you can stay safe."

Walt wanted to talk her out of it or offer something useful. But the sense of defeat and hopelessness, coupled with exhaustion, stopped him. He didn't know this woman, but her conviction was clear and he hadn't the will to change her mind. He knew he'd regret it, but he would let her go.

"Send them home," Walt said. "Send them all home."

They nodded to each other knowingly. He helped her stand, propping her up by an elbow while she found her balance.

She ambled to the door at the end of the morgue and looked back briefly. "Don't you dare follow me, young man," she said, then disappeared into the darkness.

Walt stayed, staring, compelled not to leave yet. Maybe it was curiosity, wanting to know what would happen down there. To her, to Mnemic, to this machine she mentioned. Or maybe he was afraid of seeing how far the town had sunk now.

The humming grew louder and more high-pitched, like the engine of Earth revving, implying that time was short. The sickening green light surged rhythmically.

He decided not to follow her or to leave town as she'd ordered him. Instead, he would go home and sit with Cowboy, waiting to see if his hometown would stop sinking, or not.

MYRTLE DIES

Down, deep into the catacombs she trundled, grasping her injured thigh, heading toward the Dead Rooms. Through shifting layers of darkness, she was guided only by the thrumming sound of Mnemic's machine and the green light. That light, though always dim, would surge and waiver, teasing her vision and making it more a hindrance than a help. Her sense of touch shared only the cold, slick feel of the walls along her palms and the clamminess of the stagnant air. All her focus directed at the sound, Myrtle analyzed the tapestry of mournful voices. She discerned dozens, perhaps hundreds of voices calling out in the dark, endless tunnels.

And she would set them all free. Send them all home, like Walt had said.

As she descended stair after stair after stair, she knew Mnemic could be anywhere lying in wait. Maybe he could scuttle along the ceiling or burrow through the walls themselves and access branches of the tunnels that she could not. She was on his turf again.

But there was only one way to go: straight down and turn right when she reached the bottom of the near-endless stairs. She didn't expect to find her way back out a second time, but she was confident she could find the chamber where she'd seen the machine.

Onward she strode, following the sound and trying her best to hurry. After an unknowable time passed, there were no more stairs down, and the sound had grown both louder and more insistent. The light had either bloomed brighter or her eyes were adjusting.

She headed down the tunnel, vague recall telling her she was close. Soon, the sound was near-deafening and the light would flash so bright she had to squint around it. Then it would fade until she felt blind before pulsing back again. The machine was almost within reach.

Then her struggling senses told her she'd found the large chamber where the machine was. The sound was loud and close but had more open space to travel around her, morphing and reverberating. The light dimmed completely, leaving her in utter subterranean darkness. She moved forward, a half-step at a time, her good hand tentatively leading the way.

Then, without warning, the light returned and Myrtle saw Mnemic's Infernal Machine, inches from her face. The green glow illuminated the closest section of it, bare arms and legs flailing with furious speed as the whole mountain of flesh wailed and screamed.

Myrtle cried out, too, her sound lost in the cacophony. She like them, them like her.

It towered before her, stretched beyond her sight in all directions. The machine watched her with ten thousand mournful eyes, clutched at her with a million desperate fingers, gnashed at her with generations of shattered teeth.

And in the center of its closest section was a person she recognized.

Not the whole person, though.

Only one part of him.

Myrtle was face-to-face with the boy she'd murdered. And the agony in his eyes was enough to break her.

She dropped to her knees in front of him.

"No! No. I'm sorry. I'm so sorry. I didn't mean . . . didn't—" Her words devolved into a sound that blended seamlessly with the thrumming of all the other wretched voices.

She clenched her hands in submission, defeat. She wasn't strong enough for this world. Never had been. She couldn't help.

When she relaxed her hands, though, her bad hand sang with renewed pain. And once more, in that pain, Myrtle found her strength, thinking of everything she had withstood. She was still here, still trying to live with good intentions. Trying to do right. The pain lifted her, and she stood back up, wiping tears from her eyes as she closed them tightly to focus more on the hurt.

She couldn't take back what she'd done to that poor, innocent boy. The misery she'd caused was permanent, like her own. But she could relieve him. Could set him free. And she would.

She'd end it all.

Myrtle took the scalpel from the pocket of her sweater.

She opened her eyes, and the light was bright enough to reveal that the mural of human parts had shifted. The boy's face no longer visible, replaced by another.

At first, Myrtle thought she'd found the face of her doll this time, the doll she'd stolen and left outside for the girl she'd mistaken as her daughter. This detached face had porcelain-smooth skin and perfectly formed features.

The light grew brighter, and she saw it was the face of a real girl, one about Rosita's age (her imagined age). Struck by the coincidence, Myrtle almost dropped the scalpel. Then she straightened herself and kissed the first two fingertips of her good hand while the torturous noise of the machine's blended voice built to a murderous, protesting crescendo.

"Goodbye, sweet child," she said. "I'll see you in another world."

She cut a deep gash into the palm of her bad hand, reached out and swiped it across the girl's forehead, forming the symbol Walt had shown her, and waited.

For a moment or two, nothing happened, nothing changed.

Then, a brief interruption in the sound, like it was coming through a radio with dying batteries. Another interruption, this time the body parts stopped moving at the same time. A rotting smell came, followed by a series of wet thumping noises that Myrtle guessed were limbs dropping loose from the conjoined mass.

She saw the girl's eyes go milky, then draw closed. Darkness grew, silence within it.

A flash of blinding green light, followed by a forceful wind that knocked Myrtle back. She hit the ground harshly and all remaining strength was knocked away.

Myrtle Fallsworth smiled, closed her eyes, and slept.

THREE
MONTHS
LATER

WALTER LIVES ON

Walter took another spoonful, trying to get more of the crushed walnuts and whipped cream this time. He'd arrived just a few minutes ago, and already it was in the running for the most banana-y Banana Split Festival he'd ever attended. Cowboy loped beside him, keeping pace easily as they weaved through the crowd together.

The signature fruit abounded, and Walt wondered if Myrtle liked them at all. He knew so little about her. Had she ever been to this festival? Was she from Oak Hollow? If not, how long had she been here before she sacrificed herself for it?

What was her last name?

There had been many quiet moments over the last few months where Walt thought of her, the woman who had saved his life and his home, along with hundreds or maybe thousands of souls, none of whom knew what she'd done.

He didn't know what she'd done either. Just that it had worked. The town had stopped sinking, but Walt would never know what happened down in those tunnels.

Myrtle's pivotal final moments would be a mystery for the ages.

All Walt could be sure of was that they'd driven Mnemic back underground. The house at 432 Asher Street had been swallowed completely in his wake, but the town's destruction stopped before much permanent harm was done. Which amused Walt in a nihilistic way, having wished in the past for a sinkhole to take Oak Hollow down because of his love/hate stance toward the place. Now the lot was being excavated to make room for a new apartment building, but the construction halted when human remains were found. The authorities hadn't released many details yet, but Walter fully expected those remains to come from a score of bodies. He'd bet his house that Katherine Yost's were among them. He also suspected that some would be very, very old.

He didn't expect any of them to be Myrtle's, though. Not because she wasn't down there, but because they would never dig deep enough to find her. They'd probably never find Finnegan's body either. Walt had been questioned about his disappearance because he was one of the last people to see Finnegan alive, and he had done his level best in telling the truth, but he'd stopped short of explaining how Finnegan had been killed. Just that Mnemic attacked and Walt had fled before seeing much else (which felt like merely a small lie of omission). Then the pair of detectives asked him not to leave town. That was weeks ago, and he was thinking he'd heard the last from them.

So far, he had neither seen nor heard anything about Myrtle's disappearance, though. An act like hers deserved a statue or memorial of some kind, and yet here they all were, eating and wearing and selling banana-themed garbage with no idea how close Oak Hollow and its entire population came to . . . to . . .

Walt tugged lightly on Cowboy's leash, leading him toward a seating area. He picked a table and sat down to catch his breath. Walking and eating together was taxing. His broken ribs had healed, but on hot days he still felt them.

In a silver lining sort of coincidence, the sinking that occurred around the town's borders and the damage it caused had brought significant federal economic relief. Now a venture capitalist firm (heralded by none other than Shawn Yost's brother, Martin) was interested in revitalizing a section of Main Street. A gentrified paradise, right here in Oak Hollow.

Plus, there was a rumor buzzing about Amazon being interested in moving into the old BSL air park. Time would tell, of course, but it was the first time in years that things were looking up for the town's economy.

He knew they would make it too. One thing that prolonged grief had taught Walt was the extent to which people can adjust to new norms, provided they have the strength and patience.

This new dawn for Oak Hollow was all thanks to the events at 432 Asher Street. Walt was glad it was gone, though.

He had reached a sort of terminus in his own growth in that he no longer wondered what Dad truly thought about him.

The *unspoken* had become the *written*.

While he was sitting at home, anxiously awaiting his fate as Mnemic Family Funeral Home became Ohio's largest sinkhole, he'd read through most of Dad's notes. Now they were compiled into a volume that he hoped would match Dad's vision for the finished book. And the best part was that on damn near every page was a line or two praising the man his son had become. Dad had drawn frequent parallels between the steady reliability and boundless strength of symbols and similar qualities that he saw in Walt, using examples that ranged from childhood until a few days before his heart attack cut the project short.

Throughout the pages, he described Walt as having *a quiet, unassuming confidence that springs forward when faced with adversity* and *being adept at working through complex problems by patiently waiting for the right moment to act*. Statements like that, while certainly validating to Walt, were not even the most meaningful ones. He appreciated them in great measure, and they already loomed large in his mind. But they read like something taken from a job referral. The bits that hit him hardest were more personal, more heartfelt. More simple.

Stories about Walt's childhood, moments in their life which had mattered to Dad. Many of which Walt had cherished as well.

Dad had said how proud he was of Walt over and over in those pages, almost too many to count. Proud of his actions, his qualities, his words, his accomplishments. It was everything Walt had hoped existed in the unspoken, now firmly in his grasp forever.

Walt had memorized his favorite example, which oddly enough had been on a Post-it note at the very bottom of a box (perhaps stuck fast so it wouldn't be lost).

It read: *My son is the strongest symbol of them all because he stands for everything I've ever tried to do.*

Walt was tearing up again, thinking about that. He looked around the crowd at the festival, a solid turnout. His ball of grief stirred, knowing Dad would have been pleased to see the town still standing, on the verge of a major comeback. It had now survived prolonged economic hardship and a supernatural infiltration, coming out the other end fighting and capable.

Nothing could stop it now. Oak Hollow would live on.

Walt took one last bite of ice cream, then threw the half-full dish in a nearby garbage can, his appetite gone.

"Come on, boy," Walt said to Cowboy. "Let's get the hell out of here before it gets dark." He patted the dog's head and led him to the car, hoping no one would stop him to chat on the way out. That had always been a mild-grade fear because of the anxiety that came with small talk. But this evening, it was a true phobia.

He'd come here to keep a promise to Dad (in the notes, he'd practically begged Walt to keep going to the Banana Split Festival every year).

Hell, he'd stayed in Oak Hollow primarily to honor Dad's memory and to keep an eye on Shawn's kids. *Keep telling yourself that, old man, we both know running wouldn't do any good anyway.*

But coming here was a mistake. A massive one.

He was too exposed.

As a precaution, Walt rolled up a sleeve, exposing dozens of intricate tattooed symbols, many still fresh and tender, peeling like a sunburn. Then he touched the small pistol concealed in the back of his waistband, which was also adorned with a variety of runes carved haphazardly into the metal and the tips of the bullets themselves.

Once he'd finished with Dad's book, Walt had turned his attention to finding out more about the monster that called itself Mnemic.

Whatever Mnemic's true nature or history, it had stayed well hidden over its endless lifespan. So Walt's research took time, lots of diligent digging, and while he'd learned a few points that seemed reliable, mostly what he had was suspicion or hunches. And none of it was comforting.

Walt's best guess, Mnemic was some manner of ancient insect. It looked like a massive beetle when it finally revealed itself, and he'd since learned that some species of beetles are older than dinosaurs and damn near everything else on Earth.

Older than sharks.

Older than trees.

Hundreds of millions of years old.

Billions.

Something that old . . . what frame of reference was there?

How could he protect himself?

Not only that, beetles were everywhere, he'd learned. Which was more alarming because you never notice them. A quarter of all known species across the planet were beetles, for Christ's sake. That meant if you went out and grabbed a hundred living things, twenty-five of them would probably be some kind of beetle.

Beetles were ancient, they were all around, far outnumbered every other living thing, and they seemed harmless, so he'd almost written off that theory. Then a simple Google search had underscored it.

A week after Mnemic had almost killed him, too terrified to sleep yet, Walt was thinking about how effortlessly Mnemic had messed with Finnegan's body. And everything Myrtle had said about the machine made of human bodies. He had searched the three-word combination of "beetle human flesh."

The results had all but convinced him that the beetle theory was accurate. It had to be.

He'd sat at his computer until the sun came up, reading about Dermestidae: a specific family known as "skin beetles" that consume dead flesh and hair right down to the bone. Humans included. And in that family alone, there were nearly two thousand species.

Two thousand species of carnivorous beetles that could have existed since a time when there weren't even trees yet.

That's what Mnemic was, surely. Some prehistoric ancestor of the skin beetle. And Mnemic had implied there were others like it out there somewhere.

It could shapeshift, manipulate fear, and move freely through underground tunnels. It had eons of knowledge and experience. Sure, it had been hobbled by that brand on its wrist, but it figured a way around that once. Even if it couldn't come after Walt above ground itself, how long until another budding psychopath like Preston showed up? Some days he wondered if being embalmed alive would have been a mercy.

At least then, it would have ended months ago.

This way, he'd never be sure until it was too late.

Walt and Finnegan had exposed it. Walt and Myrtle had stopped it. Now it was just Walt left, the only person with any notion of what had happened here.

All day, every day since . . . two questions nagged at him.

What if Mnemic was still out there?

What if it was ten feet below him right now?

Maybe it was time for another tattoo.

You have one too.

KENT NOTICES

"Hey," Carson said from the back seat. "That's a red light up ahead, moron."

"Oh shit," Ethan replied, mashing the brakes and jolting all three passengers forward.

"What the hell? Pay attention up there," Kent urged. He was sitting next to Carson, on the passenger side.

"My bad. I was looking at that old house."

"Which one? Over there?" Andy asked.

He pointed out his window, though he didn't need to. There was only one house on Stephens Avenue worth looking at. Bellevue wasn't a big town, especially with its population shrinking, and everyone knew that house.

They had all heard the stories.

It was dark out, lending an extra level of mystique to the place.

"Yeah," Ethan said. "I heard about this guy who was a few years older than my sister . . . he stole the mailbox on a dare last summer."

"Oh, I heard that, too," Andy agreed. "Did they ever find him?"

"No," Ethan replied. "Never did."

"It's bullshit, you realize that, right? People just make stuff up about that house because it's spooky and abandoned," Carson said.

No one responded, but there was a note of uncertainty in Carson's voice.

Ethan's car sat idling at the red light, all four teenage boys glaring at the ominous building across the street with wide eyes. None of them noticed the traffic light change until the car behind them gave a short beep.

As they started moving forward again, Kent's gaze stayed fixed on the house. He narrowed his eyes, squinting and turning his head against the car's progress for a longer view.

"Looks like it won't be abandoned much longer," he said.

"How do you know that?" Andy asked from in front of him.

"I just saw a sign in the window," Kent answered. "They're turning it into a funeral home."

END

July 3, 2023–November 19, 2023

Acknowledgements

The quality of this book, though already questionable, would be considerably lessened if not for the contributions of many people who abide my idiosyncrasies and persistent awkwardness. I'd like to thank them all properly, but hope what follows will suffice for now. I'm certain I've forgotten some, but I suppose that's what second editions are for.

Lauren, my primary source of confidence and drive since we first met (thanks for fixing the ending of this). Welles, who currently has no concept of the term "unspoken." Dad, my greatest role model, who eagerly reads everything I write, even if I can't get it published. Mom, the most selfless person I know, who has fed and preserved my love of books for decades. The rest of my family is okay, too. Love you all ya dinguses. Deb Bixler, Mark and Emily Kenner, and everyone at Racing to Retirement Greyhound Adoption for introducing us to the most wonderfully weird breed on earth.

Lisa Breanne (whose timely input rescued this book from being abandoned halfway through) for the fascinating conversations about the terrible things one can do with mortuary tools and the finer points of bodily decomposition. Don Noble, for crafting a stunning cover even though I gave him nothing to work with except mud and indecision. Lauren Humphries-Brooks and Danielle Yeager for cleaning up my messes. Edmund Stone for luring readers past the first page. Leigh

Kenny for her keen Irish eye and a blurb that leaves me flabbergasted. Ben Farthing for his input and support (and having the same first name so I can, on occasion, be mistaken for someone successful), plus an equally flabbergasting blurb. My beta readers: Kat Guterman and Joseph Polinger (both of whom should be writing so I can repay the favor soon), and Barbara Drake (who keeps the best book journal I've ever seen). Taylor Gibbs for gifting her time and talent to make merch depicting the best character in this tale (tail?).

Everyone in Books of Horror, always and forever, for encouragement beyond measure. Fellow authors I've met since joining BoH (listed in no particular order and without repeating from the last time I did this): Patrick McNulty, Matt Wildasin, Lance Dale, Dan Franklin, Jay Bower, James Seamone, Sean McDonough, MJ Mars, Matt Lutton, Colt Skinner, Kyle Rolinatis, Ian Gielen, William Gray, Stephen Barnard, Carver Pike, Kayla Frederick, JS Bailey, Elford Alley, Brittany Miller, Mike Salt, Asia Brito Guerrero, Jason Nickey, E.L Giles. There's more, but I plan to do this again. If I missed you this round, please yell at me so I remember next time. By the time any of you see this, I will probably have been voted out of the brawl.

Everyone foolhardy enough to follow me on social media or subscribe to my infrequent newsletter, what can I say except 'sorry.'

And once more, to every reader choosing to join me on the trek. I'm glad you're here, and hope you'll hang around for the next leg. It promises to be terrifying for us both, but if we stick together, we just might make it.

(There were also a number of books, both fiction and non-fiction, which were helpful as I made up all the weird shit you just read: The Auctioneer by Joan Samson, Needful Things by Stephen King, Savannah Shadows by Tobias McGriff, Confessions of a Funeral Director by Caleb Wilde, Stiff by Mary Roach, Smoke Gets in Your Eyes by Caitlin Doughty, Powerful Secrets of Fortune Telling by Paul McTaggert, and This is Who I Am by Colonel A.E Bob VonHolle. I even kept a few issues of F&SF close at hand.)

ALSO BY BEN YOUNG

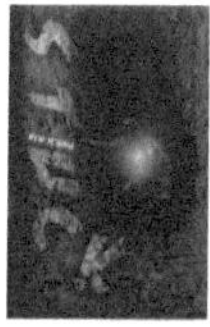

STUCK

Each death is unique.
Will you recognize when yours begins?

John Camden doesn't realize he's dying, yet the physical signs are becoming more clear, and he's having recurring visions where he is trapped in a tight space.

Everything changes when his best friend Robbie convinces him to go on a poorly planned caving trip as a form of immersion therapy.

Soon the lines of reality blur as John finds himself lost and alone, deep underground where all is not as it seems, and the person he trusted most may have sinister intentions.

About the Author

B en lives in the Cincinnati, OH area with his family and dogs, where he is slowly working on another novel or two, along with a prickly smattering of shorter works which may or may not ever see the light of day.

He does not like writing about himself, particularly in the third person like this, even if it is considered *de rigueur* (which he just had to Google).

Find him online at *www.benyoungstories.com*

(Oh, and whatever you do, please don't *follow him on social media*. He hates that.)